all we have left

we have

left

Wendy Mills

BLOOMSBURY

NEW YORK   LONDON   OXFORD   NEW DELHI   SYDNEY

For Zack and Gavin
and all the children who were too young
to remember the day the world changed

First published in the United States of America in August 2016
by Bloomsbury Children's Books
Paperback edition published in August 2017
www.bloomsbury.com

Bloomsbury is a registered trademark of Bloomsbury Publishing Plc

For information about permission to reproduce selections from this book, write to
Permissions, Bloomsbury Children's Books, 1385 Broadway, New York, New York 10018
Bloomsbury books may be purchased for business or promotional use. For information on
bulk purchases please contact Macmillan Corporate and Premium Sales Department at
specialmarkets@macmillan.com

The Library of Congress has cataloged the hardcover edition as follows:
Names: Mills, Wendy, author.
Title: All we have left / by Wendy Mills.
Description: New York : Bloomsbury, 2016.
Summary: In interweaving stories of sixteen-year-olds, modern-day Jesse tries to cope with the
ramifications of her brother's death on 9/11, while in 2001, Alia, a Muslim, gets trapped in one
of the Twin Towers and meets a boy who changes everything for her as flames rage around them.
Identifiers: LCCN 2015037717
ISBN 978-1-61963-343-8 (hardcover) • ISBN 978-1-61963-344-5 (e-book)
Subjects: LCSH: September 11 Terrorist Attacks, 2001—Juvenile fiction. | CYAC: September
11 Terrorist Attacks, 2001—Fiction. | Interpersonal relations—Fiction. | Conduct of life—
Fiction. | Muslims—Fiction. | Love—Fiction. | BISAC: JUVENILE FICTION /
Love & Romance. | JUVENILE FICTION / Social Issues / Friendship. |
JUVENILE FICTION / Historical / United States / 21st Century.
Classification: LCC PZ7.M639874 All 2016 | DDC [Fic]—dc23
LC record available at http://lccn.loc.gov/2015037717

ISBN 978-1-68119-432-5 (paperback)

Book design by Colleen Andrews
Typeset by RefineCatch Limited, Bungay, Suffolk, UK
Printed and bound in the U.S.A. by Berryville Graphics Inc., Berryville, Virginia
4 6 8 10 9 7 5 3

All papers used by Bloomsbury Publishing, Inc., are natural, recyclable products
made from wood grown in well-managed forests. The manufacturing processes
conform to the environmental regulations of the country of origin.

2001

Alia

Travis draws my face into his chest as the smoke engulfs us.

The other tower fell, it fell straight down like a waterfall of concrete and steel, and, oh God, please help me, because is this one going to fall too?

Travis tightens his arms around me, shielding me as parts of the ceiling fall. It doesn't feel like it will ever end, and I hold on to him with all my strength.

Eventually the terrible roaring, clanking noises subside, and Travis unwinds his arms. I sit up, coughing and spitting. The smoke has begun to clear, and I can make out the corner of the desk, and then the chair, and then bookcases farther away as the smoke continues to spiral out the window. I rub my eyes with the palms of my hands, and Travis coughs, his forehead on his knees.

"No, no, no, no, no," I keep saying, but I'm not sure if I'm saying it out loud or if it's in my head. I feel numb, and somehow unattached from myself, as if my mind has floated free like a balloon.

There's Alia in her favorite yellow shirt, sitting next to a boy with mismatched eyes who reaches for her hand because she looks like she is going to shake apart, just fall into a million pieces.

The smoke above us swirls slowly out the broken windows. We are hundreds of feet in the air, and as much as I wish I could just fly out the window, I'm not a superhero, and the only way I'm going to survive is to get up and walk down hundreds of steps.

"Gramps always used to say that they would never fall," Travis says, but he's not really talking to me.

I remember when I was a kid writing notes to God and hiding them around the house, little things like *Please let Nenek get better soon* and *If it's your will, I would like those pink shoes with sequins for Eid.* If I could, I would write a thousand, a million, notes to God right now saying, *Please, please, God, let us get out of this office alive*, and hide them in drawers, under the mouse pad, inside the pages of the splashy brochure flapping wildly on the desk.

Travis starts crawling across the floor, pulling me with him. He is leaving tracks of blood on the floor, and when I glance down at my hands, I see my palms are speckled with glass. I don't feel any pain.

"We need to get out," Travis says. "If the other tower fell, this one could too."

I crawl faster, trying to keep my head below the smoke, but it's still so thick that I have to stop every couple of seconds to cough. Travis reaches up to a desk and grabs a vase. He yanks out the flowers and, before I can protest, puts a hand to my hijab.

"What—? No!" I grab the ends of the scarf and clutch it to my head.

"You need to wrap it around your face so you can breathe," he says hoarsely.

I shake my head back and forth, tears spilling down my cheeks.

It seems forever ago that I put it on, even though it was only a few hours ago. I'd give anything to go back to earlier this morning when my biggest worry was what to *wear*, before planes started crashing into towers, and entire buildings dropped out of the sky.

Without speaking, Travis lets go of the scarf and dumps the water at the bottom of the vase over the front of my shirt.

"Pull it up over your face, then," he says, his voice husky with smoke. "Come on. We're going to get out of here alive, okay? We're going to make it."

2016

Jesse

The car comes closer, and I dig my feet and fingers into the crumbling brick wall and freeze. A stupid voice in my head whispers, *If you don't move, they can't see you.*

The car continues down the road, and, holy crap, maybe Nick is right. Maybe we *are* invisible. People see what they want to see, and it's not a girl hanging on the side of a building at two in the morning.

"Jesse, you need to hurry!" Nick's standing in the alley below me, his hood pulled over his dark hair as he stares up at me.

"I told you she was all talk," Hailey says. "She's chickening out. I told you she would."

I look down at the two of them and have the almost uncontrollable urge to squawk like a chicken, but I know it's just nerves.

I pull out the first spray paint can. My fingers are so cold I can barely hold it. It may be the end of March, almost spring, but tonight it still feels like the cold, dead middle of winter.

I push my feet into cracks between the bricks, take a deep breath, and sweep the paint can down the wall. The smell of paint clouds the air around me.

I finish the first letter, *N*, and it's big and bubbly, the way Nick does it. Stretching one foot over to the right to find another foothold, I start on the next letter. My arm is already shaking, but this one's easier, and soon I have the *O*. As I move over for the next letter, my rope jerks, and I immediately grab for the wall, the paint can falling to the pavement with a loud clatter.

I clutch at the bricks, feeling their coldness seep into my numb fingers. A dog yaps, but no one comes running outside yelling, *Hey, what are you doing up there?* Moving slowly, I look up and see that one of the carabiners making up my anchor is dangling loose.

"You can do it," Nick whispers, and when I look down at him, I see the promise in his eyes from late last night when I'd shown up crying at his house: *No matter what, I won't leave you hanging. Get it? Hanging?* He'd laughed, and I'd felt hurt, because I needed him to be serious. He'd pulled me in for a hard kiss and said, "I won't leave you. Ever." I'd been so upset with Nick after what had happened after the pep rally, but at that moment he was the only one who understood the anger that was burning me from the inside out.

Gingerly, I tug on the rope, but the other two anchor points seem to be holding. I move over for the next letter.

By the time I've worked my way to the corner of the building, I've dropped two empty cans of paint into my backpack and I'm on the last letter. I didn't judge my wall canvas accurately so my letters are like a kindergartener's first attempt at writing, lopsided and all squished up at the end of the page.

I do the last stroke on the *G*, grab the rope, and lean back away from the wall so I can see the whole tag.

NOTHING

It's just a word, but it's our name, mine and Nick's, and Dave's, and even Hailey's. It's what we have painted on the side of dozens of buildings across town in the last six weeks. The word feels exactly right, like it comes from that place squashed down at the very core of me, where all the unsayable things are written in invisible ink on a crumpled sheet of my heart.

The streetlight begins fizzing with snow, and I shiver as I pull myself back to the wall, and grab a handhold.

"What about the rest?" Nick calls.

I shake the can, and then, quickly, without thinking about it too much, I write the next words just the way we talked about. They aren't bubbly, and pretty, but I'm running out of time. I try not to think too much as I paint the hard-edged letters, but I can't help it. This is about me, my father, 9/11, my dead brother, all that hurt and anger spilling out of me onto the wall. It feels good and bad at the same time, like screaming until you're hoarse inside a stadium of empty seats.

I lean back again to see what I've written.

Terrorists go home

"Cops!" Dave yells from where he's standing at the road as lookout. They've stepped up patrols lately. Looking for us. For *us*.

"Come on, Jesse!" Nick yells.

I drop the paint can and let the rope through the belay device, grabbing at it to control my descent as the blue police lights wash over me in a skittering spray of light.

Even as I slide toward the ground, I see a police officer is already running toward me, and I know I'm not going to make it.

September 11, 2001
Events at the World Trade Center

8:46 a.m.   American Airlines Flight 11 hits the north tower

9:03 a.m.   United Airlines Flight 175 hits the south tower

9:59 a.m.   The south tower collapses

10:28 a.m. The north tower collapses

Chapter One

Alia

I wake that morning thinking about what to wear, the taste of candied dreams lingering even after I open my eyes. I slide out of bed and grab my clothes, accidentally kicking a stack of comics piled beside my desk, sending *Elektra* and *Batgirl* skidding across the floor.

I freeze, stuck with one leg in my pants. The ice maker thumps, and I can hear the gentle whir of the fan that Ridwan aims at his face while he's sleeping, but nothing else.

Moving carefully, I slip my other leg into my pants and tie the drawstring at my waist. I go quietly toward the door and open it a crack, and then slap the light switch off as light pours out. I hurry to the bathroom, twisting my crazy-curly hair up into a makeshift bun to keep it from attacking my face, trying to be as quiet as possible. When I've finished, my skin tingling and damp, I go out into the living room, letting my eyes adjust to the dull, gray light trickling through the front windows. It's almost dawn, and I need to hurry.

I wind my way through the furniture to the front door, patting my pocket to make sure I have my key. Carefully, I unlock the deadbolt and slip out into the carpeted hall, shutting the door softly behind me.

I see the light through the window at the end of the hall begin to brighten, and I start to jog, feeling the smooth pull of my muscles. My head is full of messy, jumbled thoughts, and I wish so badly that yesterday had not happened, but that wish has never come true for me or anyone. Not even Lia with all her superhero powers can help me change what happened. But now everything is messed up, and I don't know how to make it right.

I reach the door at the end of the hall and open it. Not caring about the noise now, I let it slam shut behind me and race up four flights of stairs, feeling the pleasant burn in my thigh muscles. I reach the top and fumble for my keys and then step through the roof door into the quiet, luminous dawn.

I stand for a moment, just breathing. Rainwater puddles under my feet, and the air feels cool and clean. There were storms yesterday, but today the sky is brightening into a soft blue and gold, decorated with just a few high lacy wisps of clouds. It's going to be a beautiful day.

Traffic rumbles gently on the street below, and a flock

of swallows dart by in absolute silence, as if they too are in awe of the perfectness of the morning. A waft of wind brings the smell of the river, wet and salty, and I inhale all of it, the river, the faint smell of exhaust, the honey-gold air. I walk across the pebbly concrete and stand near the rail, gazing out at the Manhattan skyline. It's an imperfect view, but I can see the blocky buildings across the river, the Twin Towers soaring high into the sky, the dawn soft and gold in their mirrored surfaces.

It's getting late, and I still need to get ready for school. Already, the evidence of a waking city is all around me, the smell of coffee, quiet, sleepy voices through open windows, the sound of bus brakes screeching briefly before the bus accelerates.

I pull the scarf out of my pocket, and it unfurls in the hushed air. I slip the silk through my fingers for a moment, smelling the wax that my grandmother used to design the intricate patterns. I miss Nenek, suddenly and fiercely. I miss the girl I was when we lived in California and how simple everything was then.

I quiet my breathing and my heart, making my intention known to God. Raising my palms to my shoulders, I whisper, *"Allahu Akbar."*

God is the greatest.

Peace seems to flow into me, and I stand for a moment, eyes closed.

As I go through the familiar motions of prayer, bowing

and then kneeling, so I can press my forehead, palms, and knees to the old prayer rug my father stores up here for just these occasions, I feel serenity and quietness fill me.

> *"Say: I seek refuge in the Lord of the dawn,*
> *From the evil of what He has created,*
> *And from the evil of the utterly dark night when it comes,*
> *And from the evil of those who cast (evil suggestions) in*
>   *firm resolutions,*
> *And from the evil of the envious when he envies."*

I chose this particular surah this morning because of the dawn, and because sometimes it seems like being who I want to be is so hard.

I begin to unwind the scarf from around my head, but my hands still. Can I do it? Is it time?

Something deep and irrevocable inside me says *yes*.

With shaking fingers I coil the scarf back around my head, letting the ends flutter behind me. I'll have to find some pins to make sure it stays in place, but for now it'll do.

While I was praying, the sky has turned a deep and almost endless blue. It stretches taut over the city buildings, and it seems like the tops of the Twin Towers will rip right through the rich fabric of the sky and reach all the way up to the stars. In that moment, I feel infinite, like I can be anything, and do anything, and I wish I felt like this all the time.

౬

I let myself quietly into our apartment. My father, slim and quiet, is folding up his prayer rug as I come into the living room.

"Alia," he says, his quiet eyes taking in my crumpled shirt and wet feet. My scarf.

"Ayah," I say.

We stand for a long moment, and I wonder what he's thinking. I used to be his Lala, the little girl who said and did anything, who would put my arms around his smooth neck and whisper, *I love you, Ayah. Forever and forever.*

There's a galaxy between us now, hung thick with stars of hurt and disappointment. I don't want to hurt him, but there are so many things he doesn't understand about me. I'm not that same little girl anymore.

"Have you changed your mind?" I ask simply.

Last night the argument had been fast and furious. Mainly between me and my mother, because even though we are both small, our words never are. Ayah had walked into the apartment while the words were flying, looking tired and drawn as he slowly pulled off his tie and folded it into a perfect square.

Mama wasted no time telling him that my principal had called to tell her that Carla Sanchez and I were caught in the girls' bathroom smoking a joint. While some of this was true—yes, Carla and I had been in the girls' bathroom, and, yes, there was a joint involved—my mother has not given me a chance to explain.

"I'm trying to tell you," I had yelled a thousand, a million, times, but my mother had talked right over me, and *I'm trying to tell you* was left spinning alone and unheard in the air between us.

In the end, it didn't matter.

"You understand," my father says now, and his words sound like coins dropped into a cool, quiet wishing well, "that we are talking about trust. We need to trust you. And you, Alia, you need to be able to trust yourself, *inshallah*."

For Ayah, words are precious. Measured and weighed, and then shared as carefully as water rations in a desert.

"What have you decided, Ayah?" I'm already tired, and the day has barely begun. I feel a deep pit of fear in my stomach, because I think I know what he is going to say and it is going to ruin my life.

"Your mother and I talked," he says. "We will meet with your principal this afternoon and ask that she not expel you. That is the first thing."

I let out a small breath, because this is good, better than I expected. My mother and father were never happy with my choice of schools. They thought I should go to a more academic school, not one that focused almost exclusively on the creative arts.

"But," he says, "you will come home directly every day after school for the next three months."

My heart stops.

"You're grounding me?" I ask, my voice shaking. "You know what this means?"

He gazes at me steadily. "I know you are disappointed, Alia."

"Only fifteen people made it into the program, Ayah. I was one of them. If I'm grounded, I'm going to lose the best opportunity I've ever had."

He shakes his head. "You are only sixteen. There will be other opportunities, other chances. This is not the end of the world."

"But it is," I say, and turn around and walk out before I can say anything else, because all the words in me are hurtful and angry.

I don't say good-bye to him, and he doesn't mention the scarf on my head.

Chapter Two

Jesse

Up until that bitter-cold February morning when he comes in late to class, Nick Roberts was just the skinny kid with dark hair who always sat in the back, the kid people made fun of for being too quiet, too weird, too unwilling to fit in.

It's the first day of Entrepreneurship, a semester-long block, so you always wonder who you're going to be stuck with for the rest of the year. I'm a little surprised to see him, because I never thought of Nick Roberts as the type of guy who says, "Hell *yeah*, I want to start a million-dollar company someday."

Not that I'd ever thought about him much at all, but when he comes in ten minutes late and heads for the back of the room, which is my favorite territory, I see his face. I give him a sideways glance, and then again, because he looks the way I feel lately, bottled up and trying not to explode like a can of shaken soda.

He sits in the empty seat next to mine and drops his backpack onto the floor. Out of the corner of my eye, I take in the silver hoop winking in his eyebrow, and his eyes the color of a cold winter sky. He's dressed all in black, including clunky black boots, and he's got plugs through both of his ears.

Something else: Nick Roberts is hot. I don't know why I'd never noticed this before.

Mr. Laramore, who is passing out syllabuses, looks at Nick. "Nice of you to join us, Mr. Roberts," he says, and his voice is a just-right mixture of friendly and edgy. A couple of girls behind me sigh, and I can just imagine the hearts they are doodling all over their notebooks.

That's when I see the tattoo snuggled up under the arm of Nick's black T-shirt. It's hidden by his sleeve, but I can see it is a word. *What is it?*

A muscle twitches in Nick's neck before he leans back in his seat, but he doesn't say anything. I'm still staring at his tattoo. I can make out an *N* and an *O*. "No" something? But it is all one word. My fingers itch to slide the sleeve up so I can see the rest of it.

"Do you have anything to say for yourself, Mr. Roberts?" Mr. Laramore is not going to let it go.

Nick stares at our teacher for a long moment. "My dog was sick."

If there was one thing I had noticed about him before, it was *this*. He says things in a low voice, most of the time so the teacher never hears, which are so blatantly *eff you* that you don't know whether to laugh or be horrified. He usually says it so quiet you wouldn't hear him unless you're really listening.

This time we all heard him. I don't think any of us knew why we broke into giggles because *his dog was sick.* Mr. Laramore continues passing out the syllabuses, and there's a general murmur of disappointment, because school is a contact sport and some people get a kick out of seeing blood on the field.

Nick leans his arm down to his backpack, and for just a moment I see the word tattooed on his bicep. It says "Nothing."

All righty, then.

He sits back up, and pulls his sleeve down, covering the tattoo entirely.

"I trust he has recovered," Mr. Laramore says, stopping in front of Nick and putting the syllabus square in the middle of his desk. Nick stares at him with no expression; you can see the anger coming off him in waves, but maybe only if you're a pro at surfing anger like I am.

I twine my blond ponytail around my finger, pulling and pulling until it hurts my head.

"She," Nick says, and it takes me a minute to realize that he's still talking about the dog. And then he shrugs, an extravagant *whatever, dude,* and says, "She'll either be kicking or stone cold dead when I get home."

Nobody laughs this time.

I glance over at him, and there's something in his eyes that makes me want to smile, or cry, or say *I'm sorry.* Emi is frowning, and she rolls her eyes at me. She takes school very seriously and hates it when less-serious students disrupt her class zen.

I, however, am intrigued.

❦

This all goes on for a week. Me, turning in my homework on time and acing Friday's quiz like the good girl I've always been, and Nick Roberts baiting Mr. Laramore under his breath and nodding his head the rest of the time to the music playing in his earbuds.

I've started noticing the way his soft, dark hair sweeps over his eyes, that his long fingers are covered with paint and always in motion as he taps them on his thigh, twirls his pencil, or plays with the thick plugs in his ears.

I wonder what he sees when he looks at me, those fleeting glances out of the corner of his eye. A completely ordinary girl, not cute, not awful, just *there.* My blond hair is always pulled back in a long ponytail, and my pale blue eyes look like they've been through the wash too many times. Nothing special, so lusterless that I wonder sometimes if I could just fade away without anyone noticing.

But Nick has caught me staring at him more than once, and he's nodded a couple of times, like, *We're the same, aren't we? Even if you don't show it on the outside, we're alike, you and me,* and I think that he sees me, even if no one else does.

I don't know if it's true, but it makes me feel good, when nothing has been feeling good lately. It's as if every nerve in my body is shrieking and no one hears it but me.

The bell rings on a cold, shiny February day, and Emi and I rush with the others toward the hall after class.

Entrepreneurship counts for college credit, which is the reason Emi and a bunch of the smart kids are taking it. I'm taking it because I figure if anybody is going to take over my dad's climbing shop one day, it'll have to be me. Some girls take it just because Mr. Laramore is hipster hot, if you like angsty guys in their thirties with thick black glasses, skinny jeans, and high tops. It's a pretty diverse crowd that battles for the doorway and the freedom of the hallway.

I'm watching Nick as he slips through the door, and Emi nudges me.

"Why are you so into him?" she asks as we jostle together, caught in a bottleneck at the doorway.

Emi Yamada has been my best friend since the sixth grade. She is dedicated and somber, skinny and gangly, with short, spiked black hair and a row of rings along her earlobes. Her narrow amber-colored eyes light up the most when she's talking about apples, clouds, and streams, which might make you think she really likes nature, but only as wallpaper on her tablet screen.

"I was thinking I should mix it up, trade in my earrings for some plugs," I say, fingering the small gold hoops in my ears. I'm not serious, but I really don't know how to answer her.

She shakes her head. "They wouldn't look good on you," she says.

Because it's Emi, I can't tell if she really thinks I want a pair of ear plugs like Nick's or if she's trying to tell me something else.

As the jam breaks and we swirl out into the hallway, Emi and I get separated. I'm heading for Teeny's locker when a group of mimes come down the middle of the hall, the drama kids doing live art. People laugh as they goof off, acting as if a windstorm is blowing them around the halls, and then walking a tightrope, with expressions of terror on their faces. I step to the side to let them pass.

But instead they surround me and start to pat the air all around me.

"Uh . . . ," I say, because *what the hell?*

People are starting to gather around, and suddenly I realize that the mimes have me in a box. They are feeling along the side of it with their hands, and Jenny Knowles jumps up to feel the top of it, catching my eye and winking as she lands back on the ground.

I don't have freaking time for this, but it seems rude to just walk away, so I stand there as they press their palms against the box that only they can see. The box is getting smaller, and I instinctively duck my head as Jenny pats the air above my head. Their palms are getting closer as the box shrinks and I pull my arms in tighter to my body.

I feel stupid as the crowd gets bigger and someone starts clapping as the box starts getting smaller and smaller. Soon I'm sitting on the floor, my face red as I half laugh with exasperation, and it's then that I catch Nick's eye.

He's leaning up against a locker, and as I watch, meathead Lawrence Jenson catches him with his shoulder and laughs, but Nick just steps away, his eyes trained on me.

"Really, guys?" I say to the mimes, but they ignore me, and the box just keeps shrinking. I duck my head down between my shoulders. When I look back up, Nick turns his hand palm up and brings his fingers together. As I watch, he snaps his fingers back and then mouths four words at me.

I don't get it, but then I do.

Blow up the box.

When he sees that I understand, he turns and disappears into the crowd.

"What on earth are you doing to my girl?" Teeny cries, and suddenly she and Emi and Myra are there, and they catch me by the arms while Teeny scolds Jenny and the other mimes. I let them fuss over me, but in my mind all I can see is Nick as he walked away.

Chapter Three

Alia

I resist the urge to slam the double doors behind me as I go into my room. I've never been able to be like that with my father, even though Mama and I slam doors on each other on an almost-daily basis.

I wait until I'm inside the safety of my bedroom before I let myself cry. I unwind the coil of silk from around my head and hold it to my face, feeling my tears wet the scarf that Nenek made for me.

Lia wouldn't be sitting here crying. Lia would force her parents to understand, save the world on the way to Star-bucks, and make it to school on time with her deodorant and her saucy smile intact.

I look over at my desk where Lia's life is laid out in half-inked panels of pencil drawings and bubbles of gutsy dialogue. Having a superhero for a friend doesn't do anybody any good when that friend is only real on paper.

I put the scarf on the bed and look at the permission slip that sits prominently beside my panels, pencils, and ink. If I don't turn in the slip today, I won't be able to go to the highly selective eight-week program at NYU for talented high school artists. My portfolio beat out hundreds of others, and I was over the moon when I received the acceptance. But though I've had the permission slip for two weeks, it still remains unsigned. My parents needed to talk about it, they said.

I know what they were thinking. They were thinking that they wished I would focus more on my studies instead of sketching. They wished their daughter wanted to be a doctor, or a lawyer like her mother, not a comic book artist. At least my parents are progressive enough that they aren't using the Quran as an excuse to keep me from drawing comic books, but in the end it amounts to the same thing.

And now I gave them the perfect opportunity to say no. They never had to say, *No, Alia, we think your dream is stupid and juvenile.* Instead, I handed them the perfect excuse on a silver platter.

∽

Yesterday afternoon, in the girls' bathroom.

I knew I'd have to run into Carla eventually. I hadn't seen her since the end of tenth grade, and it was already the second week of my junior year. Maybe a part of me even wanted to run into her, wanted to yell, *How could you do it? I thought you were my friend!*

"Hey, Alia, you want a hit?" Carla says when I come into the bathroom. Her voice sounds all squished, and smoke trickles from her nose as she holds the joint out to me.

Inside my head Lia shouts, "Pot is for losers, Carla!" and gives a roundhouse kick that knocks the joint out of Carla's hand and fries it to a smoldering heap with one point of a lightning-tipped finger.

I go to the sink and stare at my plain, non-superhuman face in the mirror.

The bathroom is empty except for us, which is rare in a school with thousands of people, but this bathroom was always Carla's and my favorite. It's tucked down a dead-end hall on the third floor, and it's always cold, even when it's warm and sunny outside. The sound of faraway clanging pipes always used to make us jump, thinking it was the clickety-clack of a teacher's heels in the hallway, and we'd giggle and make fun of each other for being scared.

"Are you serious, Carla?" I ask. "Are you trying to get kicked out?" I look back at myself in the mirror: too-round face, skin the color of lightly stained wood, and brown eyes with thick, dark lashes, which I thank God for every day. I sigh when I see my hair. It's gone positively Medusa, despite the coconut cream I smoothed into it this morning.

"Who cares if they kick me out?" Carla exhales sharply from the corner of her mouth, a big, nasty bubble of smoke rolling toward me.

"Grow up, Carla." I run my fingers through my hair, watching in disgust as the curls bounce back up and say, *Why, hello there!* It's hopeless. *I'm* hopeless. If nothing else, wearing the hijab would save me from bad-hair days for the rest of my life. But I wasn't brave enough to wear it today, just as I'm not brave enough to tell Carla what I really think about what she did to me.

"You used to be *fun*," Carla says. "What happened to you, Alia?"

I turn back to her. "And you used to be my friend," I say evenly. "I guess we *both* changed."

"Aw, girlie, you can't take stuff like that seriously. Mike? He didn't mean anything."

"He meant something to me." *Or I thought he did anyway.*

Carla takes another big hit off the joint, and her voice comes out all squeaky. "Remember how much fun we had last year? What changed?"

"Me," I say, because I hope that it's actually true.

Carla and I started hanging out the beginning of our sophomore year when I'd just moved to Brooklyn from California. She was cool and fun, which is exactly what I needed at the time. We laughed at the tourists on the promenade as they sighed over the view of Manhattan, hung out under the bridge at night and watched the strobing headlights of the cars, and snuck over to Times Square to see our favorite bands on *TRL* at MTV Studios.

I had a blast with her until she totally betrayed me, and

my parents grounded me all summer except for two weeks of camp. I wish it were easy to write the real Carla out of my life, the way I'd written her twin out of Lia's story.

I glance at my watch and see that it's time for Anatomical Drawing. There are no bells—my school is big on personal responsibility—so it's up to me to make sure I get to my next band on time. At first that freedom felt too big, like I was a pet bird bursting out of its cage for the boundless sky.

"Come on, girl," Carla is saying. "You're like me, you know you are. I'm sorry about all that before, I really am."

I stare at her face in the reflection of the mirror, and see that she probably *is* sorry, but that doesn't change anything, does it? Do I want to be friends with her again and go back to being like I was last year?

"Look, Carla, it just doesn't matter anymore. Here." I take the joint from her, which is about to drop ash all over the bathroom floor. We both hear the familiar clickety-clack of the pipes and sort of smile, like old times. I put the joint out in the sink with a hiss and go to hand it back to her.

Ms. Donaldson walks in.

Of course she does. This is me we're talking about, where Lia lives only in my head, and my actions spill like dark ink across my hastily drawn life.

She takes in the swirling cloud of smoke, and me holding the joint. "Ms. Susanto, Ms. Sanchez. Go to Ms. Julio's office. *Now*."

Chapter Four

Jesse

"I've seen the way Nick looks at you," Teeny says, shoving her Health book into Emi's locker a day after the me-versus-mimes incident. "I suppose he *is* cute, in a kick-ass nerd-boy kind of way."

I'm not sure whether to be offended or not, so I shrug. It's not surprising that Teeny picked up on the vibe between me and Nick; she's always been good at seeing the compli-cated webs of connections between people and groups. She laughingly says she plans to use her powers for good when she becomes a psychologist. Pretty and curvy, her real name is Christina—which she hates—and though she claims to have hit five foot even, no one believes her.

"I heard Hailey Brinson is all into him," she continues. "You know, Hook-Up-Hailey?"

"*Teeny*," Emi says disapprovingly.

"What?" Teeny shrugs. "If she doesn't want to be called that, she shouldn't get drunk and try to hook up with every guy she meets."

Hailey isn't in any of my blocks, but she's one of those girls everyone knows about. She arrived at our school last year and immediately made herself notorious—you know the type: flashing Mr. Johnson's tenth-grade Algebra 2 class when he had his back turned, kissing Michael Higgins with full-tongue when he won class president.

"Are they going out?" I ask, and Teeny bursts out laughing.

"Jealous?" she hoots, and nudges me with her hip.

"Me, jealous of Hailey Brinson? Right," I say, but I can't help but grin as I hip-bump her back. Because, yes. Yes, I am.

I don't tell them that I have Nick's number in my pocket, that right before we left class he slid it across my desk with an expression of feigned indifference, though the number burns against my leg for the rest of the day. Emi, Teeny, and Myra are my best friends, but this is something I'm not sure they would understand, because I'm not sure I understand it myself.

❧

That afternoon, I weave my way through Dad's climbing shop, waving at Grill, the shop manager. I go through the door marked No Entry and climb the narrow staircase to our apartment. Dad is watching TV in the living room. I know he should be working, know it because of the exasperated look Grill threw at me, but it's not like it's unusual lately.

"Hi, Dad." I open the fridge and pull out a jug of OJ. Mom's got dinner in the oven, so she must be off to another committee meeting, or whatever it is she does to make sure she's not at home as much as possible.

"Keep it down, will you?" Dad says, his attention fixed on the screen.

Being as quiet as possible, I rinse my glass and put it in the dishwasher.

Mom comes into the kitchen, a whirl of motion as she checks the casserole, sends a quick text, and then turns to me.

"Hi, honey," she says, but her gaze slides off me as if I'm a big stick of butter. She doesn't really see me. She hasn't for a long time.

"I have a school meeting tonight." She adjusts her dress, which used to be her favorite and is just a little too tight, and runs her hand through her silvering blond bob.

When I meet her former students, they rave about her. She's the best, most conscientious, most inspiring fourth-grade teacher on earth. She must be a great mom, I'm so lucky.

Right, okay, if you say so.

I think about how, over Christmas break, I found her asleep with her head on the kitchen counter, her well-worn

Bible in her hands. In front of her was a perfect chocolate cake with thirty-three candles on it, all burnt down to smoky nubs, the cheery red wax melted all over the top of the cake.

I must have made a sound, because my mother woke up and looked at me blearily, and I wondered how much of the bottle of wine beside her she had drunk. She's a lightweight, and I hardly ever see her drink. My dad takes care of that for the both of them.

She saw me staring at the cake. "He should have been here," she said. "He should have been here to blow them out."

It hit me then that it was Travis's birthday. My brother Travis who died in the Twin Towers almost fifteen years before.

Part of me wanted to yell, *But* I'm *still here. Doesn't that count for something?*

She got up unsteadily and went to her bedroom, and I was left staring at the smoldering cake.

Of the three children my parents brought into this world, one is dead, the second is in Africa, and then there is me. The unwanted, invisible kid they still have to act like they give a damn about.

I haven't been able to get the picture of my mom and that sad melted cake out of my head, and it makes me want to scream until someone hears me, but the screaming is only in my head.

"Gerald," she says now, a little sharply, and my father looks over at her. "I'll be back late."

Their eyes lock for a brief moment, and some sort of private conversation flows between them, and it could be, *Gerald, maybe you should cut back on the beer* and *Susie, when the hell was the last time you were actually* here *for dinner?*

As a kid, I used to bounce up and down and demand the "bike story" from my mother, because when you're five, stories about your fledgling parents seem like something out of a fairy tale.

It was the story of how they met. Dad was finishing up college and working as a bike messenger in the city, and Mom was doing her first student teaching assignment. On her way home one afternoon, she saw a group of older kids start messing with one of her students. Mom, young and fearless, jumped into the fray and stared down the group of hoodlums. Enter Dad like some sort of freaking superhero. He had no brakes because he had stripped them off his bike so he could go as fast as possible. He rode right up to Mom and a cowering Juan Arias and jumped off. His bike flew into a nearby van, and Dad told the hoodlums to go packing. In the story, they actually do, and in the story, it was love at first sight. Mom's hero.

It wasn't until I was older that I realized that Mom always told the story fast and bitter, as if by then she was having to convince *herself* that the younger her and Dad had existed, that they weren't just a young couple in a love story.

There were no other Mom-and-Dad stories, but in my mind I've filled in the rest. They were married, moved from the city to the Gunks, and had two boys, first Travis, then three years later, Hank. Everything was fairy dust and perfection. Then, almost seventeen years after Travis was born, an accident came along and they named it Jesse. Two years later Travis died in the Twin Towers and Dad decided to hate everyone and Mom started running so fast she left the rest of us behind. Hank just fell off the freaking page completely, and sometimes I wished I could follow him.

The end.

My dad mutters something, and my mom stands there for a moment, her face perfectly blank, and then she drops a quick kiss on my forehead and is gone.

"I'm going over to Teeny's. We're studying for a Statistics test." I feel like I'm whispering, though I'm pretty sure I'm not.

"Why can't you be friends with normal people?" Dad doesn't look at me.

"They *are* normal people." But I say it under my breath. Avoiding confrontations is my specialty.

I feel myself shrinking, like the atoms inside me are deflating one by one. I think of Nick then, his face shining with something like sympathy as he watched the mimes put me in the box. Then I think of what he mouthed:

Blow up the box.

Chapter Five

Alia

I hold up my favorite long-sleeved yellow shirt against my chest and eye myself in the mirror. The yellow fabric does nice things for my dark hair, but it just isn't right. *Nothing* seems right today.

I flop down on my bed and stare at the ceiling. Grounding me so I can't attend the NYU program might not seem like a big deal to my parents, but to me it feels like the continuing game of Whac-A-Mole I play with them. I dare to dream, and they wallop it into oblivion.

I'm lying on a pile of clothes, and I fish out a silky blue shirt and hold it up in the air above me. Superheroes get to wear masks and capes and pretty much anything they need to keep their identity a secret and kick some major butt in the process.

I wish dressing for school was that easy.

I throw down the shirt and roll over to look at the white scarf covered with swirling yellow designs and delicate flowers in green and crimson. Finding something to wear with it is harder than I thought it would be. Tanjia got a party and a new wardrobe when she started wearing the hijab, and the thought of a hijab-themed shopping spree with Tanjia and Kaitlin cheers me up a tiny bit.

I jump off my bed, dislodging piles of clothes and tripping over my track shoes as I lunge for the radio.

Music. Music is what I need.

I flip through radio stations until I find a good song, Blink-182's "The Rock Show," and turn it up as loud as I dare. I dance around, jumping on the bed and off again, knowing that Ms. McGillicuddy downstairs will probably "have a word" with my mother about my thumping around, but not caring. I might not be the best dancer in the world, but I have dancer friends, and I've seen their moves. I shimmy my hips and wave my arms around and then catch sight of myself in the mirror and collapse on the bed, because it. Is. Not. Working.

Lia in a dance club, really breaking down her moves, while the people who are talking about her all mean just stand around with their mouths open.

I can see the panel in my mind, and I almost grab my notepad, but I don't have time, and besides, Lia would never be caught dead in a nightclub. She knows better.

I wonder again if it's worth wearing the scarf today. There's so much going on, but if I don't do it now, then when? I've thought about it for months, since camp, but when the first day of school came, I put on my regular clothes and marched off to the subway, pretending I didn't notice the disappointment in Tanjia's eyes.

"Alia! Turn down the music, you're going to wake the entire building!" my mother yells through the French doors into my room, which used to be a dining room until my parents turned it into a bedroom for me.

I want to turn the radio up and up until I don't hear the disappointment and frustration in my mother's voice.

"Alia!" Mama smacks her hand on the outside of my locked bedroom door.

"Yeah, okay, I heard you."

I turn down the radio and glance at my desk. Lia's face, confident and strong, stares back at me, and I swear she winks.

"When I was stuck at the bottom of the Hudson River after the Evil Mad Doctor turned me into a squirrel and locked me in the trunk of a Camry, who was there to save me? That's right. No one. It was all me, baby."

"Easy for you to say," I mutter, picking up the yellow shirt.

I need to get going or I'm going to be late for school.

〰

When I walk into our narrow kitchen, my mother is sitting at the small table by the window overlooking the fire escape, sipping her milky tea. She takes one look at me and narrows her eyes.

"Is this a joke?"

Somehow I never think of her as short because when she opens her mouth all the words are tall and imposing. She's pretty in her gray pantsuit and white silk shirt, and her dark hair is pulled back into a perfect braid with not a single hair daring to misbehave. Her face is serious and unrelenting unless she smiles, which hasn't happened a lot lately, at least at me.

"No, Mama," I say. "It's not a joke." I nervously finger the scarf that covers my hair and drapes loosely around my shoulders. I know I did a crappy job of fastening it. It keeps slipping off my head, and the pin has it all bunched up on one side.

She stares at me, her eyes unflinching, and I can just see her in the courtroom, one of her Bangladeshi or Pakistani clients by her side, giving that stare to the opposing counsel. Which is all well and good, except *I'm her daughter*; why does she want to make *me* feel like something she needs to wipe off her shoe?

"Today? This is the day you choose to wear the scarf?"

Since this is what I was basically thinking fifteen minutes ago, of course it just pisses me off even more.

"Yes, Mama, today's the day," I say evenly, opening the refrigerator and grabbing my lunch bag.

"I'm sure you will understand that I find your timing suspicious," she says. "Do you think that because you have decided to wear the scarf, that your father and I will change our minds about the NYU program?"

"No, *Mother*," I say. "I did not think that at all." Though the permission slip crinkles inside my pocket. I hate it when she does this, makes me feel young and obvious and stupid. And while my timing may not be ideal, deciding to wear the hijab full time is a pretty big deal and why can't she give me some credit?

My mother takes a deep breath, and stares out the window. I can hear cars going by and the excited shrills of children on their way to school. She's not seeing them though. She's trying not to lose it on me.

She turns back to me. "Of course it is your decision," she says, "and I support you." Her tone is cold and formal, as if she's reading directly out of the "How to Be a Good Muslim Parent" handbook. My mother has been speaking English since she was four, but she also speaks Indonesian and Arabic, which gives her English a lilt that people find charming. When the sound of her voice isn't playing hopscotch on my last nerve, I wish I had her accent. I speak English just like everyone else, and no one smiles when I talk.

"Good." I grab an apple off the basket on the counter. "That's nice of you. I'm sure Nenek said the same thing to you when you decided to *not* wear the scarf."

I meet her gaze for a moment, and then turn my attention to the apple.

The silence stretches.

We weren't always like this. Before we came to Brooklyn, Mama and I used to be close. I remember us putting on puppet shows, making bead bracelets, and pretending to batik on strips of old bedsheets, dripping crayon wax in a splatter of colors. When we moved away from California, something cracked between us, like the delicate shell of an egg that even Humpty Dumpty couldn't put back together.

"You think I'm going to embarrass you, don't you? You don't think I'm a good-enough Muslim to wear it." The fridge and the counter have grown monstrous, squeezing me so tight that there's no room to breathe.

"It is your decision, Alia," she says again. "But if the only reason you are choosing to wear it today is to somehow convince us that you have changed, then God knows what is inside you."

"I *have* changed. Why can't you see that?" I know that I sound like a whiny little girl, and I take a deep breath and try to calm down so she will listen, so she will *hear* me for once. When did her words get so much more important than mine?

"After you were caught smoking marijuana in the girls' bathroom yesterday, Alia?" She sounds like she just heard the funniest thing *ever*, and it makes me want to scream. "Have you forgotten your father and I have an appointment with your principal this afternoon, and that you might be expelled?"

"Just because I got into trouble with Carla yesterday doesn't mean I'm some sort of criminal. It was her joint, not mine!" I fling my arm out dramatically, and Mama sighs, like *Really, Alia?*

"You never think before you act," she says as if she knows me so much better than I could ever know myself. "You told us after you ran away last year that you didn't think about how we would feel, how much it would hurt us. You did it without thinking. You need to think about the consequences of your actions, Alia!" Mama sets down her cup hard enough that the milky tea splashes out onto the counter.

"That was months ago!" I say. "I've told you again and again how sorry I am. It was a horrible, terrible thing to do, and I regret it, but that doesn't mean that I can't be a better person *now.*"

She wipes up the spilled tea with hard, angry swipes of a napkin and glances at her watch. "It's not like you've given us a lot of reason to trust what you say, Alia," she says with finality. "It is time for you to go to school."

As usual, she's ending the conversation before I have a chance to say any of the things I want to say.

I take a deep breath. "This is the last day to turn in the permission slip for the NYU program," I say, but she has already gotten up to put her cup in the sink.

"We have made our decision, Alia," she says, her back to

me, and I know that while it's Mama and I fighting, she has my father's iron will behind her. "We will see you today in the principal's office."

Lia would not be standing here dumbly as her mother ignores her. Lia would say: *I may not be the person you want me to be, but I am trying to be the person I want to be, and isn't that good enough?*

"I hate you!" I say, and run out of the room.

Chapter Six

Jesse

"I called him," I announce as I come into Teeny's room.

Three faces look up at me with identical expressions of surprise. I sit on the bed next to Emi and fight the urge to cover my ears and start *la-la-la*-ing. I debated all the way over here whether or not to tell them, but this is big, and these are my best friends in the entire world.

"You called Nick?" Teeny asks, the first one to get it.

"I called Nick," I confirm.

"But why?" Emi asks, genuinely confused.

I hesitate, because it's hard to explain, and I know that steady, rational Emi will never understand. Emi is insanely smart, which makes it sometimes hard for her to understand us mere mortals.

"He gave me his number, and I thought: Why not?" It

doesn't come close to explaining the way I felt when I was doing a repeat performance of my own personal live art with my parents this afternoon—*Invisible Kid*—and how I thought, just maybe, Nick might understand.

"So are you meeting him?" Myra asks from the chair in the corner where she is busy on her phone. She's probably already looking up "What to do when your friends act like fools," because Myra is constantly googling *something.*

"Yes." I glance at my phone, and feel a wild fluttering in my belly. "In like forty-five minutes."

"Okay then." Teeny stands up and goes to her closet. "We need to get you outfitted."

"I thought we were studying Statistics," Emi complains.

"Really? Myra and I aren't even *in* your Statistics block, so if you really thought you and Jesse were going to study AP Statistics at my house then you were seriously mistaken," Teeny says over her shoulder to Emi as she starts rifling through her closet.

As smart as she is, Emi falls into this trap all the time. She doesn't understand just hanging out with friends, so the only way to get her out of the house is to promise her a study date.

"This one's cute." Teeny holds up a filmy, low-cut top. The tag still flutters off the sleeve, and we all know it's something her aunt sent her, willfully ignoring the fact that Teeny's parents won't let her wear filmy, low-cut stuff.

"Um . . . ," I say, not wanting to sound ungrateful.

Teeny sees my face, and shoves back her mass of black

hair so she can more effectively narrow her eyes at me. "Stop looking at me like I'm feeding you to the lions. Pure laziness is not an excuse to dress like a slob."

I obediently hold out my hand, because you don't mess with Teeny when she sounds like that.

"You know, Hailey's going to go ballistic if she hears you're seeing Nick," Myra says, putting down her phone as I pull the shirt over my plain white cotton bra.

"We're just going to be working on our business plans," I say, trying to tie the sash behind my back. Teeny comes over and brushes my hands away so she can do it.

"Yeah, right!" Teeny and Myra say at the same time. I can't help but laugh with them because when Nick slid the note across my desk and said, *Maybe we can get together on our plans* with that sidelong look, we both knew he meant something else, something that made my heart race and my mouth go dry.

"I'm assuming you'll be doing about as much studying as we are right now," Emi says, rolling her eyes, but then she smiles.

"He's cute, right?" I say.

"Sure," Teeny says. "Just not your style. Don't take this the wrong way, but he's . . ."

". . . more than passingly weird," Myra says, wrinkling her nose.

Myra is plump and pale, kind and generous, and unswervingly loyal. She takes a lot of things seriously, including global warming, listening to humpback whale songs, and fighting for the ethical treatment of frogs. But let's face it, she's not exactly my barometer when it comes to whether or not something or someone is weird.

"Nice." Teeny surveys me with satisfaction. "She looks nice, doesn't she?" Teeny turns to Emi and Myra, and they nod dutifully.

"You look hot, girl." Teeny turns back to me and sees my face. "Why do you find that so hard to believe?"

Emi rolls her eyes, and Myra is back on her phone, probably searching: "What to do when my best friend wants to date a guy who looks like an ax murderer."

"All we're saying is that Nick Roberts is a far cry from Jayden Sweeny and Dalton Hodges," Teeny says. "You know?"

"*I* wouldn't date Nick," Myra says, glancing up from her phone. "He looks like he's about to rob a bank or something. What about Jerry Horbensky? He's hot, don't you think?"

"Seriously?" Teeny says. "Isn't he the kid who ate his boogers all the way up to middle school?"

"I want a boy all my own, who writes me poetry and holds my hand and gives me flowers every week on the anniversary of our first kiss." Myra looks around at us defensively. "It could happen."

"Uh, Myra? I'm pretty sure guys like that don't exist," I say. "And if one did, he probably keeps a collection of girls' underwear under his bed."

"I wouldn't care. Nothing would get between me and my Jerry Horbensky," she says dreamily.

"Anyway, are we going to study at some point?" Emi says, shrugging it all off, the boys, the hormones, all the silly high school stuff that plagues the rest of us. I sometimes think that it's not fair that it's Teeny who doesn't date, because if it were Emi, it wouldn't bother her at all.

"*No*, Emi, you can study later," Teeny says patiently. "We're discussing Jesse and Nick. Nick and Jesse. Nessie. Isn't that the nickname for the Loch Ness monster?"

"Nick could be that kind of guy," I say. "Like Myra said. Not the roses-on-your-first-date kind of guy, but the kind that I can talk to, who will actually listen to me."

I ignore the look they exchange. I can hope, can't I?

I don't want to listen to their concern, or even acknowledge the niggling feeling in my own stomach that is whispering: *danger, danger, danger. He's not safe.*

I feel like I'm getting ready to rappel down a big cliff and I haven't tied a knot at the end of my rope. If I rap right off the end into free fall, I don't even *care*.

I'm tired of safe.

∽

By the time we leave though—Teeny is on her way to Bible study, and Emi and Myra to Starbucks—I'm having serious second thoughts. But then I think about Nick's eyes burning into the *me* that no one else seems to see, not even my friends.

I slide down the narrow, icy sidewalk of Main Street, ducking the snow sliding off awnings. The shops are all closing, people pulling doors shut on jewelry and antique shops and hurrying toward home in the freezing dusk. The college kids, the ones old enough to drink or resourceful enough to have fake IDs, laugh inside the bright warmth of bars.

In the distance the white cliffs of the Gunks glow pink and yellow in the light of the setting sun, and I take a deep, burning breath of frosty air. Winding through back streets shaded by skeletal ash trees, I head into a more rundown part of town, where people put cars up on blocks and forget them, and the snowmen are slumped and despondent. I stop in front of Nick's small clapboard house, the blue, peeling paint dull in the waning light.

I'm nervous. Big time. My attraction to Nick is different than what I felt for Dalton or Jayden. I can't seem to stop thinking about him, like he's a glittering shard of glass lodged in my brain. It's strange and unexplainable, and deliciously painful. I shiver and break a small icicle off the railing, holding it in my fingers until it starts to melt.

The front door slams open, and a bunch of guys, big and bulky in coats and hats emblazoned with Greek letters, come crashing out of the house, most carrying beers.

"Why, hello there," one of them says to me, doing the up-and-down thing with his eyes. I wish I could paint a tunnel in the air behind me and step through it.

"I'm, uh, here to see Nick," I stammer, unnerved by his smile, which reminds me of rusty nails, dirty needles, and wingless flies.

"Baby brother's upstairs," he says, jerking his head toward the front door.

I escape into the house, feeling shaky.

Inside, I take off my coat, but I don't know where to put it, so I fold it over my arm. The sounds of rowdy, pumped-up guys die away, and the house is silent. The stairs are right inside the front door, and I make my way up them, already feeling sweaty in the too-hot house.

I hear loud music coming from behind the door closest to me, and I knock on it.

"Come in," Nick yells from inside.

He's lying on top of his unmade bed, staring at the ceiling. One arm is stretched behind his head, his clunky black boots crossed at the ankles.

He picks his phone up off his chest and hits a button. The music suddenly stops, though the silence roars, like the air particles are still bombarding off one another.

"You came," he says, and for some reason I think of a little kid saying, *I didn't think you'd come to my birthday party.*

I try to smile, but my mouth does a weird twisty thing, so I gaze around instead. His room is a mess, but the walls and ceiling are covered with an elaborate, shadowy mural, full of people and blood and a horse with wings.

"Wow," I say. "Did you do this?"

"Yeah," he says. A scruffy-looking dog lies beside him, watching me.

"That's the sick dog?" It's totally inane, and I wouldn't blame him if he said, "No, it's a porcupine dressed up like a mangy mutt who looks like he fought with a pair of garden shears and lost."

"My brother likes to get her drunk and watch her fall down the stairs," he says and yawns.

"Oh." Because what else is there to say?

He swings his legs over the side of the bed and stands in one smooth movement. He walks to me and I watch the rise and fall of his chest until I finally find the courage to look up into his eyes.

"I'm glad you came," he says in a quiet voice, and something trills inside me like a happy songbird. We stand so close that for a long, searing moment I think he's going to kiss me.

Then he steps back.

"Come on, we're late," he says. He drops a gentle pat on the dog's head, and then grabs a black jacket and a bulging backpack off the floor.

"Late? Where are we going?" I follow him to the door.

"Bombing," he says, throwing me a grin over his shoulder. *Bombing?*

Like that explains freaking anything, but I'm all in, and I have a pretty good idea he knows it.

Chapter Seven

Alia

My hijab flutters uneasily around my head as I rush out through our building's mosaic-tiled lobby. I'm fleeing my mother and all her words that make me feel small and unsure. Her doubt makes me wonder if I have changed as much as I think I have. But how will I know unless she lets me try?

"*Damn*, girl," Ridwan says when he sees me. He's lounging on the steps by the front door in his trifecta of plaid boxers, blue gym shorts, and a larger pair of orange baggy shorts, topped with an oversized Dodgers jersey. "I was laying bets with myself if you were going to make it out alive."

"She is such a pain," I say. "Why doesn't she go after you? You're the one who got drunk last summer, and you're always coming home late."

"Unh-unh, we're not hating on Ridwan. This is all about

you, little sister. You're the one who got caught smoking pot yesterday—"

"I was not—"

"And ran away for like two weeks last year—"

"Two days—"

"I'm just saying you give her a lot to worry about." Ridwan stares at me seriously. My brother takes after my father, slim and handsome in an unassuming aw-shucks-you-think-I'm-cute? kind of way, and laid-back to the point that I think I could set his shoes on fire and his only reaction would be a mild "Damn, girl." He prefers to slide under the radar, which is why he goes by Ricky at school, and a lot of people think he's Hispanic. I know he's got a new girlfriend, a pretty Filipino girl with long black hair and a swaying walk who my parents do *not* know about.

"I don't mean to," I say. "I'm just trying to . . ." I don't even know how to finish the sentence. Survive? It's like someone put me down in a jungle with nothing but the clothes on my back. That's how I feel most days.

"You'll get through it," he says. "Just, maybe, chill out every once in a while, okay?" Ridwan grins, a quick flash of white teeth, and punches my arm.

"Ow!"

"You're such a girl," he says. "Since you've gone all native, do you want me to take you to school, or are you good?"

He's supposed to ride the subway with me to my school, even though we pass the stop for his school on the way and he has to leave early to go with me. He's only a year older, but my parents have always acted like he's my BIG brother, with capital letters. They expect him to protect me, like someone is going to throw me down on the subway and Ridwan is going to fight for my honor. We both get a big laugh out of that.

"I'm fine," I say.

"Suit yourself," he says. "Let me know if anyone gives you a hard time. I'll take 'em out for you."

"Thanks, Ridwan," I say.

He saunters off while I try to fix my scarf. After a minute of struggling, I screech and throw the pin on the pavement and stomp on it.

"Alia?" a voice says behind me, and someone giggles.

"What?" I snap, and snatch the pin off the ground. It's bent and useless, and of course I didn't think to bring another one.

I turn to find two girls standing behind me. Tanjia, with her pretty green eyes, neat hijab, and stylish clothes, and Kaitlin, in an adorable sundress with big yellow flowers that matches her mop of curly blond hair.

"Problems?" Tanjia laughs again, but not in a mean way. Her dad is from Trinidad, and her mother is American, and she always knows exactly what she is doing and where she is going. She's one of the hijabi girls I met at camp, and we've become pretty good friends.

"What does it look like?" I retort, and then smile sheepishly.

"Hey, Alia, did you have a fight with a scarf and lose?" Kaitlin grins. She is one of Tanjia's best friends, which is how I met her.

"Here, let me." Tanjia pulls a pin out of her purse. She puts it in her teeth and pulls the scarf tight around my face over the green headband I'm wearing to keep the silky fabric from slipping too much.

"Say 'ohhhh,'" she commands, her voice muffled by the pin.

I open my mouth in an O, feeling like an idiot, and she wraps the long end around my chin and over my head and pins the scarf by my ear.

"There," she says. "I tried not to do it *too* tight, 'cause you don't want a hijab headache your first day."

"Thanks, Tanjia," I say.

"So today's the day?" Kaitlin says, eyeing me and nodding approvingly. "Accessories are rocking, girl."

"Today's the day, and I think I picked the worst day *ever* to wear it. Ayah was so upset about what happened yesterday he barely noticed, and my mother thought I was wearing it for the sole purpose of pissing her off. And no one even mentioned going shopping!" I wail and they both laugh.

"I want to commemorate the moment," Kaitlin says, pulling a camera out of her bag. "The day of the scarf. Smile!"

"I don't want to smile," I say, and then Tanjia tickles me and I start laughing and Kaitlin snaps the picture.

"You'll burn it if it sucks, right?" I say.

"Okay, diva. But, yes, I cross my heart to burn it if it sucks." Kaitlin mouths *no I won't* to Tanjia.

"Come on, you're late," Tanjia says.

We link arms and head off down the sidewalk toward the Borough Hall station, the early September sun pouring down on our heads. None of us go to the same school, but we've been walking together to the subway every morning since classes began.

"What did they decide?" Tanjia cuts to the chase. We had a marathon phone session last night, me curled up with the cordless in my bedroom, long after I was supposed to be asleep, dissecting the argument with my parents about Carla and the joint, and talking about whether I really had the guts to start wearing the hijab.

"At least they're not using the whole joint thing as an excuse to make me switch schools, but they've nixed the NYU program," I say gloomily.

"Oh, girl, I'm so sorry." Tanjia squeezes my arm in sympathy.

"So, Alia, when are we going to see the next installment of Lia? I'm jonesing for my favorite Muslim American superhero," Kaitlin says, trying to cheer me up.

"Just because you don't get to go to the NYU program doesn't mean you have to give up on Lia," Tanjia says.

"Your fans are not patient. You left us hanging with Lia's mom stuck in the Arctic ice and Lia trying to decide whether she was going to rescue her or save the world from the Evil Mad Doctor," Kaitlin says encouragingly.

"She's still deciding," I say, thinking of the crumpled-up pieces of paper covered with sketches piled in my trash can.

"At least you wore the scarf today," Tanjia says. "That counts for something."

"I think you guys are brave. I'd be scared what people would say," Kaitlin says. "I get worried sometimes when I wear a new pair of shoes."

"Listening to what ignorant people say is like listening to a dog fart," Tanjia says. "You ignore it and hope it'll go away."

"Sure, for *you*," Kaitlin says. "But it's like people see a woman in a scarf and think she's all repressed or something, and believe me, I've known you both long enough to know that it's *not* the case." She laughs. "So, so not the case."

"I think she's calling us opinionated loudmouths," Tanjia says to me.

"That's what I heard," I agree. I spot a street vendor. "Caffeine! I've *got* to have caffeine."

I buy a coffee, waiting impatiently as the man slowly puts my five in his money belt and fumbles for change. The *New York Times* is lying on the counter, and I glance at the lead story about the mayoral race, and then skim the story about school dress codes, highlighted with a picture of a schoolgirl sporting a bare stomach.

How would you like it if I went to school like that, *Mama?*

All of a sudden, it hits me what day it is.

"Oh no." I clutch my change and steaming cup of coffee as I turn back to Tanjia and Kaitlin. "I have gym today. I totally forgot. And I have *no* clothes."

Some girls hate gym, but I love running and I'm pretty coordinated, so I didn't want to skip it, and I didn't want to get into trouble either for not dressing out.

"Maybe you can call your mom from school and have her bring your gym clothes during her lunch break," Kaitlin says.

"Sure, okay, *not* going to happen." I pull away from them. "I'm going to go back and get my stuff."

Tanjia frowns. "You'll be late." She is always on time, wherever she goes, and she doesn't get why I'm always five minutes late to everything in my life.

"Not if I hurry," I say. "I can't afford to get in trouble today, not with the whole joint thing hanging over my head."

We say our good-byes, and Tanjia calls, "Good luck!" as I head back down the wide sidewalk toward my building.

Chapter Eight

Jesse

Nick and I walk in silence to his car, snow crunching under our feet, and I'm wishing I had the nerve to grab his hand, wanting to feel his warm fingers on my cold ones.

Nick nods at an old beater, and I get in, hugging my arms to me in the icy interior.

"Your brother's dead, huh?" he says after he pulls out onto the road.

People ask about Travis sometimes, usually around 9/11 when the yearly article about him in the local paper comes out, but it's always with a note of awe, as if somehow having a brother who died on 9/11 makes me special.

I think about my mother and the wax-covered birthday cake, and shiver.

"Yes, he's dead," I answer.

"I wish mine was," he says, and I look at him in surprise, because this is not the way these conversations usually go, but he doesn't say anything else.

A few minutes later, Nick pulls the car off the road under some trees, and we walk toward the baseball fields. Two figures step out of the darkness.

"What's up, brother?" a guy says, coming up to Nick and giving him a fist bump.

"Dave, Jesse. Jesse, Dave," Nick introduces us briefly, the cold vapor of his breath fogging the space between us.

Dave is shorter than me, muscular and scrappy like a wrestler. He looks familiar, and as he turns to flick out a cigarette, I see in the dim light that he's wearing an oversized camouflage coat, the name "Tucker" sewed onto the front of it.

Tucker. Craig Tucker. Three or four years ago Craig Tucker came home from Afghanistan with only one leg. I remember now that Dave's his brother. He and I share something then, a brother who makes us memorable for all the wrong reasons.

We nod at each other without speaking.

"You know Hailey?" I realize with a small shock that the other shadowy person is Hailey Brinson. Hook-Up-Hailey, who reportedly has a thing for Nick.

What the . . . ?

Hailey comes slowly over to us. She is all wavy blue-black hair and dark eyeliner and breasts. They are roughly the size of the Grand Tetons and are on display in a low-cut tank top barely covered by a flannel shirt, despite the cold.

"Hey," she says, and her voice is unenthused.

"Hey." My voice is equally unenthused.

"She's coming with us?" Dave nods at me. He doesn't seem unfriendly, just sort of surprised.

Nick seems completely unaware of any awkwardness. "Yeah, she's coming with us."

Hailey gives me a measured stare, shakes her head, and looks away.

"Let's start at the bathroom. They've already buffed us out from last time," Nick says. "Jesse, be our lookout, okay?"

I go where I'm told, though I have no idea what I'm supposed to be looking out for. Shooting stars? Clowns doing magic tricks? An exploding bathroom?

The park is empty, and I stand under a tree. Nick, Dave, and Hailey are in the shadows near the restroom, and I hear bags unzipping, and then the unmistakable *shk-shk-shk* of a can being shaken rapidly. A few moments later I smell paint.

I get it now, and my palms go sweaty. I look across the baseball field, blanketed in snow, but I don't see anyone. Cars are moving on a nearby street, and I watch them, hoping one doesn't turn into the park, police lights flashing.

I've never done anything illegal in my life. I've always been the good kid, the take-up-as-small-a-space-as-possible kid. What have I got myself into?

It's over in a couple of minutes. The smell of paint fades, and I can hear bags being zipped back up.

"Wanna see?" Nick calls softly, and I go toward the back of the restroom.

A word in big, black bubble letters covers the side of the building. It's dark, so it takes me a minute to get it.

NOTHING

Just like Nick's tattoo.

"What does it mean?" I ask.

"Mean? It's our tag. It's our name. Haven't you seen it before?"

I shake my head. I'd noticed some graffiti here and there, but I'd never paid much attention to it. The scrawled words were usually cleaned up by the store owner by the next day, something ephemeral and loud, but quickly silenced.

Nick seems disappointed. "That's why we're bombing tonight," he says. "The goal is to do as many tags as we can. Eventually they'll *have* to notice."

~

Nick has it down to a science, so it takes him only a few minutes to do each tag. Hailey and Dave carry the paint, I act as lookout, and Nick does the tag, writing "Nothing" over and over again, on the side of a bank, a bus, on the sides of closed shops. Behind a Mobil gas station, I watch him. He's so intense, his teeth indenting his lower lip as he concentrates on the long, sure strokes. I am imagining him focused on me like that when a car pulls into the parking lot.

"Go, go, go!" Dave yells, and he and Hailey grab the bags and take off. Nick stays a moment longer to finish the tag, and then grabs my hand. He pulls me down an alley toward a fence at the far end, and we both duck to avoid a window AC hanging precariously out a first-story window.

"Hey! Hey!" someone yells, and I can hear the sound of heavy footsteps.

Nick and I hit the fence together with a clatter of squealing metal. Dave has already made it to the top and leaps down. Hailey is having more trouble, making mewling sounds as she climbs. I swarm up the fence, Nick right behind me. I stop and look down at Hailey. Her face is panicky and pale as she stares up at me, and I reach my hand toward her. She hesitates a moment.

"I'm so tired of you kids!" someone yells from behind us. "I'm calling the cops and you're going to PAY!"

Hailey grabs my hand and I pull her to the top of the fence and we jump together. I land lightly, feeling a thrill of something unexplainable and addictive. We head down the road, and I hear the guy chasing us hit the fence and a dog barking frantically. I put on another burst of speed.

Nick is laughing as he runs.

We duck down another back street and eventually emerge onto Main Street. Music blasts out of a coffeehouse hosting open-mic night, and a group of college kids tumble out like big colorful turtles in their heavy coats.

"Hell *yeah*." Nick grabs my hand and pulls me close as we climb the steep hill. I can't tell whether he's doing it because he wants to seem like a couple of kids just looking for a bar or because he wants to be that close to me.

A black-and-white cop car cruises by, and slows near us. I hold my breath, and Nick runs his hand up my back and into my hair. He pulls my head over and gives me a casual kiss, but it's enough to make sparks shudder through me.

He doesn't seem to notice.

"Still watching?" he says out of the corner of his mouth to Dave.

"Nah, he's gone," Dave says, glancing over his shoulder.

Nick doesn't let me go though, and I snuggle close to his side as we walk up the steep sidewalk. I see Hailey's face, and for a moment I feel sorry for her. Then Nick pulls me in for another kiss, and this one is longer. My head is swimming when he lets me go and keeps walking.

"Where are we going to hit next?" he says.

∽

Emi and Teeny are in A lunch block with me. I slide into the seat across from them with my tray of chicken bites, even though it's barely 11 a.m., and I'm not even remotely hungry. I'm still jittery from last night, but I force myself to open my milk with steady hands. Then I realize they are both staring at me.

"What?" I say, feeling guilty and buzzy at the same time.

"You look . . . weird," Teeny says. She flips her hair behind her shoulders and leans in. "So, spill. I texted you like fifteen times last night during Bible study, and you never said peep back."

"I did too," Emi says sourly. "I wanted to know if you got the answer to number fifteen on our Statistics homework."

"I wanted to know if you made out with Nick Roberts," Teeny says, and grins at me. "I'm going to take a wild guess and say yes."

"Maybe," I say, but my smile gives it away.

"What did you do? Did you go anywhere?" Teeny asks.

"Did you get the answer to number fifteen?" Emi says.

Teeny and I stare at her and burst into laughter.

"What?" she asks defensively. "Statistics is next block."

"We just . . . hung out," I say, because it feels disloyal to talk about the bombing run that put the word "Nothing" on sixteen different buildings last night. And while Teeny is pretty open-minded, she is really only a good girl who pretends to be bad. I know she would be shocked. And Emi . . . Emi would never understand.

I should be shocked too, but for some reason I'm not. The thrum of illicit excitement still courses through me.

"Hung all over each other is more like it," Teeny says with a smirk. "Is he a good kisser?"

"Um . . . *yes.*"

Teeny starts to laugh, then glances up over my shoulder, her eyes widening.

I feel a hand on my shoulder and turn to see Nick standing behind me.

"Do you want to eat with us?" he asks, looking adorably uncomfortable.

I throw a glance at Teeny and Emi. "You guys want to come?" Something like pleading creeps into my voice, because I know what they're going to say. It feels like a moment when you think, *I bet I can beat that train* or *That dog looks friendly*, but Nick is looking at me with those eyes that seem to see the small, scared part of me that doesn't want to feel that way anymore.

"No, you go on, girl," Teeny says, eyeing Nick narrowly.

I get up and take my tray. "I'll see you in Statistics," I say to Emi.

"Okay," she says, and mouths *be careful*, but it's too late.

Nick and I don't talk as we walk to the other side of the cafeteria to where Dave is sitting. I don't know whether Hailey is in this lunch block or not, but she's nowhere to be seen. In the fluorescent lights of the cafeteria, Dave has obvious zits and his gray "Two Time World War Champs" T-shirt is stained and straining across his broad chest.

Nick, on the other hand, looks just as good as the laughing boy I remember from last night, the silver ring in his eyebrow flashing, the smell of paint still on his hands.

"Okay, so what I want to know," Dave says as I sit down, "is where did you learn to climb like that? You went up that fence like it was nothing."

"I climb," I say. "You know, the Gunks and stuff? My dad

has owned the climbing shop for like thirty years, and I've been climbing since I was a kid."

"You must really be into it," Dave says. "I've gone out a couple of times, but it was never my thing."

"I'm pretty into it," I agree, though it's a far cry from how I really feel about climbing. It's the best thing in the world.

"I think she did good last night," Nick says, sneaking one of my chicken bites.

"You going to help get us some paint?" Dave asks.

"What?"

"We have to be careful about the paint," Nick explains. "We can't just go down to the hardware store and buy a case. So we either find someone to buy it for us, or steal it." Nick watches for my reaction, and I carefully keep my face blank. "She'll help us get paint," he says to Dave.

I nod, because of course I will, and he knows it. I'm blowing up the box, and it feels dangerous, and wonderful, and completely necessary.

"Hailey is not going to like it," Dave says.

"Hailey's just going to have to deal," Nick says. "Jesse's part of the crew now."

Chapter Nine

Alia

As I walk back toward my building, the trees sway in the light breeze, occasionally sending down a single gold leaf or a sprinkle of drops left over from last night's rain.

I walk slowly, stepping aside to let a group of clean-cut Jehovah Witnesses pass. Unless I want to run into my mother again, I'll have to wait until she leaves for her office. A part of me whispers, *Lia wouldn't be hiding down the road from her building. Lia would breeze in and face her mother with her head held high.*

As if on cue, my mother comes out of our building. She's talking on her cell, and she balances it against her ear with her shoulder as she stops under the green awning and fusses with her bag.

She has to pass me to get to her office, and I dive between

two parked cars and crouch down. I wish I had Lia's camouflage burqa; I'd just drape the voluminous folds of the cloak
around me and I'd magically fade into the car behind me.

I hold my breath as my mother gets closer and duck my
head. Mama's almost even with me, but she's so caught up
in her conversation—I wonder which auntie she decided to
call to complain about me—she's not paying attention to
anything else. She almost steps in front of a cab, and then
steps back onto the curb, waiting for the morning traffic to
lighten up so she can cross the street.

She's past my hiding place, so unless she turns around
she won't see me. I can hear her though, her low, musical
voice agitated as she punctuates each word with a quick jab
of her hand.

"That's what I told her, Maysan, but did she listen? Of
course not."

Maysan. One of my aunties from California. She's my
mother's best friend, with an easy smile, long brown hair, and
beautiful eyes. Not actually a relative, but one of the big circle
of aunties and uncles that make up my extended family.

I was fifteen when Mama landed her dream job in Brooklyn
as an immigration lawyer. Dad is a computer whiz, so he
can find a job anywhere, and I remember long conversations
between them on our sunny porch, my mother talking fast,
her hands flying, and my father nodding, saying, "Asmara, if
you need this, we will go." So it was *her* fault that we moved
here, so far away from everybody we knew and loved.

After we moved, I began hanging around Carla Sanchez and her girls, and Mama and I went from not fighting, ever, to having these epic blowouts that blew up the walls of our apartment.

Mama glances at the traffic and looks down at her watch. "I just keep thinking of her running away last year, Maysan," she says, and really? *Really?* Why does her voice suddenly sound watery, as if she's trying not to cry?

When Mike Stanley asked me out near the end of my sophomore year, I made the big mistake of telling my parents, instead of making up some fake story like Carla told me to do. I don't know why I thought they would say yes, maybe because they'd never made a big deal about me not dating before. It was just understood that I wouldn't. Things spiraled out of control, and I fled to Carla's for two nights. But I learned my lesson, I came home, and *why does it sound like she's about to cry?*

My mother's voice fades as she heads across the street. I remain crouching between the cars, knowing it's safe to go back to the apartment to get my gym clothes but suddenly wanting to hear what else my mother has to say about me. So many of the words lately have been brutal and hard; hearing her talk about me in that soft voice felt like peering into a secret part of her that has been closed to me for a long time.

I stand and watch my mother, a short, determined woman even in heels, her head held high, disappear down the street.

Part of me wants to run after her, give her a hug, tell her I'm sorry.

Sorry for what, though?

I mean, I'm sorry for running away, but I've apologized for that over and over again.

Now it seems like I should be apologizing just for being Alia.

Instead of going after my mother, I throw my half-empty coffee cup away and head for home.

◠

Our corner apartment is in an old prewar building, full of high ceilings and pretty decorative molding, and stacked with colorful paintings. It's smaller than where we lived in LA, but I love being able to go up to the roof. Sometimes my father will come up when he gets home from work, and we'll stand in the soft silence, taking in all those buildings. My father would breathe "Allahu Akbar" as the moon slipped into view, and I would slide my hand into his.

In my room, I gather my clothes and tennis shoes, already dreading the conversation with my new gym teacher about why I can't wear the issued shorts and T-shirt. Wearing the hijab full time means that I will also be wearing clothes that cover up my chest, arms, and legs, at least while I'm in public. I sigh as I look at my closet full of cute short-sleeved tops.

The end of my scarf catches on the corner of the desk, pulling it across my face. I blow out in exasperation, the silky material puffing away from my mouth, and try to fix it. I wish Nenek were here to help me with it.

I wonder what my grandmother would think of me today. I miss her warm hugs, sweetly pragmatic wisdom, and bakso soup, full of golf-ball-sized meatballs and garnished with fresh shallots and boiled egg. Most of all, I miss her love, which is big enough to embrace me and all my mistakes. It's not that I think my parents don't love me, no matter how many mistakes I make, but it's their job to teach, to judge, to correct. I know this because they've told me enough times.

My grandmother's job is just to love.

I go into the kitchen and pick up the phone, dialing the familiar number.

"Nenek?"

"Lala!" my grandmother says, and I feel her love for me flooding through the telephone line. I realize belatedly that it must be super early in California, but she sounds wide awake.

"I decided to wear the scarf today, Nenek."

I imagine her sitting in her cozy kitchen, her round, wrinkly face framed by a scarf the color of sea foam. I used to be so embarrassed walking with her when I was a kid. Not that anyone seemed to pay any attention to her scarf, but I didn't understand why she wanted to look different from everyone else, why she wanted to stand out.

Now I understood. Because I *am* different, but the same, and it's all mixed up in my head.

"I am proud of you," Nenek says. "I know it can be a very hard decision."

"Were you mad when Mama decided not to wear it?" I ask, settling my butt against the edge of the counter and twirling the phone cord through my fingers.

"Mad?" she asks and laughs, melodic and tinny with distance. "Why would I be angry about a choice that was your mother's alone?" She is silent for a moment. "I suppose," she says, "in some ways it felt as if she was letting her culture slip away like sand through her fingers. But I understood. And she is a good Muslim, and that is what matters."

I know that there are some women who believe that wearing the scarf is their duty, that God asks it of them. There are also Muslim women like my mother who think that wearing the hijab is a personal choice, and that the tradition of covering a woman's hair is a cultural interpretation of the Quran. It's all pretty confused in my head, and I really don't know what to believe. But I think wearing it will make me a better person, and that's what I want desperately right now.

"Everybody is so mad at me," I say softly as I wind the cord so tight around my hand that the tips of my fingers turn white.

"And why is that?"

I tell her what happened with Carla yesterday, and she lets me talk, lets me tell my side of the story, and when I am done she doesn't start talking right away. I'm thinking about how my grandfather used to carve masks out of wood. When I was younger I would try on the different masks, royally nodding as Princess Candra Kirana, or clowning around as a jester in a half mask with a big black mustache. In the end though, I always had to go back to being ordinary Alia.

"I have never told you the story of how I came to be in America," my grandmother says after a moment.

I know my family is from Indonesia, and that my grandmother and grandfather had come here when my mother was just a kid, and that my father and mother married soon after college. I didn't realize that there was more to the story than that.

"The country we come from is beautiful," Nenek says, "more beautiful than I can put into words. Thousands of islands strung like pearls on a necklace, pink petals floating in the rain puddles, and the water touches the sky. Your mother was only four years old when everything went bad. There was a coup, and your grandfather was thought to be a sympathizer. We had to go into hiding. Thousands of people died, and the streets ran with blood. Literally, I am saying. Your mother wandered out one morning before I was awake, and when I finally found her, her feet were red with the blood of the people who had been murdered and left in the street. I scrubbed and scrubbed them, but even when they were pink and clean, I cried, because I knew it would never come off.

"Your grandfather was able to bring us to America, and I remember walking around that first year feeling like I was in a dream. Everything was so normal, while in my home country, people, my friends and family, were still dying. I felt guilty for living in peace. It was hard adjusting at first. I could not speak English, and everything was so different here. But I learned the language, and eventually your mother was old enough to go to college, and we were so proud. A lawyer! Imagine! We wanted to make sure she never felt powerless, that she had a secure place in this country."

We are both quiet after she stops speaking. It's a horrible story, and I almost want to cry thinking about my mother's little-girl feet covered in blood. I can't imagine living in a place where things like that happened. I have only been to Indonesia once, and it *is* a beautiful country, but who would I be if my grandparents hadn't come to America? Those teenage girls I saw in the streets of Jakarta seemed so different from me.

But were they really?

"I think you need to understand where you came from, that these bad things that happened have shaped your parents. Remember, Lala, that to love is to be frightened every minute of every day."

"I don't know what they expect from me! I don't *want* to be a lawyer like Mama, and I think I might want to write comic books, but that won't ever be good enough for them."

"You are afraid too, Lala. You are afraid of disappointing your parents, but you cannot let fear keep you from being the person you need to be."

We sit in the rich, light-filled silence for a moment, thousands of miles apart but still in the same place.

"I need to get to school, Nenek," I say eventually.

"Yes," she says. "What I wanted to say is this: you are stronger than you think you are. We all are."

"I've made so many mistakes, Nenek. I'm not sure my parents will ever be able to forgive me," I say.

"Of course they will forgive. It's harder to forget though. I love you very, very much, Lala. So do your mother and father."

Chapter Ten

Jesse

I'm in the shed, searching for my boots and ice tools when I find the photo album, hidden under a pile of tarps on the top shelf.

My phone rings, and I dig it out of my pocket.

"Hey." I balance the phone between my ear and my shoulder as I lift the silver-covered album down from the shelf, wondering why it's here.

"What are you doing today?" Nick asks.

"I told you, remember? I'm going climbing. Want to come?"

He laughs. "I was thinking more like huddling up under a blanket with you and watching dirty movies. It's freaking cold outside."

"I know," I say. "Isn't it great?" I lean my hip against the wall and listen to Nick laugh, low and deep. I like it when he laughs. We've been inseparable since the night I went out bombing with him a month ago. It all happened so fast, and I'm not even really sure how we became Nick-and-Jesse so quickly, or Nessie, as Teeny called us when we first started going out. I suppose running from the cops on your first date has a way of bonding people.

I flick open the album with one finger.

Nick says something else, but I'm no longer listening.

A picture of my brother Travis stares up at me.

"All right," I say to Nick, having no idea what I'm agreeing to, but suddenly needing to get off the phone. "I'll call you when I get back, okay?"

I slip the phone back in my pocket and take the album to the workbench.

The first pages are the news articles that our local paper does every year on the anniversary of 9/11. They all say the same thing, that Travis was eighteen when he died in the attacks on the World Trade Center, that he was a recent graduate of our town's high school, and that he played in a popular local band. There's not much else, because as far as I know my parents never talk to the reporter when she calls every year. The articles always show the same sly-eyed graduation photo of Travis in a tux, like it is the only picture ever taken of him.

No one in my family ever says much about Travis. Hank used to talk about him some, before he decided to drop an arsenal of bombshells all over Christmas three years ago, and the resulting Dad-sized explosion blasted him out of our lives for good. But he only talked about Travis as a big brother, funny stories like the time Travis chased Hank so high up a tree they had to call the fire department to get him down, or how they used to play football with me when I was a little kid, and *I* was the football. But he never said a word about what happened to Travis on 9/11.

As far as I know, no one knows what Travis was doing in the towers that day. It's never mentioned in the articles that I secretly read every year, and once I heard my mom on the phone with a friend saying "What on earth was he doing there? Why was he *there*?" And then she'd started crying, and I'd shut the door gently without her seeing me. I pretended I'd never heard her, and how effed up is that? Except in my house it was totally normal.

I flip through a few more pages and see that every one of the yearly articles about Travis has been neatly cut out and painstakingly glued into the album.

I think about my mom and Travis's birthday cake and know that the album must be hers. But why has she hidden the album away? Who is she hiding it from?

Me? My dad? *Why?*

I hear the back door to the shop bang open, and my mom's voice calls, "Jesse?"

I hurriedly shove the album back where I found it and grab my boots and ice tools.

∾

I'm standing at the base of the frozen waterfall with a couple of other kids from our climbing club. I try to pay attention to Drew, the young hippy-dippy adjunct professor who organizes our climbs, but my thoughts keep wandering back to the photo album in the shed. It's bugging me, like an unsolvable problem your physics teacher gave you solely to amuse himself. I wish I'd had time to go through more of the album.

"This is Adam," Drew says as a new guy walks up. "I climbed with him last weekend, and he knows his stuff."

"Morning," the guy says easily and nods at all of us.

Holy heck, he's gorgeous. Dark, wavy hair that curls across his forehead and over his collar, a skim of beard on his lips, chin, and cheeks, and eyes so blue it's like they swallowed the sky whole.

Not that I'm noticing.

"Jesse, why don't you and Adam pair up? Neither of you has a partner here today," Drew is saying.

The guy, Adam, catches sight of me and for a moment his face goes still. Then the smile is back and he eyes me lazily.

"Think she can keep up?" he says to Drew as if I'm not standing right-freaking-there.

"Um . . . ," I say, which is my way of saying *anytime, anywhere, you cocky jerk.*

"She's good," Drew says. "You guys will make beautiful mountain music together."

Adam laughs, and I stand there with my face flaming as Drew keeps talking.

"It's warmed up a tad over the past couple of days, so the ice is maybe sketchy—"

"Ya think?" a guy named Gary says, because he broke through the ice on the creek bed on the way in and is soaked up to his knees.

"Yeah, well, here's your sign," Drew says, unfazed. "It's not like any of us are going to win any Darwin awards, right?"

We all laugh, drunk on the strong morning air and joy of it all, because climbing waterfalls is not exactly the safest thing in the world to do. We do it because it's so damn hard to stay on the ground during the cold winter months when it's tough to climb rock.

"There are six pitches, topped with ledges, so it's like six short climbs," Drew continues. "The last one is the crux, so save up some energy. Double up on your screws, and we'll see you at the top."

I watch Adam walk toward me, his gear *clink-clink-clinking* on his belt, crampons—metal spikes on his climbing boots— scuffing in the snow. I try not to notice the assured lilt of his walk, and instead assess his rack. Ice tools, which are basically skinny axes, screws—Black Diamond and all sizes—and no Grigri. Not a gym rat then, and his gear appears extensive and well used, not bought yesterday.

"Hey," he says.

Up close I see he's even cuter than I first thought, which is like saying the sun *can* get hotter, or the ocean deeper, or reality shows more annoying.

"Hey," I say, forcing myself to look away from him and up at the first step of the frozen fall above us. Sheets of white ice cascade down over rocks and a fallen tree, and the ice is puffy like cauliflower in spots, stringy in others, and in some places just plain slick. I've always wanted to watch a waterfall thaw. Does it happen all at once, the rushing water just gushing down all of a sudden, or does it happen slowly, one molecule at a time?

I look back at the guy standing next to me. Around us, partners are talking pitches and deciding who will lead.

"You done this before?" I ask abruptly.

"Looks like no big deal." White, white teeth flash against his tanned face, and his black hair rustles in the cold wind. He radiates confidence, sharp and bright.

"I don't know where you're from—" I begin.

"Michigan. Born in New York, but we left when I was three." His face shuts down for a quick, slicing moment, and I can tell there's something more there, but I can't imagine what it could be to make him appear so closed-for-business all of a sudden. "My dad travels a lot though, and I go with him. I've climbed in Utah, Wyoming, and Colorado," he says, all affable again, and I wonder if I imagined that beat of anger.

He's named a few of the best climbing states in the country, so he *should* know his stuff. I sigh. I don't like climbing with strangers. But the thing about climbing is that you need a partner, unless you're a show-off with a death wish, and since Maggie, the girl I usually climbed with, moved to Arizona, I've been left without a steady partner for months now.

"Okay, so maybe you've climbed some," I say. "All I meant is that some of the pitches here are harder than they look. So tell me honestly, can you do it?" Climbing is the one thing I can talk about without getting all clammed up. It's the one thing I know.

"Yes," he says, and grins widely. I get the feeling that he's trying not to laugh at me.

I resist the urge to smack him, hoping he's telling the truth.

"I'll lead," I announce. "I've climbed this before."

He shrugs. "No problem."

Nick would never let me lead. The traitorous thought slithers through my head and I slice it in two and bury the pieces.

"Okay." I turn away from him and check my gear. I step to the bottom of the falls, thinking about the best line to take and where I can set screws.

"Am I on belay?" I ask, looking back at Adam, who is pulling on a pair of heavier gloves, tucking his lighter climbing gloves in his pack at his feet. He has anchored himself with webbing to a nearby tree, which is probably overkill, but I'm glad to see he's being careful even if he is a cocky jerk.

"Belay on," he answers.

"Climbing," I say, kicking my crampons into the ice.

"Climb on," he answers.

∽

He surprises me by being just as good as me, if not better. Thoughts of the photo album and my brother are banished for the duration, because when I'm climbing I disappear into feeling, moving, doing, and there's no room for anything else.

We don't talk much, but after the first pitch we alternate leading until we reach an echoing amphitheater of ice right below the last fall. We've made good time, and other than Drew and his partner who have already disappeared up ahead of us, the rest of our group are below us, splashy beetles on the side of the ice.

"Easy as pie," Adam says just as we both hear an ominous rumbling.

"Are you trying to jinx us?" I smile though, the sheer exhilaration buzzing in my veins. "You should see the falls in the summer. It always feels strange to be here when they're frozen and you can't hear them, or feel that boom in your chest as the water hits the rocks. It's like they're holding their breath right now."

"Such a basic geological process like water flowing over rock creating something so *beautiful* that you feel it in your soul." He waves an arm at the falls, his eyes intense with nerd passion and I swallow a giggle.

"You're a rock geek, aren't you?" I ask. There are a lot of them here in the Gunks.

He grins. "Something like that. I'm going to work as an intern for a geology firm this summer. That's what I'm planning on majoring in."

"Knew it." I roll my eyes.

He shrugs. "My dad used to bring home rocks from all these places, and I got interested in rocks, mountains, the whole shebang. When you see a mountain, you either want to go around them, climb over them, or, I don't know, blow holes in the side of them." He laughs. "But the one thing you never can do is ignore them."

I look at him, feeling something unfurl in my chest.

Who is this boy who has the ability to say the words I feel but never can put into words?

I see he's watching me, the dimple flirting in his cheek. It flusters me, makes me feel guilty, makes me think of Nick. I look away and fumble in my pack for my water bottle.

"You ready?" I ask, after taking a gulp of water.

"Sure," he says.

Does he have a girlfriend? The thought pops out of nowhere, and I frown, because it's none of my business.

I've got to stop.

We're all business as we talk about who should lead, and lines to follow. I'm not as gung ho about leading this time, but when he arches an eyebrow at my hesitation, I grit my teeth and say, "I'll do it."

He smiles, and it's so sweet that I just want to stand and look at him. Or strangle him. One or the other.

I start up the final pillar, kicking the metal crampons of my boots into the ice and setting the thin ice tools. I stop for a moment when I hear a loud *crack* and watch a chunk of ice fall and crash onto the ground, rainbows of glittering snow puffing out like smoke.

"Okay?" I yell down at Adam, though he had known not to stand directly beneath me. When he nods I push myself up, using the ice tools as a grip.

About halfway to the top I realize I'm in trouble. My arms are shaking, and I'm seriously out of breath. I've been spending every free moment with Nick and haven't had time to work out, and the proof is in my rubbery, quavering arms. I clip into a screw, feeling the ice shift underneath me, and grab for my ice tool to steady myself. I'm breathing in big gasps, and I'm suddenly not sure I'm going to make it.

"Hey." Adam's voice floats from below me. "I've got you, okay? I won't let you fall. Just concentrate on the next move."

I put my forehead against the ice, feeling the rough, cold edges, and then I look back up at the top.

"You can do this, Jesse." It's the first time he's said my name, and something about the way he says it gives me the strength to kick in another foothold, and push myself up. Step by step, with Adam yelling encouragement, I make it to the top and collapse.

"You okay?"

"I'm okay!" I force myself to get up and secure an anchor for him.

He comes up, and it's like he *flows* up the mountain, like a waterfall going backward, and then he's at the top with me, and we're both laughing up at the sky, not thinking about anything but right here, right now.

Chapter Eleven

Alia

I'm almost running as I head toward the subway. I pass a group of kids being ushered along by a nanny pushing a stroller, and sidestep a deliveryman feeding boxes through a metal hatch onto a conveyor belt that slides deep into the bowels of a shop. I feel reckless and impatient, like I've left something important unfinished, and the permission slip crinkles in my pocket. It's a constant reminder of the dream that I am letting slip away.

Because it's my fault I did not make my parents hear me. I let so many opportunities pass when I could have told them what this NYU program means to me.

What can I do though? Both my father and my mother have said no, but if I don't turn the permission slip in today, then I won't be able to go to the NYU program. Maybe it's not the end of the world, but if I let them do this to me, what else will I let them talk me into? Will I wake up one day in college, studying to be a doctor or lawyer and wonder how I got there?

I drop an absentminded pat on the head of a coin-operated horse outside a shop. I remember there was one like it down the street from where we used to live in LA. I would beg Ayah to drop quarter after quarter into it and sit in the saddle and clutch the reins while it bounded up and down.

Ayah is the one I need to convince. As in-your-face as my mother is, she listens to my father. Like when I chose a creative arts high school, instead of one of the more academic ones, and my mother and I screamed and yelled for an entire week. Finally I went to Ayah and told him how much it meant to me. He somehow poured water all over my mother's raging inferno, and in the end I got to go to the school I wanted.

Ayah didn't listen to me this morning, but all of a sudden I don't want to give up.

Maybe he will listen, if I try one more time.

∽

I barely catch the crowded express train going to Manhattan. A girl, older than me, probably in college, gets on and stands across from me. She's dressed in jeans and a long-sleeved blouse, with a beautifully patterned purple scarf over her head. She catches my eye.

"*As-salaam alaikum,*" she says in Arabic, the universal

greeting among Muslims. Her voice is as American as my own.

Peace be upon you.

"*Wa alaikum as-salaam,*" I answer automatically.

And upon you be peace.

She nods at me in sisterly camaraderie, and I smile, feeling a small glow of warmth and acceptance. I sit back on the hard, plastic seat I was lucky to get this time of the morning as the train rocks back and forth. Pulling my notepad out of my bag, I sketch the girl in broad, quick strokes, capturing her slender face and the delicate edge of her scarf, and write the dialogue bubble above her head:

Lia, I want you to know that the entire world is counting on you. I know you can do it!

I finger my Hand of Fatimah amulet on its thin gold chain around my neck as I consider Lia's response to her newest fan. I sketch Lia slowly melting into the wall of the subway seat as she pulls on her camouflage burqa. I draw a cloud shape with smaller circles going down to Lia's head to indicate a thought bubble:

I wish I were as sure as she is that I can win this battle.

The train accelerates as it slides under the river, and I sit with the notepad in my lap, thinking about what I will say to Ayah.

I know he's worried about me making bad decisions. And really, after what I did, how can I blame him?

∽

My sophomore year, Mike Stanley sat behind me in my Humanities band, and he sailed paper airplanes with messages over my shoulder, saying stuff like: *My eyes are crossing. Are your eyes crossing?* and *I'm pretty sure it's possible to die of boredom.* It was funny, and I thought he was cute with his deep brown eyes and strong dancer's legs. Pretty soon he started walking with me after class. We talked on the phone, and I told myself we were just friends, that it was okay if we were just friends. Carla thought he was hot and said if I didn't grab him, she would. And then he asked me if I wanted to go see the new Pearl Harbor movie with him, and somehow I didn't just say no. Two hours before he was supposed to pick me up I went into the living room and told my parents.

"It's not a good idea, Lala," my father said, and at least he *sounded* sympathetic.

Mama just shook her head and said, "Have you lost your mind, Alia?"

That set me off, and before long Mama and I were trading words so fast it felt like we were in some kind of raging ping-pong game.

"You don't want me to be happy!" I yelled. "I hate it here, I want to be in LA, and you *don't care*! You want me to be miserable!"

"Don't be so dramatic, Alia," my mother said. "Of course we want you to be happy. It's because we want you to be happy that we are asking you to believe that we know what's best for you."

"How could you possibly know what will make me happy?"

Eventually my father intervened, telling me gently that faith was a road map to happiness, God willing, not a road-block to fun, and asked me to go to my room to calm down. I burned with embarrassment when I heard the door buzzer a while later, hating them, *hating them*, and wondering what they had told Mike when he showed up at our door.

Later that night, I packed a bag and snuck out while my parents were sleeping. It was wrong, it was stupid, but I'd felt so powerless. It felt like if I stayed there even one more night I would wake up as a puppet, dancing to my parents' commands. Carla's mom was out of town, so we had two glorious days of freedom, or at least that's how it seemed at the time.

The second night, Carla threw a party on the roof of her building. She lent me some clothes, and we giggled and laughed as we dragged chairs from her tiny apartment up two flights of stairs to the roof. I was trying not to think about my parents, who had called Carla over and over again. Every time she lied smoothly: "Oh gosh, how *terrible*, Mr. and Mrs. Susanto, but I haven't seen her!"

It was the first Saturday in June, and at first it was damp and foggy. The only lights we could see were the twinkling, colored strands of Christmas lights I'd helped Carla put up. A bunch of people were there, chilling and talking, and we watched as the damp fog rolled back and suddenly we could see the lights of the buildings around us, shining like stars on the ground. Carla cranked up the Beastie Boys' "No Sleep Till Brooklyn," and we all yelled the refrain at the top of our lungs.

I was standing at the edge of the roof when a paper airplane landed on the wall beside me. I knew who it was, even if I didn't see him arrive. Without turning around, I opened the note: *I missed you last night.*

I turned around and Mike was standing there, his hands in his pockets, wearing a tight blue T-shirt. He was so handsome I felt my pulse jump a little. Okay, a *lot.*

"Here," he said, and handed me a beer. "What happened last night?" He leaned up on the wall next to me, and I felt his warm closeness against my arm.

"What did my parents say?" I asked in a small voice, feeling so stupid.

"They were real nice, actually—wow, you look just like your mom, did you know that?—but they said there was some kind of misunderstanding, and that you couldn't go. I was hoping I'd see you here."

I looked down at the beer, and put it on the wall without drinking any.

"They are the *worst*," I said, and my voice was shaking. "They want me to act like some sort of, of *nun*, or something. It's like I'm in prison."

"That sucks," he said, and put his arm around me, drawing me close. I stiffened, but it felt so good that I leaned into him, smelling his cologne and the stuff he used in his hair. He took a sip of his beer, and we stood like that for a while, as our friends laughed and drank. It was almost the end of the school year, and even though we had finals coming up, it felt like summer was so close.

"Do you want one?" Mike asked as we watched Carla on Harry Mercado's lap chugging a purplish drink.

"No, I—" But he was already gone, and I immediately felt cold and alone. When he came back, he was holding two cups of the drink and handed one to me.

"Cheers," he said, tipping it back. I hesitated, and then I did it too. I was expecting it to taste terrible, but it didn't, just sweet and fruity. My parents didn't drink—most Muslims don't—and even though Carla and her crew did, I never had before.

"Watch out, it'll sneak up on you," Mike said. We sat on the wall together, and he put his arm around me. I was feeling warm, and somehow disconnected from myself. I found myself taking his hand, felt his strong fingers clasped over mine.

"You know I like you," he said in a quiet voice. I could smell the sweetness of the drink on his breath as he leaned down toward me, and his lips just grazed mine, soft and gentle.

I was so startled that for a moment I didn't react. Truthfully, I didn't want him to stop as waves of sensation slid through me whispering and hot. But then the wrongness of it crashed down on me, and oh no, *what was I doing?*

"No," I murmured, and tried to pull back, but he just drew me closer. His hands were slipping under my shirt, and I wasn't liking it anymore, because I really didn't know him that well, not really, and how could *this* be my first kiss, with some guy I barely knew? It wasn't supposed to be like this, and *why won't he stop?*

"No!" I cried, and finally got my hand free from his and pushed against his chest.

He blinked at me, fuzzy and bewildered. "Wha . . . ?" He was drunker than I had realized, and his expression took a moment to change from confused to angry.

"What the hell?" he said. "You wanted it. Don't act like you didn't. Come on, girl—" He tried to pull me back to him, and I struggled away from him.

"Stop it!" I said. "I told you *no*." I stood up, breathing hard and almost crying. There was another couple nearby, moaning and kissing, and I saw it was Mary Naradan and some guy from another school who I knew she just met tonight. Was that the kind of girl I was?

"I never pegged you for a tease," Mike said, his voice hard. "You hang out with Carla and her crew, so I *know* you can't be that uptight. So, what? I'm not good enough?"

"You don't understand," I said. "I wasn't trying to lead you on. I *wasn't*."

I'd been so caught up in the flirtation, I'd never really thought about where it was going. It's not like I didn't know what guys want; Carla and Mary and the others were always talking about how far they'd gone with what guy. *You really need to get it over with already, Alia.* But I didn't *want* to just get it over with. I wanted the guy that I was with to be important to me, and for my first kiss, my first *whatever*, to be special, with a guy who really loved me, and who I would marry.

"I'm Muslim," I said, though he already knew that. I was really saying it to myself, because, yes, I'm Muslim, but sometimes it was hard to be all the other things I wanted to be too. "This isn't right. None of it is." I gestured to the empty cups beside us, at him, at the party where girls and guys were hooking up in dark corners, or out in the open, not caring who saw them. "This isn't who I want to be," I said in a low voice.

"You could have fooled me," he said, and walked away without looking back.

Later that night, I was curled up on Carla's couch bed when I heard her come in. She was talking to someone, and she didn't see me when she opened the door. I watched as she reached up and kissed Mike, long and slow, pressing her body against his.

"Forget her," she said, slurring her words, and somehow I knew she was talking about me. "She's just a stupid girl who doesn't know what to do with a guy like you."

I sat up. "Stupid girl? I'm not the one stumbling drunk, Carla!"

I felt so hurt, so betrayed by both of them. In my mind,

I jumped out of bed and took a swinging kick at the two of them, driving them apart. The girl wasn't me, but a stronger, better version of me, who always knew the right thing to say and do. I imagined her blocked in a panel, eyes narrowed as she said, *"The best path is not always the easiest,"* which was something Ayah was always saying. My fingers itched to draw this superhero-me, who would never be sitting here silent, not knowing what to do.

For a moment Carla's eyes looked sorry, but Mike just stared at me, like I was nothing to him.

Without speaking, Carla pulled Mike into her mom's room, while I shook with anger and humiliation.

I went home to my parents, and they grounded me for the summer, and forbade me from seeing Carla. I didn't even care, because I didn't want to see her, or Mike, or any of them, ever again anyway.

I wasn't like that. I didn't know exactly what I *was*, but it wasn't that. That's what I thought about all summer, as I inked Lia, my new Muslim superhero, in panel after panel of frenzied world-saving activity. I went to camp and met the cool confidence that was Tanjia, and I began to see what I could be, if I tried.

∽

I'm still trying to formulate the perfect words that will make Ayah listen, to make him understand, as I change at Chambers Street for the local #1/9 and get out one stop later at the

Cortlandt Street station. I climb the narrow brick staircase and enter the light modern hall above. People are hurrying in all directions, and I sidestep a woman carrying a green-and-white Krispy Kreme Doughnuts box, and go through glass doors past a sign reading 1 World Trade Center.

The lobby is white marble, soaring windows, glass and metal. I stop next to a potted plant, feeling small all of a sudden as people hurry past me, their voices crisscrossing across the echoing space. I scratch my head, because my hijab is *itchy*. A guy in a suit standing on the balcony ringing the second floor points at me, and for a minute I think it's because of my scarf, but then he starts smiling and waving and a woman behind me calls, "I'll be right there."

Feeling silly, I bypass the line of employees swiping their ID cards at the turnstiles, and hurry over to the security line. The line moves in fits and starts, but thankfully, there aren't a whole lot of visitors this time of morning. When it's my turn, I give the guy in a blue blazer my school ID and best smile, and with some sweet-talking, he hands over a visitor pass card.

Then I go to stand with a crowd of people waiting for an express elevator to take me up to my father's offices, high up in the north tower.

Chapter Twelve

Jesse

The Monday after I climb with Adam, I head toward my locker, thinking about a plane flying toward the Twin Towers one ordinary morning. It makes me feel precarious, as if anything could happen at any time. Which tower was Travis in? The first tower hit, or the second? I've been thinking about him a lot since I found the photo album, and wondering why no one seems to know—or wants to talk about—what my brother was doing there.

I literally bowl into Adam as I turn a corner by my locker. He is talking to one of the basketball guys, and I see his eyes widen, but it's too late and I crash into him. I feel the soft musky wool of his sweater on my cheek as he catches me by the elbows.

"Sorry!" I say, my cheeks flaring a three-alarm fire. He

smiles, the dimple flashing in his cheek as I step back from him hurriedly.

"I thought . . . I thought you were in college. I've never seen you in school," I say.

"No, I just moved to town. My parents moved here last summer, and at first I wanted to finish at my old school so I stayed behind. But then it got boring being the hot, popular valedictorian"—he yawns dramatically—"so I figured, why not see how the other half lives?" He leans his arm up against the wall, and I try to ignore the shivers that race down my arms.

"Really?" I say. "Can you be any more conceited?"

He nods. "Yes. Yes, I can."

I swallow, because it would be so much easier if he didn't go to my school. Immediately, I think of Nick, and turn toward my locker, brushing against Adam by accident.

He steps back to give me room to work on my combination.

But even as I'm trying to ignore the tug of attraction between us, I wish I could ask Teeny about him. She would know all his vitals, like why he *really* changed schools so close to the end of his senior year; but there's a coolness between Teeny and me lately, a thin film of ice on our friendship which neither of us has been able to break. And it's not just Teeny. None of my friends are talking to me much, and I can't really blame them because I've been avoiding them too, mainly because I know if I tell them what's going on with Nick and all the tagging they'll tell me to stop.

"You're a pretty decent climber," Adam says. "Not on par with the awesomeness that are my own climbing skills, but close."

"I'm guessing when you were a kid you thought you were going to grow up to be Superman." I know I need to cut this, whatever it is, short because Nick will be here any minute.

"Naw. Spidey all the way. Have you seen that boy climb?"

"You're nuts."

"But I've managed to make you smile. Why don't you smile more?"

"Do I look like I'm smiling?"

"I see a sparkle, a twinkle of a smile, longing to escape."

My mouth twitches. "You need glasses."

"Smiling is good for the soul. Laughter is even better. Volcanoes feel so much better when they let it all out."

"Do I look like a volcano?" I ask, trying not to laugh.

"Yes, you do," he says, and I can't tell whether he's joking or not.

I glance over my shoulder. *Where is Nick?* He's usually here by now.

Adam looks at me curiously, picking up on my unease. "I . . . uh . . . I was thinking about going back out next weekend, if the cold snap holds. Do you, maybe, want to go?" His words stutter, which is such at odds with the confidence he usually wears like a bright neon sign that I glance up at him.

My gaze is trapped by the endless blue of his eyes, and I feel sparks like fireflies fluttering through my veins.

This is not good, I'm thinking, but I can't seem to look away. Neither, evidently, can he. We stand like that for a moment, until he finally backs up a step, his cheeks turning red.

"I can't." I stare down at the lock, which will *not* cooperate. I've already gone past my first number twice.

"Okay, then," he says finally. "I'll see you around."

"Okay, sure," I say, keeping my eyes on the lock.

He stands for a moment and then without a word, he turns and walks away.

"Who was that?" Nick comes up and snakes an arm around me.

"No one," I say.

∽

That night I sneak past my parents' bedroom, stopping for a moment as I hear the reassuring rumble of my father's snores, the slight murmuring of my mother. She hums when she sleeps, and sometimes it sounds like a lullaby. I wonder what baby she is singing to in her sleep. Travis, the dead child? Hank, the one who ran away? Or me, the one who is still right here?

I slip out of the apartment and down the interior stairs into the shop below, winding my way through the display cases and racks of coats and boots. The bells attached to the door jingle softly as I lock the door behind me.

Nick, on the steps outside the shop, stands when he

sees me. Without speaking, he pulls me in for a kiss. I relax against him, feeling my heartbeat slow as he rubs my back and drops gentle kisses on my jaw and neck. It's best when it's just him and me, like when we lie curled together on his couch and he talks in a soft voice about the graffiti business he wants to start, about his mother who left after getting hit one too many times, the fight he had with his brother that broke his collarbone. I talk too, about my parents and Travis, and the anger that seems to build and build inside me.

"It's just us tonight," he murmurs into my hair. My pulse skips, because it'll be more dangerous with just the two of us. Nick grabs his pack, and I follow him down the icy sidewalk. It's late, and the traffic on Main Street is light, the hiss of tires slow and sleepy in the wet spring snow.

Nick stops in front of Lila Danver's cheese shop, and I say, "Nick? Here?" because this is the first time we've ever done anything fronting Main Street. Even though there isn't a lot of traffic this time of night, there's still some. He starts unpacking his bag without answering.

Lately, he has been getting reckless, and it's scaring me how he's taking more and more chances. But I know he's frustrated that no one seems to be noticing our tags. At this point, we have painted "Nothing" on literally hundreds of buildings, and except for one small mention in the paper, and a few more police patrols, no one seems to care.

"Jesse, it'll be fine. Trust me."

I nod without speaking, hating that at this moment I

feel with Nick the same way I feel with my dad, like there is something I should say but don't.

I hand Nick the cans of paint, and keep watch as he starts the tag. He's halfway through when I see a car.

"Nick!"

He pulls me back into the shadows next to the doorway, and even though we are plainly visible if anyone looked, the car drives right past us.

"See?" Nick says. "We're invisible. No one sees us."

He's almost done when I see the cop car. It's cruising slow, like a shark, as it comes down the steep hill toward us.

"Cop!" I say, and Nick glances over his shoulder, and then back to his tag.

I stand for what feels like an eternity and then at least another week as the cop gets closer and Nick finishes the tag.

"Got it." Nick grabs his backpack and we run. A quick burst of a siren follows us, and I feel the burn of headlights on my back as the cop accelerates.

"He's going to catch us!" I yell, and Nick darts down a side street and across someone's lawn. I can hear the siren in earnest now. Nick ducks behind an old shed, pulling me down into the bushes with him.

I sit on the wet, squashy ground, and Nick draws me close, his arm around my shoulders.

"They'll have to notice us now," he says, and presses a quick kiss to my temple.

○∽

But they don't. By the next morning, a fresh coat of light yellow paint has obliterated Nick's tag. The cops must have woken up Mrs. Danver to tell her what we had done, and she painted over the "Nothing" by the glow of the streetlights.

Nick is so pissed that he's barely speaking to me, or anyone, and when Adam flashes a dimpled smile at me in the halls, I look away. I feel his puzzled stare long after I've walked off.

That afternoon when I get home, the shop is super busy and has been all day, according to Grill.

"I need help, Jesse," he says. "Your dad went upstairs for a liquid lunch, and I haven't seen him since. This is getting old."

"Let me get changed, and I'll come right back," I promise.

I walk up the stairs, making my feet as light as possible, but my heart sinks when I hear Dad screaming at the TV.

"Damn terrorists! We ought to nuke those towel heads back to the Stone Age!" he yells as I come into the kitchen. "See what they're doing? That's what they want to do to every one of us." Dad doesn't bother to look at me, his eyes trained on the TV.

It's another beheading. I see the man in an orange jumpsuit on his knees, a man in black standing behind him with a sword.

My stomach clenches, and I avert my eyes and try to make myself small as I head for my room.

"They won't stop until we're all dead!"

Dad doesn't like anyone he considers a foreigner, but he carries a bottomless well of hate for Muslims, which he often vents in a rage-filled rant at the TV. I've learned to stay as far away as possible from him when he's like this.

The buzzer for the door downstairs sounds, and I jump.

"Tell Grill he can damn well handle it on his own," Dad says, his eyes fixed on the TV. "Tell him that's what I pay him for."

I don't tell him that Grill has told me emphatically that Dad doesn't pay him anywhere near enough to put up with his crap, and when the buzzer sounds again, I abandon my plan to get changed. The sound of my father's continuing tirade rings in my ears as I escape down the stairs.

At the bottom landing, I yank open the door and find Teeny, Emi, and Myra standing there.

"What . . . ?" I'm surprised because I haven't seen a whole lot of them lately, and anyway they almost never come to my house. They've met my dad.

"We need to talk," Teeny says grimly.

"What's up?" I say, trying for normal, though I can tell already that this is anything but normal. I shut the door behind me and lean against it, hoping they can't hear my dad's screaming. There's a line at the counter almost ten people deep, and Grill frowns as he catches my eye.

"Guys, this isn't the best time in the world," I say, knowing I need to help Grill or he might walk out.

"There's never a good time with you anymore," says

Teeny, who evidently has been elected spokeswoman of the group. Myra is on her phone, probably searching, "How to talk to your best friend when she won't talk back," and Emi just stands there looking uncomfortable and fidgety. She hates emotional scenes.

Teeny, however, thrives on them.

"You talk to us now," she announces. "Or else."

Or else? Really? But whatever is going on is clearly important to them, so I sigh and lead them through the door to the shop office. We stand awkwardly next to my father's overly neat desk.

"This is an intervention," Teeny says. "We don't understand what's going on with you and Nick, but we're here to tell you that we are your *friends*, that we'll be here long after Nick bites the dust, and you need to remember that."

"Can't you hang out with us and Nick too?" Myra asks plaintively.

I don't know what to say. I share so many secrets with Nick, Dave, and, yes, even Hailey Brinson that it has just been easier to avoid my friends than to lie to their faces. I'm still hyped up about our close call last night, and the whole thing has gotten a lot more serious than I bargained for. I'm scared a lot of time that the police are going to show up at my door. So how am I supposed to study Statistics with Emi or ooh and ahh over Teeny's newest batch of clothes from her aunt?

"Nick isn't good for you," Emi says, but she won't meet

my eyes. "I miss studying with you." For her, it's basically a declaration of love, and my eyes sting.

"I'm *sorry*." There's nothing else I can say. I can't tell them what's going on, because if I do, I'll lose Nick, and he's the only one who seems to understand the anger that feels like it is burning me up from the inside out. I'm not sure if all that mad is going to just leave me a dry, burned-out husk, or explode outward at the people around me.

But these are my best friends, and I don't want to lose them either.

"We're worried about you, Jesse," Teeny says, and while her words are sweet, her tone is not. She is glaring at me.

I nod, because I'm worried about me too.

"Aren't you going to say anything?" Myra asks. "How can you just stand there?"

Somehow that has become the story of my life, and I'm still standing there silent as they turn to leave.

"Don't call when it all comes crashing down," Teeny says over her shoulder, and her tone is spiteful, but I see the dark pain in her eyes.

Emi pauses at the door, and she stares at me for a long moment.

"Is he worth it?" she asks quietly.

She turns to go without waiting for me to answer.

Chapter Thirteen

Alia

I notice him in the crowd waiting for a local elevator in the seventy-eighth-floor sky lobby. He's tall and lean, and his straight blond hair is too long, and he's got a hip-hop thing going on with his baggy pants and oversized Giants shirt.

I'm not sure why I start watching him, maybe because in the mass of people in suits and dresses, he's the only one close to my age. But that's not the only reason. He looks like one of those guys who could pop off at any time. You watch people like that because you never know what they're going to do.

As if to prove my point, the guy reaches out a hand toward the back pocket of a maintenance guy holding a bucket and squeegee.

In my head, Lia yells, *"Stop right there, buster!"* and slaps his hand away from the maintenance man's pocket.

"Hey!" I say, and the guy and several other people glance over at me curiously.

I'm staring right at Hip-Hop Boy, and he knows why.

He looks at me for a long moment, and I notice that he's actually *cute* in a bad-boy, I-just-got-busted-trying-to-lift-some-guy's-wallet kind of way. His wheat-colored hair is silky and appears as if it was chopped with a blunt instrument, and his eyes are a light greenish hazel shadowed by strong eyebrows. And then he smiles, and his whole face is transformed from kind of cute to *wow*. He stands there grinning at me, like he knows I saw and thinks if he's going to be busted by anyone in the world, he's glad it was me.

I glare at him, and he shrugs, like "What can I say?"

I remember then that I'm wearing the hijab, and that I shouldn't be flirting with some punk. Not that I was *flirting*, I was preventing a crime, and if I happened to notice the would-be thief was cute, well . . . Just because I definitely don't want to date anyone, I'm not dead.

Still, I avert my eyes from him. I'm blushing, and for some reason I think he's still looking at me. I back up and run into a sign on a metal easel, knocking it over with a clatter. I scramble to pick it up, feeling stupid.

The local elevator opens, and I'm pushed forward with the crowd. The boy doesn't get on, but I find myself thinking about him as we go up. I wonder if he was just waiting for me to leave so he could continue his wallet-snatching without a witness. Lia would go back down, this minute, and confront the boy. I pull out my notepad, accidentally elbowing a few people in the crowded elevator. I sketch the scene quickly: Lia dragging him out of the building by his collar, her dialogue bubble reading, "Why don't you steal from someone your own age, Hip-Hop Boy!" and all the while, tiny hearts are coming from his head because he can't keep his eyes off Lia.

I hurriedly tuck the pad back into my bag as the elevator opens on my dad's floor. I head for his office, practicing the words I want to say to him so they don't get all jumbled up, like they did with my mother.

Ayah, I need you to understand how serious I am about this NYU program. My drawing means so much to me. This isn't one of my crazy impulses, and I really think it's what I want to do. I hope that you will change your mind and give me your blessing.

It sounds good. Hopefully he won't notice that I should be in school. Somehow I thought wearing the scarf would make me feel grown up, strong, like Lia, but so far all I feel is young and silly.

Inside my dad's office, I thank the receptionist for telling the security guy downstairs to let me up, and she smiles and gestures for me to go on back. It's not yet nine, and there are a lot of empty cubicles, but my father always gets there before everyone else to run reports from the day before.

But when I get to his desk, he's not there. His computer is on, the tiny fan clipped to the side of it running, and there are stacks of paperwork and a few diskettes lined up neatly with my father's slanted handwriting on the labels.

But no Ayah. I wait for a couple of minutes, nodding at people as they pass me, staring through an office door out the windows at a thin slice of blue sky. I asked Ayah once why the windows were so narrow, and he told me that he'd heard the towers were designed by an architect who was scared of heights, which made me laugh.

I tap my foot. Where the heck is Ayah?

I know sometimes he will go upstairs to pray with some of the restaurant staff from Windows on the World when he doesn't have time to go to the other tower to the prayer room. He told me that they spread tablecloths and use flattened cardboard boxes as prayer mats on the stairwell landing. But he's already prayed the morning prayer, and it's not time for the noon prayer, so that can't be it.

"Alia?" Mr. Morowitz says. "Is that you?" He's holding a cup of coffee in one hand and a bagel smeared with cream cheese in the other.

Mr. Morowitz is big and puffy, and always reminds me of a balloon in his tight suit, but he's really nice. He's often part of the group my parents invite to the apartment to eat dinner. They always end up talking about religion, and the world, and how we all fit into it. My parents don't believe in sheltering me from other religions, and I've been to synagogue with Mr. Morowitz's family, and church services with our Christian friends.

I wonder for a moment why he isn't sure it's me, and then I remember the scarf. Do I look that different with it on?

"Hi, Mr. Morowitz," I say. "Do you know where my father is?"

"You just missed him, honey," he says with his mouth full, a smudge of cream cheese on his chin. "He was in earlier, but he left to go vote, and then he's got a training seminar across town. Bagel?" He offers me an American Café bag. "They're kosher, halal, for you."

I shake my head. "No, thank you."

What am I going to do now? I'd felt so sure that this was the right thing to do. Now, the next time I see my father will be when we all meet in Ms. Julio's office, and I can't imagine that he will be in the mood to sign my permission slip after *that* meeting.

"Alia?" Mr. Morowitz is saying. "Are you okay?"

I focus on his kind, concerned face. "Uh, sure. I'm fine," I say, and smile reassuringly.

He blinks, and then smiles back. "If I see him, do you want me to give him a message?"

"No," I say. "I'll talk to him later."

I check the clock on my father's desk and see that I'm going to be late as heck for school, and I don't have a thing to show for it.

Chapter Fourteen

Jesse

The pep rally is in full swing, pumped-up teenagers screaming and yelling at the cheerleaders who are doing a dance that honestly looks like they should have some sort of pole to go with their shake.

"She was putting them up earlier," Dave is saying. "You wouldn't believe this crap . . ."

I can't really hear what Dave and Nick are talking about, though I'm sitting on the bleacher row just below them, leaning back between Nick's legs. His hand is twined in my hair, his fingers rubbing the base of my neck. Every once in a while, he pulls my head back and leans down to give me a kiss, as if saying, *See, she's mine.* It's been a couple of weeks since we almost got caught by the cops, and if anything Nick has gotten even more reckless. More and more lately, I've wanted to call Emi, or Teeny, or Myra, and say: *Help. I'm in too deep.* But it's too late. I made my choice and now I'm on my own.

Even with Nick's fingers warm on the back of my neck, I find my thoughts wandering a well-worn path to Adam. I've seen him a couple of times in the halls—a nod, a flicker of dimple—but we haven't talked again. I've been thinking a lot about the way I felt when I was on the mountain with him.

"See, she's putting up another one," Dave is saying as the pep rally roars around us. Hailey is all over him, her hands under his army jacket. They'd started going out soon after Nick and I hooked up. I think she did it to make Nick jealous, not that he seemed to notice.

I finally look around to see what Dave is talking about. Jade Grimsky and Hal Jones are busy putting up fliers. Jade and Hal are big into good works, and I assume it's another bake sale to raise money for some cause or another. Why does Dave care so much about two-dollar brownies?

The pep rally finishes, and we get up, everyone jostling and yelling as we stream toward the doors. Nick has his arm wrapped around my shoulders, and even then, with my boyfriend's arm encircling me, I find myself looking for Adam. Dave is in front of us, and slows as we near the blue flier that Jade and Hal were putting up. It says: Islam Peace Center, and there is a date for a grand opening this Saturday, and an address in town.

My stomach turns, and before I can help myself, I think: *It was Muslims who hijacked those planes and drove them into*

the towers of the World Trade Center and killed all those people.
It was Muslims who killed my brother.

"See?" Dave says. "Can you believe this crap? My brother
got his leg blown off over there, and they want to open up a
freaking *peace center*?"

Nick reaches out and rips the flier off the wall. Dave
follows suit and rips down another sign nearby. As we head
down the hall, they tear down every blue sign they see.

$\backsim$

The four of us walk a long, circuitous route home. We usually
take Nick's car, but it's in the shop, so we're walking today.
I'm not paying much attention where we are going, because
my thoughts are spinning like car tires caught in the snow.
My dad has gotten worse, and, as promised, Grill has quit,
leaving me and a few newbies to run the store. Mom has
never had much to do with the shop—as far as I know, she's
only climbed once in her life, right after my parents moved
here, and she swore she'd never do it again—so she keeps
zipping along like a deranged bumblebee pretending everything is peachy, while I try to keep things together.

We've stopped on the sidewalk, and Nick, Dave, and
Hailey are staring up at a building. We're at the bottom of
a stretch of antique shops just off Main Street, and the last
building in the row, which used to be a chocolate shop, has a
new sign reading: Islam Peace Center.

"You'd have to tag it up high," Nick is saying, and I finally tune into the conversation. "If you didn't get up there"—he gestures to the top of the wall of the brick building, up on the second floor—"no one would see it."

It takes me a minute to figure out what they are talking about: tagging the Peace Center. But there's a fence running along the side of the building on the corner, and unless you got up high, the tag wouldn't really be noticeable.

"A ladder?" Hailey suggests.

"Nah," Nick says. "You'd have to move it every letter and it would make too much noise. We need a climber."

They all turn to look at me.

"Uh . . . What? Me?" I squeak. Nick is the one who does the tagging. Though I've practiced our tag on paper, I've never painted it on the side of a building.

"You're the only one who can get up there and do it," Nick says.

I check out the old wall, with bricks jutting out here and there. Lots of cracks to place gear. It would be a breeze.

"I don't know," I say uneasily. *I don't want to!* I'm thinking.

"We have to tell them," Dave says furiously. "We have to tell them that they should go the hell back to where they came from."

"Chill for a minute," Nick says to him and turns to me. "Jesse?"

He stares at me seriously, ignoring Hailey and Dave, who are grumbling and throwing what-the-hell? looks at me. Nick shakes his head a little to clear the hair from his eyes. "Look,

I don't want you doing anything you don't want to. Just think about it, okay?"

Before I can answer, a girl comes out of the Peace Center with a handful of blue fliers. She's wearing jeans and boots, and a green head scarf tucked into her thick jacket.

The girl stops at a car with a "Just Dua It" bumper sticker and grabs a staple gun out of the trunk.

"Come on," Nick says, and we trail after the girl as she starts up the street, putting up the blue fliers with a brisk *thump-thump* of the staple gun as she goes.

The girl in the scarf meets up with Jade and Hal, and they continue along the street, laughing and talking as they continue putting up the blue fliers.

"What the hell?" Dave yells at them as we get closer. His face is red, and he's breathing hard. For a moment, he reminds me of my dad. It's not the first time. When he gets going about the "freaking A-rabs" that cost his brother his leg, I keep my mouth shut. I know from experience the slightest word will set him off even more. Nick thinks it's funny, and will egg him on into a frothing frenzy, but it scares me.

The girl in the scarf looks at Dave, and then her gaze travels to the rest of us, and I realize that I'm carrying some of the blue fliers that Nick crumpled up and handed to me at school. I want to shrink back against Nick, but he steps up so he's standing next to Dave.

"No one wants you here!" Dave spits.

"Dave Tucker," Jade says severely. "We most certainly want Sabeen here. You, on the other hand, can go take a flying leap."

Jade, tall and redheaded in a gypsy skirt, jangles the bangles on her wrists angrily.

"It's okay, Jade." Sabeen, the girl in the scarf, looks at us. "What do you want to say to me?" she asks Dave directly. She is pretty, with dark eyeliner accenting her flashing eyes, and tiny diamond studs glimmering in her ears. A few people have gathered around, attracted by the confrontation.

"Go *back!*" Dave shouts. "If you don't like it here, go the hell back to your *own country!*"

"I'm an American," she says evenly. "I was born here, just like you." I can't help but admire her composure, but her words seem to set Dave off even more.

"*You are not like me.* You will *never* be like me."

People begin murmuring in disapproval. Someone pushes through the crowd, and I feel sick when I see it's Adam. He's out of breath, his hair damp with sweat and curling crazily over his forehead, and the dimple is nowhere to be seen.

"Everything all right?" he asks, and his tone is neutral, but his blue eyes are not as he stares at Dave and Nick.

"No problem, man," Nick says between his teeth, his breath hissing out.

"I didn't think so." Adam's gaze lands on me, cool and appraising. I duck my head, flushing.

A group of college kids come by, and in the roiling crowd of people, Sabeen cries out. Her scarf lies in a puddle on the ground, the beautiful green silk slowly turning dark as the muddy water bleeds into it.

Adam is yelling something at Dave and Nick, while people mill around in confusion. I quickly stoop and pick up Sabeen's scarf. I hand it to her, avoiding her eyes as my heart crumples.

Nick grabs my hand, and we walk away quickly. I feel like I want to throw up.

I know it's all so wrong, but I can't seem to find the words to say anything.

I try not to think about what I saw.

I try not to think about Nick grabbing the end of Sabeen's scarf and yanking it off her head as she cried out in pain.

∽

"You should hate them more than any of us," Nick says later as we walk alone under a sky of clouds full and fat with snow, crowded close to the ground.

Hailey and Dave went back to her place to hook up, and Nick wanted me to come back to his house, but I told him I had a lot of homework. Suddenly I want to tell him I have plans every day and night for the foreseeable future. But I don't know how.

"What?" I look over at him, at his handsome face, the silver ring in his eyebrow gleaming dully.

"I'm just saying they killed your brother. You should want them to pay for that," he says.

I can't stop thinking of him yanking off Sabeen's scarf, but a part of me understands what he's saying, that it's hard when you feel like there's nothing you can do or say to change anything. That someone should pay for making you feel like that.

"I don't think about it," I say finally, but it's not true, because lately I've been thinking about it a lot.

$\sim$

I go into our apartment. Mom is gone; there is an uneaten casserole on the stove with a sticky note that reads: "At prayer meeting, back at 9:30!" punctuated with a smiley face. There are eight beer bottles lined up on the counter, and I glance reflexively at Dad's recliner, but it's empty.

I move down the hallway like a ghost. My parents' bedroom door is cracked open, and as I pass, I see Dad on top of the covers, asleep. He's snoring loudly, and there's a book on his chest. I go to move past, but something makes me stop.

The day after I found the silver photo album in the shed, I went back to look at it again, but it was gone.

Now it's here, on Dad's chest. I walk over to the side of the bed and gaze down at the open album. A bottle of glue sits on the table next to Dad. He must have been gluing one of the older articles that had come loose.

I understand suddenly that this was never Mom's photo album. It's Dad's.

He stirs, and I freeze, my gaze darting to his face, but he lapses back into rumbling snores.

I step closer to him and use one finger to flip past the news articles. Behind plastic protective sleeves are childish, scrawled Happy Father's Day cards, a crayon picture of stick figures with arrows pointing at "*Me*" and "*Dad*." On another page are the pictures: a small, blond Travis building a snowman with a laughing, pregnant Mom; Travis, sledding down a hill; in the mountains, the red and orange leaves falling like rain behind his gap-toothed smile.

My stomach clenches as I catch my breath in a choking gasp. This is Travis. This is my brother.

I look down at my sleeping father. While his opinions and rage spew out of him in a hate-fueled frenzy, his silence about Travis is a void that screams louder than any words.

The only time I remember him saying anything about Travis was Hank's last Christmas when my brother yelled, "Why won't you let us talk about him? For all you know he could have been a hero!" And Dad said, in a quiet, shaking voice that was so much scarier than his usual roar, "*My son was no hero.*"

I look back at my father's face, relaxed and vulnerable in sleep. He won't talk about Travis, and refuses to let anybody else talk about him, but here he is with a secret photo album, filled to the brim with Travis.

Something breaks inside me. Something big and dark cracks open, and white-hot anger pours out. I'm shaking, though I couldn't begin to say what I'm angry at. I understand for the first time my dad's free-flowing, no-target rage. I want to scream, I want to kick something, I want to make someone hurt like I'm hurting.

I go into my bedroom and close the door carefully, my hand trembling with the urge to slam it shut as hard as I can. I fumble in my pocket for my phone and send a text to Nick. It reads simply:

I'm in.

Chapter Fifteen

Alia

I take an elevator back down to the seventy-eighth-floor sky lobby, still full of people rushing to get to work. I don't notice Hip-Hop Boy until after I step onto the express elevator. He sees me, and his eyes widen, but then he looks away. There aren't a ton of people going down, just a group of people in suits talking animatedly about commission rates, and one goes, "Hey, there's Bob. We can ask him," and they duck back through the doors, leaving just the two of us in the big car.

The boy seems worked up. His jaw is clenched, and he is jiggling his hand in the pocket of his baggy jeans.

I stare down at the slick brochure I picked up in the sky lobby, advertising a celebration of dance with a picture of two dancers staring into each other's eyes as they hang suspended between the two towers. I pretend to study it—*September 5-16 at 7 p.m., right here at the World Trade Center, why yes, maybe I will go!*—so I can ignore the agitated boy, but my gaze keeps straying to him. At first, I think he's just pissed about something, and then I see the gleam of tears in his eyes. He's upset, and mad, all at the same time.

What happened to him in the ten minutes since I saw him last?

I edge closer to him. I'm not sure why, but even with his sticky fingers and tough-boy act, I don't like that he's upset.

"Hey," I say and realize it's the second time I've said that to him, and that each time it meant completely different things.

He glances up at me as the elevator jerks. I grab the rail, panicked, then feel stupid when I realize the elevator has started going down.

He doesn't say anything, so I stare up at the red numbers, willing them to flick downward, and try to forget about him. In a manner of minutes we'll be at the lobby, and I'll never see him again.

I look up to see him staring at me.

"Do you normally stare at people like that?" I snap, figuring for sure he's looking at me like that because of the scarf.

"*You're* the one—" he says, and there's a *THUD,* and the elevator swings crazily.

Then we drop into free fall.

Chapter Sixteen

Jesse

The blue lights wash across the brick wall of the Islam Peace Center, and I see the police officer running toward me as I slide too fast, *too fast*, toward the ground.

I land hard and something pops in my ankle, and the pain is glaring and vivid. I fall to the cold, snow-slippery ground, biting back a scream.

"Nick!" I clutch my ankle and yell *"Nick!"* not even caring if anybody hears me.

I'm alone, clutching my ankle and crying, when the cop reaches me. He sweeps his flashlight over me, and then up the wall to where my rope is still lazily swinging in front of the wall and the letters.

He doesn't say anything at first, knowing that I'm not going anywhere. He just shines the flashlight over the letters that scream silently on the side of the center.

The first word, big and bubbly:

NOTHING

Below that:

Terrorists go home

The cop shakes his head in disgust and pulls out his hand-cuffs. The blue lights strobe over me as I lay with my face pressed to the icy ground, wishing I could just melt into it and disappear. The cop is saying something, but his words are disappearing into the black vacuum of my pain.

All the hot, blinding anger that has fueled me since I found my dad with Travis's album is gone, and all I feel is empty and alone.

All I feel is nothing.

Chapter Seventeen

Alia

The elevator is screaming as it drops.

Or is it me screaming?

I can't tell. I am on my knees, clutching the rail with both arms.

Orange sparks stream through a gap in the door as the car slams into the side of the shaft with a terrible scraping, grinding sound, and it gets hot, so hot I feel like the elevator rail is burning my palms.

Thoughts swirl through my head without any order, almost in slow motion.

What is happening?

And *Mama, Ayah, I love you, I love you, I love you.*

And *God, please, please help me.*

Hip-Hop Boy dives toward the front of the car. He begins

stabbing buttons, cursing in frustration as the lights flicker crazily, and the elevator bounces around like a rubber ball.

Suddenly the car crashes to a halt with a horrendous screech. I don't dare move as the elevator continues to sway. I'm convinced that if I move it will continue its plunge to the ground.

He seems to think the same thing, because he remains frozen by the console, staring up, as if somehow that is where he will get the answer to our question:

Will we fall again?

A voice starts speaking, and I jump, then realize that it's a recorded message, saying that our message has been received and help is on the way. I feel a tiny bit better, because *help is on the way.*

A curl of smoke seeps into the top of the car, and I watch in numb silence as it slides around the top of the car like a thick curious snake and then gets fatter and more transparent before disappearing. The rocking begins to subside, and finally we are still.

"What—" I clear my throat, because my voice sounds froggy and weird. "What happened?"

"I don't know. A bomb, maybe?" His voice is careful, as if even the sound of our voices might tip the elevator back into free fall.

"A bomb?" I say, too loud. But, oh my God, did he just say a *bomb*?

"A bomb went off in '93," he says, still staring up at the

ceiling. "In the basement. It killed five or six people. I heard an explosion. Did you hear it? I did. I'm thinking that's what it is, but . . . I don't know."

"A bomb?" I say again, wiping sweat off my face and fighting the urge to scratch under my scarf. It's still so, so hot.

I'd never heard about a bomb going off in the World Trade Center, right here where my father had worked for the last year. Why hadn't someone told me? Why hadn't someone told me that my father worked in a place that people liked to bomb?

"My grandfather worked here then, and he said it was pretty bad. I'm thinking that's what it is," he says again, as if saying the words aloud will make some kind of sense of this whole terrible thing.

"How long do you think it'll take before they come for us?" I ask in a shaky voice, finally daring to let go of the rail and sit up. I hold my breath, half expecting the elevator to start swinging again, or even worse, drop.

"It might be a while. There are ninety-nine elevators in this tower—and the same in the other tower—so if it was a bomb, a lot of people will be trapped like us. We just need to sit tight and wait."

Lia wouldn't be just sitting still, afraid to move. She'd figure out some way to get out of this elevator, and then, before lunch, have discovered what was going on and solved the problem without breaking a sweat.

I burst into tears. I want to go home and see my father and my mother and give them a big hug. I want them to hold me for the rest of my life.

I cry for a few minutes, head down and shoulders shaking, before I sense the boy sliding down next to me. He doesn't say anything, just sits quietly.

"I don't want to die!"

"We're not going to die," he says. "The emergency brake caught us, and there's no reason to think it won't keep us here until help comes. Crying won't change anything."

"I'm not crying," I say, though I still am.

"I don't think we dropped very far," he says after a moment.

"It felt like we were falling for *ages.*"

"But we didn't."

I think he's trying to make me feel better, but the fact is, we *fell,* and elevators aren't supposed to do that.

"What's your name?" I ask after a moment and am happy to hear that my voice is stronger. His comment about crying not changing anything has made me mad, and mad is better than sad right now. "I can't keep calling you 'Hip-Hop Boy' in my head."

"Hip-Hop Boy? Really?" He turns toward me, and I see that he has mismatched eyes; one is hazel, and the other is more green. It's not something you would notice if you weren't looking closely.

"Well, it's not like I knew your name. What else was I supposed to call you? 'Pickpocket'?"

His face reddens. "I didn't steal anything."

"Yes, because I stopped you," I snap back. Then I relent. "I'm Alia." When he gives me a puzzled look, I exaggerate my name the way I have to sometimes. "Ah-LEE-ah."

"Alia," he repeats.

He offers me his hand, and we shake awkwardly across our knees and legs.

"I'm Travis," he says.

Chapter Eighteen

Jesse

I stand outside the Islam Peace Center in a monotonous June drizzle that streaks the glass of the door in front of me. It's not cold, but I'm shaking as hard as I did the last time I was here, two months ago.

The night I got arrested.

I know I need to go in. In fact, I should have gone in ten minutes ago, but I can't seem to make myself move. What will I say? What will they say to me? But if I don't go inside soon, then I'll have to go back to court.

I deserve this, I deserve this, I deserve this.

The door opens, and a woman with bright blue eyes and a pink head scarf peers out at me.

"Are you going to come in?" she asks briskly, though not in a mean way.

I would rather rip out my toenails one by one, I want to say, but I don't have a choice, because I'm doing my community service *here,* at the Peace Center.

I was lucky, because it could have been worse. I had a good lawyer and was underage with no criminal history. I could be going to a juvenile detention center like Nick.

I nod mutely at the woman and duck past her into the cool, bright building, wincing as my healing ankle twinges in protest.

I can still smell the warm, sweet richness of candy, as if it has permeated the very walls. I remember coming here once with my dad, when I was eight or nine, and him standing patiently while I stared in happy indecision at the trays of chocolates behind the glass counter.

The counter is gone, and all that is recognizable from the candy shop days is the small kitchen against the back wall. The rest of the room is open, full of light and posters, and tables with kids my age who sit silently staring at me.

What are they all doing here?

"I'm Yalda," the woman says to me. "I think you should know that this is a no-judgment place. When we are here, we will try not to judge you, and I hope that you can extend us the same courtesy."

I nod, staring at the floor, which has been painted with feet in a rainbow of colors and sizes, all walking in different directions.

"We are doing teen outreach today," she continues. "We do it every Thursday."

She takes my arm and draws me away from the door. I try not to catch anyone's eye; I've gotten used to the disgusted looks, because it is what I've been seeing from friends and strangers alike for months.

"This is Jesse," Yalda says, raising her voice so the unsmiling kids can hear her. "There's no point pretending that you don't know who she is, and why she's here. But the purpose of this Peace Center is to bring people of diverse faiths and backgrounds together. So no snark, okay?"

I sense the lessening of tension as her words fill the chocolate-scented room.

"Jesse, why don't you sit down?" Yalda nods at a table with three or four kids, but I head for an empty table near the back instead.

I'm not sure what I was expecting—cleaning toilets with a toothbrush?—but it wasn't this. Yalda seems to have every intention of treating me like the other teens who are here legitimately, not ordered on pain of juvenile detention to be here twice a week for the next six months.

I sneak glances at the other kids who are now focused on Yalda. A few of the girls wear head scarves, but the majority of the kids look like the ones I go to school with every day. They *are* kids I go to school with. I see Jade Grimsky and Hal Jones, and a girl, Nina, from my Health block, and a few other people I recognize, and some I don't, who I assume must be in college.

"We're talking about what it's like to be a Muslim in America," Yalda says to me.

She turns to a tall, regal-looking girl with gold bangles on her wrists and a colorfully patterned scarf over her hair. "Nadifa, you were saying . . . ?"

Nadifa nods. "I was just saying that I wear the hijab because I'm proud of my Muslim identity. One of my teachers in high school asked me to stay behind class one day, and when we were alone she said in this real quiet voice, 'Sweetie, you're in America now, you don't have to wear that scarf if you don't want to.'"

Laughter sweeps through the room, and I see the scarved girls nodding.

"I mean, she was sweet and all, but look, it's *because* I'm an American that I have the freedom to wear it. Hello, I'm a feminist! I'm majoring in political science; I *know* what my rights are."

A dark-eyed girl wearing an "I love Malala" shirt says, "I'd be a millionaire if I had a dollar for every time someone asked me whether my parents make me cover my hair, or if my dad's going to force me to marry some old, fat guy. No, it's my choice to wear the scarf, and my dad wants me to be happy. But it does piss me off that they *make* women wear the veil in other countries. That they *beat* women who don't wear it, or even kill them. That's just so awful."

Yalda says, "It is awful, Maira. I think it's important to remember that in the seventh century the Quran gave women more freedom and rights and equality than most other civilized nations at that time."

"So how come people use the message of the Quran to stifle women's freedom *now*?" another girl with sleek, dark hair shouts out.

"It's cultural, not religious," Nadifa says. "There are still some villages where people are following customs that go back a thousand years. It's all they know."

"And it's not just girls who have issues," says a boy wearing jeans and a SUNY New Paltz T-shirt. "I was born here, and I think what those ISIS guys are doing is lousy, but it feels like people think we're all like that. I was trying to find a bathroom last year at the DMV, and a security guy got all suspicious on me, like I was casing the joint or something. Like I was looking for a place to plant a bomb." He shakes his head.

"Flying while Muslim. That's my dad's only crime, and he gets stopped every time he gets on a plane," another guy says.

"Everybody is mad at *us* for what happened on 9/11, and all the crap that's been going on since, but why don't they understand that we think it's horrible too?" Maira says. "God never told us to kill like that."

"They're just guys with an emptiness where their hearts should be, believing madmen who tell them to do terrible things," Jade says, her voice high and clear. "It's not the first or last time it'll happen."

"But when you see what's going on with our brothers in Afghanistan, and Iraq and Palestine, it's like America hate

Muslims. I thought we had religious freedom in this country, so why do they hate us so much?" the guy in the SUNY shirt says.

"My cousin in Afghanistan got killed in a drone attack," a girl says, and she swallows hard. "How did she deserve to die? She was only *fifteen*!"

Jade puts her arm around the girl, and whispers to her while she cries.

Yalda clears her throat and glances at her phone. "We're almost out of time, and I want to tie up some details about an upcoming presentation. Anne Jonna, a survivor of the attacks on the World Trade Center, is coming to speak to us at the end of the month. We've started putting notices in the paper, we've got the food lined up, but we need to make posters and get them out to the community. Anybody have a hidden artistic talent they'd like to volunteer for the cause?"

"What about the new girl?" one of the college girls says, and her voice isn't friendly. "I hear she has some pretty bad-ass artistic *skills*."

Suddenly, everyone is looking at me, and my face burns and I stare fixedly at the table as I try to think of what to say.

The front door opens, and a gust of rain and the smell of flowers blows in.

"Sorry we're late!" a girl calls, and her voice is full of laughter.

With a feeling of inevitability, I see that it is Sabeen in a pale yellow scarf, her dark eyes flashing.

"You could have called," Yalda says.

"Mom, we tried, but you must have your ringer turned off. Anyway, we would have been here on time but, for all his bragging, baby brother here drives like a little old lady in the rain."

Sabeen shoves her brother's arm playfully, and I recognize him, of course I do, and my bones dissolve, my heart collapses in on itself, because I didn't know.

I didn't know.

His laughing gaze falls on me, and his face freezes, the dimple disappearing, and his sky-blue eyes turn cold.

Chapter Nineteen

Alia

Travis and I sit in tense silence.

"How long will it take for them to get us out?" I ask.

"You're right, in my free time, I'm a working psychic," Travis says, and then sighs. "I have no idea. Maybe I'm wrong, maybe there's just a problem with our elevator, in which case it shouldn't be long."

This cheers me up. All his talk about a bomb seems pretty farfetched now that I've calmed down. It's way more likely that our elevator car malfunctioned in some way, and they are working hard right now to get us out.

I start fidgeting.

"Why are you here?" I ask him, because I'm not good with silence. At all.

"What?"

"I was here today to see my father." If only I'd gone to school like I was supposed to, none of this would be happening to me.

"Yeah?"

"So why are you here today? You look too young to work here," I persist.

"I'm almost nineteen," he says. "Plenty old enough to work here if I wanted."

"Okay, okay," I say, holding up my hands. "I didn't realize you were *ancient*, or I never would have asked. I'm just trying to make conversation. Let's talk about something." I can't bear the thought of being alone with my frantic thoughts.

"What do you want to talk about?"

I shrug. "It doesn't matter. World peace? Which is your favorite, Rachel or Monica? The name of your dog?"

"I don't have a dog."

I sigh in exasperation. "Can you work with me here?"

"Monica," he says after a moment. "I like neurotic dark-haired girls." He smiles at me, and my heart skips a beat, because is he *flirting*? "Where are you from?"

"I live here now, or in Brooklyn anyway. I was born in LA. Where are *you* from?" I say it challengingly. Why does everyone think that just because someone is Muslim that they aren't natural-born Americans?

He seems surprised at my tone, and I realize that maybe I read him wrong.

"A small town a couple hours from here." He rubs the back of his neck. "I hate it. I can't wait to leave."

"Why?"

"People think they know you. In a small town, they think they know everything about you, but they don't. I'm so tired of it."

I have the weird desire to touch the side of his face and make the scowl go away.

"I've never lived in a small town," I say. "But honestly, I think it's like that everywhere. I grew up in a neighborhood with a bunch of aunties and uncles who have all known me since I was born. It was exactly the same."

We hear a faraway clanging noise, and we both tense, but even though we listen hard, we don't hear it again. I'm still so hot, and the pin in my scarf is digging into my head. When I reach up to adjust it, I realize that the scarf is askew and I try to fix it, but it's hard without a mirror.

He looks at me curiously. "Why are you wearing the scarf?"

"It's a hijab. It's to show my submission to God. That's what Islam means, you know, submission, surrendering to God."

"You're Islam?"'

"No, I'm *Muslim*. My religion is Islam." I stare at him. "Really? The scarf didn't give it away?"

He looks embarrassed. "I thought . . . maybe you were a nun or something?"

"A nun?" For some reason I find that hilarious, and I

burst out laughing. He watches me, a bemused expression
on his face.

I wipe my eyes with my sleeves, knowing I'm laughing
so I won't cry. "The scarf basically means the same thing as
it would on a nun. It represents purity and faith." For some
reason, the word "purity" makes my face flame, as if I am
announcing I'm a virgin.

"Oh." He tucks his shaggy blond hair back behind his ear
like he's trying to think of something to say.

"So, what were you going to say to me? Before?" I ask.

He looks at me quizzically, his one eye just a tiny bit
greener than the other. I suddenly want to sketch him again;
I can see him on paper, with his strong jaw and messy hair,
saying something like: *Lia, we need to get out of here so we can
save the rest of the people who could be trapped just like us. Can
you help me?*

"What?" he says.

"Before the elevator fell," I say. "I asked if you normally
stared at people like that, and you said, '*You're* the one—'
but you never finished what you were going to say." I tilt my
head at him.

"Oh," he says, embarrassed. "It doesn't matter."

"Come on," I say. "Once we get out of here, God willing,
it's not like we'll ever see each other again. What's the big
deal?"

"Okay, fine." He heaves a big sigh that makes him sound
about six, not eighteen. "I was kind of upset, okay? I saw you

staring at me, and I thought you were going to say something about me . . ."

"Crying?" I supply helpfully.

"Yes," he says. "That. I wasn't really, you know—"

"Crying?"

"Man, stop it. Yes, okay, maybe I was. I just thought you were going to make fun of me or something, and then when you accused me of looking at you, I was, like, *really*?"

"I wasn't though," I say.

"You weren't what?"

"Going to make fun of you," I say. "My father says that 'tears are prayers too. They travel to Allah when we can't speak.'"

He opens his mouth to say something else, but we hear a clicking sound, and then static, before a real, live human voice says over the intercom, "There's been an explosion."

Chapter Twenty

Jesse

When I get home that evening from the Peace Center, still feeling raw and unsettled, my mother is waiting.

The apartment is dim, and I can hear the fall of rain on the leaves outside the cracked kitchen window and the gush of the gutters.

And my mother sits at the counter, not moving, not texting, not doing anything but waiting.

Usually she's such a whirlwind of energy, always talking, but only about what's happening tomorrow, what happened today, what's happening *right-freaking-now*. There's not a lot of conversation about anything important. It's like she lives her life only half-tuned to a radio station so that she doesn't have to listen to the lyrics.

"What's up, Mom?" I say, a little unnerved.

She looks at me, not speaking.

After I was arrested and taken to the hospital to get my ankle X-rayed (no break, just a bad sprain), they took me to jail, where I was fingerprinted and put into a holding cell. I couldn't seem to stop crying when my mom arrived with a lawyer to bail me out. The look on her face was indescribable. All she kept asking on the way home was "Why? Jesse, *why*?"

I couldn't answer. I had no answer. I didn't know why.

My father had refused to come with my mom to get me out of jail.

"Unbelievable," is all he said to me the next night when the local news flashed a video of the side of the Peace Center. A group of people were on ladders, busily scrubbing at my fading words with brushes and buckets of soapy water. Even then, I wondered what Nick would think. I hadn't spoken to him since I arrived home except for the one text he sent me:

Did you talk

I didn't reply.

He found out soon enough when the police arrived to pick him up.

"What, Mom?" I ask, because she still hasn't said anything.

Her face wrenches, like she's trying not to cry, and she stares at me so searchingly that I fight the irrational urge to close my eyes so she can't vacuum out my brain.

"It's our fault," she says. "What you did. We should have realized it would affect you." She sighs. "Travis was my baby boy, but when your father first stopped talking about him, right after it happened, I let him. I thought: *This is how he copes. This is how he gets through it.* And when his sadness turned to rage, I thought: *Give him time. He'll come back to me.* Because he wasn't always like this, Jesse. I remember him the way he used to be—funny, brave, smart—and it makes me so sad that the man I fell in love with is gone. All I can say in his defense is that losing a child is the worst pain a parent can experience, and losing Travis the way we did . . . it changed your father. It changed both of us."

She presses her lips together.

"Jesse, I know I haven't been here for you the way I should have been, and all I can say is I'm sorry. Sometimes it hurts so much to look at you."

I swallow hard, because this feels like a sharp, burning knife slicing into my heart. I've always known deep inside that somehow I caused my parents pain, that somehow it was easier for my mother to run, and my father to drink, than to have to deal with me.

"Sometimes it seems pointless to have anniversaries to remember something I remember every single day." She gazes over my shoulder at the rain streaming down outside the window.

She shakes her head and turns back to me. "The city is planning a memorial service for the fifteenth anniversary of

9/11. They've always done something small to remember the date, but the new town council has decided to do something bigger this year. They want to do something special for Travis, and they want us to come and speak about him."

"I'm sure Dad thought that was a spectacularly wonderful idea," I say, my voice bitter.

She smiles slightly, because we both understand Dad, whether we want to or not.

"Actually, we got into a pretty spectacular fight about it. I can't do it anymore, Jesse. I see what your father has done to you—I mean, look what you did! I still . . . can't believe it." Her voice drops. "I used to tell myself that he wasn't affecting you, the things he said, especially when you had friends like Emi and Teeny. It was like you were standing up to him in your own quiet way, befriending people you knew he wouldn't like. But now I see you *were* being affected. I've let him do this to you all these years, and I can't stand by any longer. I'm leaving. *We're* leaving. I've prayed about it, and we're going to stay at Mary's apartment until something changes. Until everything changes. Until he's back to the way he used to be. I refuse to live with him like this. And I don't want you to either."

"You're leaving Dad?" I ask, and my voice sounds young and small because *I can't believe this is happening.*

"Yes." She stands, and adjusts her skirt, a quick, determined movement. "We agreed that I would tell you. I moved my things out today. I think you should stay tonight and say good-bye to him, but it's up to you. If you want to come with me now, I'll help you pack."

"I . . ." My thoughts swirl, chaotic and hot, a fire burning out of control. "But I don't *want* to leave." Even as I say the words I'm surprised to hear them.

But it's true. My home is the only place I feel safe. I'm caught in a tornado filled with the jagged pieces of my life, and I need a place to hunker down. I can't lose that right now.

She stares at me in surprise. "You want—" She clears her throat. "You want to stay with your father?"

"It's not like that. I'm not choosing Dad," I say. "I'm not choosing either one of you. I just don't want to leave. Not now, I just . . . can't."

"I see," she says quietly, gazing down at her hands, which look like mine, except they are clean with neatly cut nails, whereas mine are chewed and raggedy. "I wish you would come with me, Jesse. What's going on between me and your father—that doesn't have anything to do with you."

I nod numbly, but I don't believe her.

"I thought you were going with your mother" is all Dad says when he comes home later.

"I'm staying here," I say.

He stops as he reaches into the fridge, just sort of freezes as if time skipped a moment or two, leaving him hanging out in space. Then he nods, and shuts the refrigerator door without getting anything, and sits in his recliner. He turns on the TV and flips past the nightly news to a fishing show.

I wait, but he doesn't say anything else. I go into my room and do pull-ups on the doorsill until my arms burn. I haven't been climbing since the last time I was on the water-fall with Adam.

Adam.

I try not to think about the way he looked at me when he saw me today in the Peace Center.

Adam is Muslim.

I squash the expression on his face deep, deep down and do more pull-ups until my arms are wobbly and I stop thinking about Adam.

But other thoughts bang around inside my head. I'd pretty much stopped thinking about everything after I got arrested. I was too busy concentrating on surviving school, avoiding the coldness in my friends' eyes, and escaping the flurry of whispers behind my back every time I walked down the halls.

Now my parents are separating. As much as I don't want to think about that either, they are splitting up because of what happened to Travis, my mother's baby boy, the laughing kid playing in the leaves and building a snowman.

Why was Travis there? Did everyone know and just not want to tell me? But, no, I'd heard Mom on the phone. *She* didn't know. Did Dad? Did Hank?

My brother's death is like this black hole that we rotate around and around, knowing that if we're not careful we could fall into it ourselves. And I don't know a damn thing about Travis except what they put in the paper every year, and how can that be anywhere *close* to the real story of who my brother really was?

All I know about him is that he died on 9/11.

That one thing has eclipsed everything else that he was. In some ways, it made his life bigger than it ever would have been otherwise. He only lived eighteen years, but how many ordinary eighteen-year-olds have their names etched in bronze at a memorial where thousands of people come to mourn every year? Not that I've gone to the memorial or museum where the old World Trade Center used to stand. My father has adamantly refused to go, and I wasn't sure how he would react if he found out I went.

Why was Travis there? How did he die?

How did he die?

Suddenly, it seems to me that the answer to that question will answer why my family is falling apart. We're not falling to the ground in an instant like the towers did, but it's like the most important parts of us are coming apart, the foundation just crumbling away beneath us.

∾

I Skype Hank, but he doesn't pick up. No big surprise there; he's almost never home. He's in Somalia, working for a relief organization, and he loves it there. He says it's uncomplicated and visceral.

After a few minutes, I call again, and this time my three-year-old nephew's face flickers into view.

"Jesse!" he crows delightedly when he sees me, his face breaking into a wide, happy smile.

"Joshua!" I say. "How are you?"

Deka, Hank's wife, smiles at me over Joshua's shoulder. She's slim and graceful in a long pink dress, her dark hair braided in hundreds of tiny braids.

"Jesse, it is so nice to see you," she says in her gently accented English. "I hope that you and your parents are doing well."

"Hi, Deka," I say. "Yes, we're fine." This is easier than the truth.

I have never met my nephew and sister-in-law in person. Hank went to work in Africa six months out of college, and never really came back. He visited for holidays for a while, but after that last big blowout with Dad on Christmas day when I was thirteen, he never came home again. That was the day he told Dad he was thinking about relinquishing his US citizenship because he couldn't stomach what America was doing in the Middle East. As far as I know, it's the last time Dad and Hank ever spoke.

"Jesse, your brother will be sorry he missed you," Deka is saying. "I do not know when he will be returning. He is out delivering tarpaulins and mosquito netting to the camps, but I will tell him you called. May I give him a message?"

I hesitate. I don't really have a message, I have a plea.

Tell me about Travis and Dad. Tell me why Travis was in the towers that day. Tell me why everything is broken, and while you're at it, can you please, please tell me how to fix it?

"Uh, yeah," I say. "Can you tell him I need to know about Travis? Everything's FUBAR. He'll understand."

Chapter Twenty-One

Alia

Travis and I sit frozen, waiting to hear if the voice from the intercom will say anything else, but there's only silence.

"What the . . . ?" Travis says, jumping up.

"Careful!" I yell, worried about the elevator.

He ignores me as he lunges for the intercom, punching buttons, saying, "Hello? Hello? Can anyone hear me?"

The intercom remains silent. Another swirl of smoke slides into the top of the elevator, and this time I can really smell it. Something, somewhere, is burning.

"They said help was coming," I say in a small voice. "Before, they said help was coming."

"Nobody *said* that. It was an automated message because I hit the emergency stop button," Travis says angrily. "A real live person just told us there was an explosion."

We both look at the intercom, but it stays quiet.

"But they know we're here, right?"

"They should," he says, and sits down on the other side of the elevator from me. "My grandfather took me to the OCC once, the operation control center, down in the basement. There are all these monitors where they keep track of stuff in the buildings. Gramps said it was like the brain of the building. They'll know we're here. They'll send someone."

"Okay," I say. "Okay." That makes me feel slightly better.

"An explosion . . . I still think it was a bomb," he says, almost to himself. "What else could it be?"

I clench my fingers. "Do you always have this cheery outlook on life, or is it reserved for times when you're stuck in an elevator with a very scared girl?"

I'm boiling with anger, but I know it's not really at him, so I clamp my lips around the words that want to blow out of my mouth.

"It was Muslims who planted the bomb the last time, you know," he says suddenly, and it's like a chasm opens up between us.

"So?" I say right back at him. "It was white Christians who used to burn crosses on people's lawns and owned slaves. Does that make all of you bad?"

"I'm just saying, my religion doesn't tell me to go out and kill people just because they don't believe what I believe," he says.

"Neither does mine," I say tightly. "In fact, mine says,

'To you your religion, and to me mine.' Just because people do bad things in the name of religion doesn't make the religion bad. People do crappy things, people do awesome things. That's just people."

His mood has grown dark though, and we sit in silence.

"It's just all FUBAR," he says suddenly.

"What?"

"It's something my dad says." He smiles slightly. "He got it from my gramps. It means 'effed up beyond all repair.'"

I'd never heard the term before, but I get it. "Okay, so this is pretty FUBAR," I say, trying it on for size. "But they'll get us out soon." It's my father's optimism coming out of my mouth, and I *need* that right now.

"No, I don't mean just this," Travis says, waving his hand around the elevator, and the alarms that are getting ready to drive me out of my skull, and the smoke sneaking in through the ceiling. "I mean all of it. The world. People. Me. *All* of it."

"You should write greeting card messages," I say, but my voice is shaky. "Like, 'I know you're feeling down today, but guess what? Life sucks.'"

"Life pretty much *does* suck," he says. "You might as well accept it."

"Bumper stickers," I say. "You could do bumper stickers: 'When things get really bad, shoot yourself.'"

He shrugs, and we sit in uneasy silence. I can't stand it.

"Does your grandfather work here now? You said he worked here during the . . . bombing."

"He worked here for a long time doing maintenance. Actually, Gramps helped build the towers back in the late sixties. He'd just got back from Vietnam and was having a hard time finding work because he got shot in the arm over there and was still recovering. He got a job as an electrician, and he said after a day of work, it was like he had sea legs when he came back to the ground because the towers swayed so much before they put in the dampers. They would all get drunk at Volk's and talk someone into climbing the towers and doing dumb stuff like paint 'Eat at Volk's' on the side of the building. He said when the crane hoisted up that last piece of steel, the American flag waving on it, it was so high up it got lost in the fog."

He falls silent, rubbing the back of his neck. I don't say anything, not wanting to interrupt whatever he's thinking about.

"He brought my grandmother here once, when they were building it."

"He did?"

"I don't remember her—she died when I was a baby. But Gramps told me he wanted her to see the towers while they were still building them. He was like that, kind of impulsive and brave and romantic. He bribed a security guard to let them in and they took a construction elevator up and walked around. He said it was like standing in a giant Tinkertoy, because all you could see was the steel skeleton. He told my grandmother, 'These are the bare bones of one of the greatest buildings in the world. It's just being born, but it'll be here a thousand years, I bet.' He loved talking about the towers. He had so many stories, and when I was a kid I would just sit and listen."

"I wish he were here," I say. "It sounds like he would know what to do."

"I wish he were here too," Travis says, still rubbing the back of his neck. "But he died five days ago."

Chapter Twenty-Two

Jesse

Adam is alone in the Peace Center when I get there. For some reason, Yalda had assigned Adam and Sabeen to make posters with me. Sabeen isn't here yet, and, oh God, I don't want to have to go in and talk to Adam, not after the way he looked at me.

I hesitate at the door. It's the first time I've really been alone with him since we first climbed together, and it feels like my tongue is swelling up in my mouth so I know it's going to be hard to say *anything*.

Adam glances up at me and his expression is unreadable. He's wearing a Rasta-colored beanie over his dark hair, and he appears dangerous, like a big golden cat just waiting to lunge at me. My palms start to sweat.

I swallow hard.

"Hey," I manage, which I consider an achievement of the highest freaking order.

"You didn't know I was Muslim, did you?" he says without preamble, no *hi*, or *hey*, or *lookie what we have here! It's the racist girl!*

He watches me, waiting for me to say something. I had a friend who stuttered his *s*'s when I was in kindergarten, and I remember the look on his face as he tried to say "sorry." You could tell he wanted to say it so badly, but no matter how hard he tried, it wouldn't come out right. Except now, for me, all the words are like that.

"I didn't believe it at first," Adam continues. "When I first heard that you were the one the police caught painting the side of the building, I told my mom and dad it must be a mistake." His gaze is direct as he leans back in his chair and laces his hands behind his head.

I try not to notice the pure blue of his eyes, or the way his dark hair curls silkily on his forehead. I put my head down and study my muddy shoes.

"I thought," he says into the silence of the sweet-smelling room, "that you were covering for that punk boyfriend of yours. Before all that happened, the guys at school said you were pretty, but real, real quiet. No one could understand why you'd hooked up with that loser. I couldn't either. I saw the way you were up on that waterfall."

He is watching me as he speaks. I know, because when I glance up from my shoes, my gaze is caught by his, and I can't look away. It's like he's forcing me to see him.

"You were so graceful and confident when you were climbing. It's like you belonged up there, but when you're on the ground, you're just a pale shadow of that girl on the mountain."

There's a clunky rock in my throat. "I wish—"

I wish what? That I never did what I did? That I was a different person, that I really was that girl he saw on the mountain? That I was brave, and graceful and confident, that I could *be* that girl, all the time, every day of my life? Do we ever get to be the person we want to be?

But all I can say is "I wish."

He's sprawled back in the chair, his eyes on me. I swallow, and my gaze skips away because I don't *want* to notice how good he looks, and how it feels like I had a glittering ornament in my hand and I smashed it to pieces without even noticing what it was.

"When you grow up Muslim, hell, different in *any* way, you get real good at reading people. You can tell the good ones, who might not end up liking you—sure, who likes everyone they meet?—but they're not going to hate you because you're Muslim, or black, or gay, or, I don't know, a blue Smurf. And then there are the other kind, the ones who feel better about themselves when they have someone to hate." He takes a deep breath, and my eyes fly back to his face, watching the muscle in his jaw clench as he stares out the window at the rain falling like a silver veil. "I read you wrong," he says simply. "I thought you were one of the good ones."

I am! I want to yell, but I know that isn't true. Not anymore. "I'm sorry," is what comes out instead. I've said this over and over, to the police as they were booking me, to my mom, to the judge. It is the one thing I can say that reflects a little of the universe-sized sorry inside me, so big that it pushes and shoves at the edges of me.

He studies me for a long moment, and then nods. I'm not sure what it means, whether it's an I-accept-your-apology kind of nod, or an okay-yeah-I-heard-you acknowledgment.

"I hate being wrong," he says, and grins crookedly.

"Me too," I say, and take a long shuddering breath.

He is staring at me, almost curiously, when the door opens behind me and Sabeen comes in with a gust of warm, rain-scented air.

"Is it *ever* going to stop raining?" she complains, stomping her feet on the mat and folding her umbrella. "Hi," she says to me, her tone friendly, but her eyes guarded. "I wanted to thank you for what you did that day."

"Huh?" My mouth drops open, and she laughs.

"You picked up my scarf, when that jerk boyfriend of yours yanked it off. I appreciate that. I *don't* appreciate a lot of other things about you, but that was nice. Maybe you are redeemable."

"Oh." I didn't think she had noticed.

"And you—" Sabeen turns to her brother. "You are not redeemable, you stinking piece of dog poop. You were supposed to pick me up. I had to take the *bus*."

Her tone is so injured that a giggle escapes me despite myself.

"Unh-uh, no way, no how," Adam says. "I had the car today. You were supposed to get a ride with Leslyn. We talked about it this morning."

"We did *not* talk about it this morning. If I said anything of the kind, you ought to have recognized that I was still unconscious, and saying anything I could think of to get you out of the very pleasant dream you were interrupting. How many times—"

The two of them continue their easy bickering about the car, about who was going to use it when Adam started his geology internship, and I am content to work and listen in silence.

～

That afternoon when I get home, I pull out my laptop and start searching the Internet for information about 9/11. I'd always managed to tune it out when it was mentioned in my classes, and when the inevitable specials came on as the anniversaries marched by, I turned the channel.

It's not that I'm unaware of the basics. I had just closed my ears to the details, following the lead of the rest of my family who so clearly didn't want to think about it.

But now I can't stop thinking about it. As I read the horrible stories one by one, I want to scream, to cry, because I can't imagine going through something like that.

Like my brother did.

As hard as I search, the only thing I find about Travis is a small obituary in the *New York Times*, and the generic yearly articles in our local paper.

I hear my dad come in, and I slam the laptop cover closed, my hands shaking. I get up, and then turn back to exit out of my search before going into the kitchen.

Dad climbed today, led a tour for the first time in months, and he's sweaty and red faced as he chugs a Gatorade, his eyes closed. I've seen pictures of my dad when he was younger, posing on top of a mountain, beside one, or hanging off one, the mountains as much a part of him as his glacial blue eyes or super-sized nose. He's bigger now, gray weaving through his disappearing hair and scraggly beard, but sometimes when I watch him climb I can see that younger Dad.

I try to gauge his mood, and whatever alert sensors I have inside me stay quiet, and I relax. He looks better than I've seen him in a while. The hush and peace of the mountain clings to him.

"I took them up 'Three Pines,'" he says, naming a popular easy climb. "The one girl was good. She reminded me of you. The other two were hang-dogging the whole time. Pretty much useless."

I remember when he took me climbing the first time. We went out on a cool morning when the Gunks smelled of wet earth, the cliffs draped in frothy pink and white blossoms, and lady's slippers quietly bloomed in the dappled fall of sunlight. Dad walked me through the basics and then set me loose on the side of the mountain, his hands steady on the belay rope as he talked me through those first terrifying moments as my feet scrabbled for purchase. I was so excited, I was trembling, and when I got stuck halfway up, Dad got a friend to take the rope and free-climbed up next to me.

"Always look down when you get stuck," he says, hanging on easily with one hand and his feet. "Figure out how to move your feet up first, and then stand up, don't pull up. Girls don't have as much upper body strength, but you don't need it. You have all the power you need in your legs."

I got through it, and when we stood together on the cliff top, hawks circling our heads, the sky so big and deep, I was untouchable.

"You're not bad," he said, and in Dad-speak that meant *you did awesome*. "Climbing isn't about strength, it's about balance and creativity; knowing what your body can do, and understanding what the rock is able to give."

It's probably lame to admit that the reason that I kept climbing at first was so Dad would look at me like that again. Later though, it was all for me.

Dad starts going through the pile of mail I brought up, using the pocketknife he always carries to slit open an envelope and pull out a bill.

Somehow the memory of us on the mountain gives me courage. "Dad, why was Travis in the towers? Do you know?"

He stops, the knife stuck in the middle of the envelope. My grandfather's initials, *HLM*, are inlaid into the handle, and I focus my eyes on the letters shining in the sun playing peek-a-boo through the kitchen window.

"My father went to Vietnam and came back with a Purple Heart," he says, and when I glance up, his eyes have turned as hard as granite. "That's what kind of man your grandfather was. I try to live my life the same way. You do what you need to do, even if you don't want to.

"What was your brother doing there that day? I have no idea. I know where he was supposed to be though. He was supposed to be at his grandfather's memorial service, but he wasn't man enough to be there."

I stare at him speechless. It's the most I've ever heard him say about my brother.

"Your mother wants to sit and chat about a boy who has been gone for fifteen years, and is never coming back. She says if I don't go to this memorial they're planning for him that she'll stay gone. Well, fine. She has to do what she has to do, and so do I. There's no point talking about it, do you understand? Nothing we say means a goddamn in the end. *Nothing matters, do you hear me?*"

Suddenly he is shouting, and I take a rapid step back.

"A group of jihad-loving maniacs took out your brother and three thousand other people and all the *talking* in the world isn't going to change that!" He's breathing so hard and his face is so red that I'm afraid he's going to have a stroke.

I turn and flee for my room, hearing his rage echo like cannon blasts in my head even after I quietly shut my bedroom door.

∽

Dad misses his shift at the shop again, and I fill in for him, trying not to feel funny that I'm in charge of two bubbly, giggling college students who spend more time on their phones than with the customers. I feel so much older than them. Thankfully, neither of them seems to know what I did, so I don't have to field the furtive glances and meaningful pauses when I walk into the room.

It's after seven by the time I get out. Even though I can drive by myself now, my birthday having passed mostly unnoticed in May, Dad has taken his truck, and Mom has her car at her new apartment. I go old-school and jump on my bike.

The darkening sky is full of neon tangerine clouds as I pedal down to the river and the cemetery. It's been a while since I've been here, one 9/11 anniversary a few years back. I came by myself that day too, but Mom must have been there before me, because there was a fresh wreath on Travis's grave.

I wonder if Dad ever comes.

I find my brother's grave, and sit on the lush green grass beside his simple headstone.

Travis Harold McLaurin

December 28, 1982–September 11, 2001

Beloved Son and Brother

I run my fingers over the cool stone.

What were you doing there, Travis?

A plane wings its way across the sky, and I stare up at it, wondering where it's going, thinking about planes that were loaded with fuel as they began trips across the country, and instead turning all those thousands of gallons of jet fuel into bombs when they hit their targets.

I sit for a while as the air darkens, and then I get up and find my grandfather's grave, which has a small "Veteran" medallion affixed to it.

In Memory of

Harold Lawrence McLaurin

June 5, 1941–September 6, 2001

Always Brave

I'd never really thought about how close together my brother and grandfather had died. One had lived sixty years, the other only eighteen, but they had died within five days of each other.

My father said Travis should have been at my grandfather's memorial service.

Why wasn't he?

Chapter Twenty-Three

Alia

"I shouldn't even be here. I'm supposed to be in school," I say after a while, just to fill the awful silence.

The intercom has remained stubbornly silent. It makes me want to hit it.

"I'm not supposed to be here either," Travis says in a muffled voice. "I should have just gone to his memorial service." This last is almost inaudible, and I lean forward.

"Your grandfather's memorial service? It's today?"

He nods and looks at his watch, and reflexively, I do the same. It's 8:58. "In about an hour."

"But why are you here then?"

He shakes his head and looks away.

"I'm sorry to hear about your grandfather," I say, when he doesn't answer. "Were you close?"

"Yeah." He fiddles with a button on his shirt and won't meet my eyes.

"I'm sure he's in heaven," I say gently, trying to ease his obvious pain. "From what you've said, he sounded like a wonderful person."

"My family goes to church every Sunday, and I thought I believed in God, but lately I'm not sure I can believe in a God who sits back and lets so many bad things happen to good people. I kind of envy people with all that faith; it would make things so much easier."

I can't imagine what it must be like to not have something to believe in. I remember lying in bed when I was younger, listening to my father softly reciting the Quran. I floated on the melodic chanting and fell asleep to the music of the words, feeling as if my very soul beat with them.

I don't pray five times a day like I'm supposed to, but I pray as often as I can. That's when God speaks to me in my heart, where there are no words, and I feel sorry for this boy that he can't feel that for himself.

The smoke is getting thicker, a cloud lazily swirling around the overhead light.

"Are you sure you don't have a phone?" I'd kill for a cell phone right now. A few kids in my school have their own, and I'd asked my parents for one, but they said it was too expensive, even though *they* both had one.

"I left it at home," he says shortly. "I didn't want anyone calling me."

"Why?"

"I just didn't, okay?" he says. "Just because we're stuck in here together doesn't mean I have to tell you every last thing about myself."

I focus on the smoke, trying not to cry.

"Look, I'm sorry," Travis says, and shakes his head. "It's just a pretty bad day for me."

"Sure, okay." I don't *want* to be mad at him. He's the only person I have right now.

He jumps up again and starts pacing around the elevator. I watch him, worried, because I still can't help but feel sudden motions are going to send us plummeting.

"Hey!" he yells suddenly, pounding on the elevator doors. "Can anyone hear me? We're stuck in here! Hey!"

He yells like that for a while, and then stops and turns to me.

"I can't stand the waiting. We've got to try to get out of here."

"But how?" I ask. "How do we get out of here?"

"I don't know." He looks up at the smoke, which has gotten even thicker. He puts one foot on the railing and then pushes himself up so he can reach the ceiling.

"Push up, don't pull," he says, and I look at him with eyebrows raised. He smiles a little. "It's a climbing thing my dad always says."

"You climb?"

"Nah. Dad was never able to talk me or my brother into

loving it the way he does. He's got one more kid to try to brainwash—maybe it'll work on her."

He feels around the ceiling, holding his breath against the smoke, but it's smooth metal panels, with no obvious way to remove them. He pounds on them with the heels of his hands.

"We need to get the doors open." He climbs down and turns to the gleaming metal doors.

"How?"

"I have no clue!" he snaps. "Instead of asking *how* every five seconds, why don't you try to come up with some ideas?"

"You don't need to yell!" I yell. I grab my backpack and dump it onto the ground, looking for something that might help. My notepad spills out, and Travis picks it up.

"This yours?"

"Yes," I say, trying to take the pad from him.

He flips forward to the last thing I drew and looks at it for a long moment and then back up at me.

My face is burning, because it's a picture of *him*, the one I sketched quickly in the elevator after I saw him in the sky lobby the first time. The one with hearts trailing from his head as he stares at Lia.

He grins, a quick flash of smile, but all he says is "you're good," and hands me the pad back.

Completely humiliated, I take it, and then shake out the rest of my backpack junk: schoolbooks, folders, pens and pencils, my insulated lunch bag. I unzip that and look at the bottle of Coke and sandwich and a Tupperware container of my mother's *nasi gila*, or "crazy rice."

Travis watches me, then reaches into his pocket and comes out with a pocketknife. Something else comes out with the knife, a small paper bag, which he shoves back into his pocket quickly.

I stare at him curiously. *What was that?* But he turns his head away and toys with the knife, so I focus on that instead. "Why do you have a knife?"

He doesn't answer, and I huddle back against the wall, realizing I don't know this guy, and I'm stuck in here with him. And how did he get the knife past security anyway?

Travis ignores me as he unfolds the knife. I notice there are initials on the handle, and I lean forward so I can see them.

HLM.

No *T* for Travis.

It's not his.

"Oh, I get it," I say. "You stole it." I feel disappointed, though I'm not sure why.

He makes a buzzing sound, his eyes on the knife. "Try again, Sherlock. It was my grandfather's. He gave it to me when I turned sixteen."

I shake my head, not sure I believe him. He inserts the knife between the crack of the doors, pries it open an inch, and then uses his fingers to pull. The muscles in his arms bulge and his face turns red as the doors slide open, one reluctant inch at a time.

"A little help here?" he says, his voice straining.

I jump up and grab the other side of the door and pull. I have no idea whether they are just heavy or if there is some sort of mechanism that is pressing them shut, but it's *hard.* The doors open a couple of inches and then stop.

"Pull!" Travis gasps.

"I . . . can't . . . pull . . . any harder!" I gasp back, wishing I had Lia's superhuman strength, but I don't, and have to let go.

"Find something to keep it open," he says, his voice straining.

I look around, and then see my thick, fat American history book. I grab it and shove it between the doors, and Travis finally lets go. The doors shudder but stay open.

But just a few inches. We'd have to be a mouse, a hamster, a ridiculously small purse dog to get through them.

He collapses to the floor, and I sit beside him.

"Now what?" I ask, my voice small.

This time he doesn't snap at me for asking unanswerable questions and instead just drops his forehead onto his arms.

I jump up and go to the control panel. I study it for a moment and then hit the intercom. "Hello? Is there anybody there? We're stuck in the elevator! Do you hear me? *We're stuck in the elevator!*" My voice trembles, and I start jabbing the intercom button over and over again.

There's a distant *boom!* and the elevator starts swinging again, like the pendulum in one of those old-timey clocks my grandmother has in her house.

"What's going on?" I look frantically at Travis. I may not know him, may not even like him very much, but he's the only human being here.

The elevator rocks unsteadily, and dust and water trickle from the ceiling.

Abruptly, the lights go out. I stand still in shock. What did I do? My finger is still pressing the button, and I slowly release it, hoping for some reason that it will make the lights come back on.

It doesn't.

Chapter Twenty-Four

Jesse

There's a large crowd at the Peace Center when I get there on Saturday night in late June. It's been a few weeks since my first awkward day here, and it's gotten better, though some of the kids still whisper about me when I come for teen outreach on Thursday afternoons. Since I'm supposed to be here two days a week, I also come in on Tuesdays and help Yalda with whatever she needs help with. So far, I've stuffed backpacks of food for needy kids, drawn posters for an interfaith meeting, and helped arrange a blood drive.

I was doing inventory on a new shipment of Rab and Sherpa jackets at the climbing shop, so I'm late and all the chairs are taken. I find a place by the wall and lean against it.

I see Sabeen and Adam, and Sabeen smiles at me. Adam

gives me a long look from under his eyelashes and then turns away without acknowledging me.

I swallow, and twirl my ponytail around my finger, around and around and around, until it pulls painfully against my scalp.

There's a screech of amplifier noise, and Yalda, dressed in a long-sleeved tan dress, her hair covered with a white scarf, taps on the microphone. She clears her throat.

"Thank you, everyone, for coming out. The fifteenth anniversary of 9/11 is coming up in less than three months, and we have a very special guest tonight. Anne Jonna was in the World Trade Center on 9/11 and has a story that she'd like to share with us here at the Peace Center. With no more ado, I'd like to present: Anne Jonna."

A thin, dark-haired woman steps up to the podium and adjusts the microphone as the crowd claps. She doesn't say anything at first, just bows her head and closes her eyes, her lips moving in a silent prayer. Around me, others bow their heads as well.

After a moment, she looks up with a beautiful, luminous smile.

"Thank you so much for your warm welcome," she says. "In September it will be fifteen years since the unthinkable happened: planes crashed into the Twin Towers and brought them tumbling down; a plane smashed into the Pentagon; and a group of brave passengers lost their lives in a silent Pennsylvania field. It is one of those rare days in history that is etched into our collective souls. That day could be defined as a day of fear and hate, but I saw something else. Inside the towers, I saw incredible acts of bravery from people of all walks of life. I saw people just like you and me doing what they could to help others in a desperate situation. To me, the bravery and basic human kindness shown by ordinary citizens that day is a shining example of what it means to be human."

She begins to describe her day in the tower, starting so innocently as she sat at her desk checking e-mails and eating yogurt, and then, bam, out of nowhere, everything changed. One plane hit, then another, and then the towers began to fall.

The towers were only half-full. A lot of people weren't at work yet, and the horde of tourists hadn't arrived to visit the observation deck on top of the south tower, or the restaurant on top of the north one. It could have been so much worse. Anne Jonna made it out, and so did approximately twelve thousand other people.

But my brother was not one of them.

∽

I stand at the edge of the group that crowds around Ms. Jonna, and listen to people thank her for her story, and tell her where they were when the planes hit—*standing at my kitchen counter drinking a cup of coffee, on a flight over California and we had to land, lying in bed cuddling my two-year-old daughter.*

I wonder why it's so important that people recount their *own* story whenever the subject of 9/11 comes up. I want to yell, "What does it matter where you were? People were *dying*, my brother was *dying*, and you were home safe in bed!"

But Ms. Jonna listens patiently, and I realize that maybe everybody's story is important, because 9/11 didn't just happen to the people who died, it happened to the entire country. People were living their lives, doing everyday things, when suddenly the planes hit, and time ripped into two pages titled "Before 9/11" and "After." With their clumsy stories, they are saying: "We all felt it. We remember where we were when the world changed."

But what about those of us who could not remember that day? I've seen the footage, watched the big, clumsy planes crash into the towers like some sort of low-budget action film. Which is worse? To know that things used to be different, or to never have known that more innocent day at all?

I'm trembling, and I tug on my ponytail as I inch closer to Ms. Jonna. I *want* to have the courage of those people in the towers, people as ordinary as me who found an incredible well of strength inside themselves that day. What would happen if I said all the words that are hiding inside me, so many that it feels like my chest might burst with them? What if I told Adam that I thought what Nick, Hailey, Dave, and I did was wrong? What if I told my dad that the things he says about Muslims are terrible and hateful and I wish he would stop?

I am standing in front of Ms. Jonna, and her face is kind and smiling. The smile fades as she looks at me.

"Are you okay?" she asks.

I stare at her without speaking. Up close, she has lines at the corners of her eyes, and silver threads running like tinsel through her hair.

"Do you need to sit down?" she asks. Around us people are picking up bags, calling good-byes.

"My brother was in the towers," I say, and it feels like something comes unblocked in my throat.

Ms. Jonna takes my arm and draws me away from the podium to a table, and we sit.

"Did he die?" she asks quietly.

I nod, and feel my eyes burn like they know they should be crying, but no tears come. I've never cried for Travis. How can I cry when I don't even remember knowing him?

"No one knows what he was doing there that day. He shouldn't have been there. He shouldn't have died!" I'm talking too fast, but now that I've started, I can't seem to stop.

"Honey, none of those people should have died," she says, and her voice is full of sympathy. "I knew several people who didn't make it out, and I ask myself every day why them and not me. I felt guilty for a long time. What happened taught me that life is unpredictable; I've considered every day since a gift."

She puts her arms around me and gives me a hug, and I lean my cheek against her shoulder for a moment.

"If you need anything, let me know," she says, patting my back.

"I want to find out what happened to my brother," I say. "His name was Travis McLaurin, he was eighteen, with dark blond hair and greenish eyes. If you ever hear anything about him, could you let me know?"

"Give me your e-mail address, and I'll ask around," she says. "I know it's frustrating not knowing what happened to him, but I need to warn you that most people never found out what happened to their loved ones in those final minutes."

"Thank you," I say, and scribble my e-mail address on a piece of paper.

She squeezes my shoulder, and I get up. I almost run into Adam, who is standing directly behind me. He looks at me, his eyes dark and shadowed, and I know that he heard.

I put my head down and go for the door.

⚬

As I bike toward home, I slow near Teeny's house, seeing Emi's car in her driveway. I wonder what would happen if I went up to the door and knocked. Would Teeny say, "Yeah, no, loser, climb back into your hole" and slam the door in my face? I'd seen my friends' faces when I went back to school. I wasn't the person they thought I was.

My phone dings, and I see that I have a message from Deka.

Hank says look in his closet, the Tupperware
container with blue lid in the back.

Dad has been different in the weeks since Mom left,
and he exploded at me for asking what Travis was doing
in the towers. While Mom has launched us into a flurry of
girl-outings and church services that have left both of us
bewildered and exhausted, Dad has gotten quieter and
quieter.

But since that night I've caught him looking at me a
couple of times, a strange expression on his face. He's stopped
watching the news, and now watches fishing shows, or ESPN,
and while he still yells at the TV, it's because someone missed
a fish or dropped a ball.

He hasn't slept in the room that he used to share with
my mother.

He's sitting at the counter doing some paperwork, a pair
of glasses perched on the end of his nose. He hates those
glasses, hates that he can't see the way he used to.

"Where were you?" he asks when he sees me.

I hesitate, surprised by the question. I can't remember
the last time he asked where I was.

"Community service," I say, which is partially true,
though I didn't have to go tonight.

"How are they treating you? Okay?"

"Okay," I say. "Everybody's been nice, actually."

He stares at me a long moment, as if there is more that

he wants to say, but then just nods and looks back down at his papers.

Conversation with Dad officially over, but at least it didn't end with him screaming.

I hurry past him and throw my bag in my room, and then continue down the hall to Hank's old room. Mom turned it into an office, and it's full of bookcases and a desk covered with fourth-grade schoolbooks and old tests. I head for the closet, which is jammed full of stuff Hank left when he went away and never came back.

Underneath his ice hockey equipment, I see the clear Tupperware container with a blue top, like the one Mom used to put cupcakes in to send with me to school on my birthday. I pull it out and set it on her desk. I glance guiltily at the closed door, half expecting to see Dad there, and then dig my fingers underneath the plastic lid. It comes loose with a pop. The plastic is old and fragile, and a piece of it breaks off in my fingers.

Inside is an answering machine.

Chapter Twenty-Five

Alia

The dark is so heavy and thick that I feel it weighing on me as I sink to the floor. I slide back against the wall, feeling the metal of the railing against my head, and the cool smoothness of the wall through the back of my shirt. Somehow I'm convinced that Travis has disappeared and it's just me in all this blackness. It feels hard to pull air into my lungs, and I start breathing in short, quick gasps.

"Travis?" I ask, panting.

"Yeah, don't move."

I hear him rustling around, but I can't seem to slow down my breathing. I'm getting light-headed.

"Alia? Just calm down, okay?" I hear his voice, but it seems like it's coming from every direction out of the darkness.

Suddenly, there's a scraping sound. Once, twice, and then I see a flare of light.

Travis holds up the lighter so I can see his face. The smoke lazes around the flame, muffling the brightness of the light. Just a few minutes ago the smoke was looping around the top of the car, but now it is circling down closer to us, like a hungry animal biting at the tender place at the back of my throat.

"Okay," he says. "Let's get back to work on the door."

"We've *got* to get out of here," I say.

"That's the plan," he says grimly.

Travis's face is eerily lit by the flame of the lighter as he pulls on the doors. This time, they slide open almost easily.

"What the hell?" Travis says. "The power going out must have unlocked it. There should be another door—"

He holds up the lighter so we can peer through the doors at what's beyond.

A white, blank wall.

"We're stuck between floors," Travis says bleakly. Then he curses, and the lighter goes out.

"Man! It's burning my fingers." His voice is muffled by the press of darkness.

"Let me have it. Let me have it!" I reach over toward him, patting with my hands until I find his stomach. He tenses, and I jerk my hands away, thankful that he can't see my burning cheeks.

"Here." He reaches out until he finds my hands, and clasps them between his own, dropping the lighter into my palm.

It's hot to the touch, and it takes me a try or two to get it lit.

"Now what?" I ask, eyeing the white wall revealed by the open elevator doors.

Travis suddenly reaches back and punches it. A small dent appears, and white powder poofs out.

"Ouch!" He holds his knuckles. "It's drywall." He coughs. The smoke is getting thicker, and it's harder to breathe.

Travis sits on the floor, ducking his head away from the smoke filling the top of the elevator, and uses his knife to cut a square in the drywall. When he pries it out with his fingers, there's another sheet behind the first.

Cursing, Travis starts punching it, but it's awkward from a sitting position. He stands and starts kicking, but immediately begins choking from the smoke.

I look over at my lunch bag and crawl toward it. I grab the Coke, unscrew the top, and pour some of the liquid on a napkin. I hand it up to Travis.

"Try breathing through this."

Without speaking, he takes the napkin and presses it to his nose and mouth. He goes back to kicking at the wall, and big holes appear. He drops to the ground again, and uses the knife to pry out another piece.

Still another layer of drywall.

"Dammit!" Travis cries.

I take the napkin from him and wet it again, and he presses it to his face as he stands up and starts kicking. He's angry, furious, and the piece of drywall disintegrates under his flying feet.

"Okay, okay!" I cry. "Stop!"

He collapses to the floor, coughing. I pick up the knife from the floor and start cutting through the remaining wall, awkward with the lighter in my left hand.

"Oh, no," I moan when I've removed the last piece.

Because behind it is a layer of white tiles.

Travis is still coughing, curled up on the floor. I pick up the soda and douse the front of my shirt. Taking a deep breath, my head close to the floor, I stand up and pull my shirt over my mouth and nose, feeling the stickiness of the soda on my lips. I begin kicking at the tile, crying out as my toes slam into the wall.

I hear a cracking noise, and suddenly there's a flash of faint light and a shatter of falling tile. I drop down to the floor, gasping for breath, and push my face close to the hole.

"It's a bathroom," I gasp. Except for the dimness of the emergency lights, everything looks so normal: clean tile, sinks, toilets. I half expect someone to be washing their hands or fixing their panty hose.

But there's nobody there. I can still hear alarms going off, quieter here in the open.

I withdraw back into the dark, smoky elevator.

"Get up," I tell Travis. "You can't give up—we're almost there."

I push my face to the hole and take several deep breaths

before standing up and kicking again. For a moment, I am in Lia's world, and I can see the scene:

Girl in charcoal gray shadows, the white glow of her scarf the only contrast, her foot in the process of hitting the wall as large chunks of tile fly into the bathroom beyond and explode onto the floor.

I redouble my efforts, because *I can do this, I have to do this,* and suddenly Travis is yelling hoarsely from where he still lies on the floor.

"Alia! That's it. That's enough!"

I'd been in a sort of frenzy, and it takes me a moment to understand what he's saying. I drop to the floor.

"Go," Travis says. "Go, go, go!"

I squirm through the ragged hole, barely noticing as broken tiles scrape my shoulders and hips before I drop onto the white tile floor.

A moment later, Travis follows me.

He's covered with white dust from head to toe, and for some reason I laugh.

"You should see yourself," I say.

"Right back atchoo," he retorts and smiles. "That's what my brother Hank used to say when he was little. I'd tease him, and he'd say, 'Right back atchoo.'"

"How old is he now?" I ask.

"Sixteen. And I have a baby sister. Jesse. She's a pain, but, man, she loves her some Travis."

I smile at the big-brotherly combination of affection and exasperation in his voice.

"Okay," I say, taking a deep breath. "What now?"

"Let's go find out what the hell is going on."

"I need to call my parents," I say. "They must be worried about me."

We turn toward the door, but it suddenly occurs to me that my parents have no idea I'm here.

Chapter Twenty-Six

Jesse

I stare at the answering machine, feeling a deep pit of awful in my stomach. I get up and go back into the closet, searching for another Tupperware container, but there isn't one. I'm not sure what I was expecting from Hank, but it wasn't this.

Hank is so much older than me that he always seemed more like an uncle than a brother. He went away to college when I was just four, choosing a college halfway across the country instead of the one right here in town. Mainly I remember him coming to visit, though I have a few memories from before he left. He gave me a pickle, told me it was a cookie, and I believed him. He used to let me ride on his shoulders, and we would gallop around the apartment, him yelling "duck!" every time we approached a doorway.

The last time I saw him, he gave me an awkward hug and said in my ear, "Don't let them get you down, Jess, okay?"

I will always be his baby sister, and he's trying to help me in his own way.

I unplug Mom's printer and plug the answering machine into the wall. When I turn around, I see that there is a red light blinking.

A message.

All of a sudden, I can't breathe.

Do I want to listen to this? *Yes* and *no* ricochet off each other in my head.

I press the Play button, and hear a guy's voice, scared, but trying not to sound like it.

"Hello? . . . there? I'm . . . World Trade Center. Hello? Anyone there?"

I realize with a cold, knifing certainty that this is my brother Travis's voice. I don't remember having heard it before, but who else could it be?

"Hello?"

"Listen . . . bad. I don't know . . ." There's a lot of static, and Travis's voice is jumbled and unclear. Then, *". . . I . . . you, Mom, and Hank and Jesse and, and . . . Dad, I know you . . . okay?"*

I shiver as he says my name. I might not remember him, but to Travis I was a cute and cuddly toddler he had already learned to love.

There's a long pause, and then I hear a girl's voice in the background, crying as she speaks.

"Tell them . . . mother! Tell . . . Ayah . . . find him . . . love . . . so much! Tell . . ."

Travis's voice again, *"That's . . . with me,"* and the message ends.

Chapter Twenty-Seven

Alia

As soon as we push through the doors into the hallway, we can smell smoke again. The hallway is empty, and a few ceiling tiles lie on the floor. I can see daylight out a window, and it seems so strange that the sky would still be blue, that the sun is still shining, that the world outside is rolling along like it always does.

"Where is everybody?"

The buildings are usually filled with people, coursing and humming through the corridors and lobbies and elevators. I've listened to summer concerts on the plaza, ice-skated in the winter, visited my father in his offices numerous times, and there are *always* people.

"Let's see if we can find someone." Travis sets off purposefully down the hall.

"We need to find a phone," I say, hurrying to keep up with him.

We run down the hall, jumping over some debris on the floor, and stop in front of the doors to the first offices we find. Even though emergency strobe lights are pulsing and alarms are going off, even though we know something is wrong, it still feels weird to just bust into the office.

Travis puts his hand on the door handle. I guess we are both half expecting to find people behind the door, working away at their desks, and we will back out with apologetic smiles, whispering, "Sorry, our mistake." Actually, I close my eyes for a moment, praying that's what we'll find. *Please God, if it is your will, make everything go back to the way it was this morning.* How could everything go wrong so quickly?

"There's so many people here that they gave the buildings their own ZIP code," Travis says, and I know he's wondering like I am where all the people are.

He takes a deep breath, and opens the door.

I know even before I peek over his shoulder that the office is empty. It's obvious people left in a hurry. Coffee still steams on a desk, a chair is knocked over, and a drawer is open, full of women's shoes, like someone hurriedly switched shoes right before leaving.

"There's a phone!" I run to the phone on the desk nearest to us.

"We should call the OCC," Travis says as I pick up the phone. "They'll know what's going on."

I don't answer, because I have every intention of calling my father and mother. It doesn't matter either way, because all I hear is a fast busy signal. I jiggle the receiver a couple of times, but it's the same thing.

"Everybody must be calling out," Travis says, after taking the phone from me and listening for himself. "I don't know what's going on, but it must be bad."

I nod, because I know he's right. Nothing less than a full-scale emergency would drive everyone out like this.

"Gramps said during the '93 bombing, there were some people who didn't evacuate," Travis says. "We'd probably find people if we kept looking, but I don't think we should take the time. Let's get out first, and then we can worry later about what's going on."

"Okay." I swallow hard. I'd hoped we could find some people to tell us it was all okay, that we were panicking for nothing.

Travis is heading for the door when he stops, his hands in his pockets, like he's searching for something.

"What are you doing?" I ask, wanting to go, to get out, right now.

"No," he says, his face tight. "No, no, *no.*" He's patting his pockets more frantically now.

"What?"

"I've got to go back," he says.

"Go back where?"

"The elevator," he says, and takes off running back the way we came.

I run after him. "Are you crazy? You can't go back into the elevator!"

But he doesn't seem to hear me.

I put on a burst of speed, thankful for my mornings spent running, because I'm determined not to get left behind.

Travis bursts through the bathroom door, and I follow right behind him.

"Stop!" I cry as I see him heading for the dark, ragged hole in the wall where we had slithered out just a few minutes ago. "You can't go back in there!"

But he is already wriggling headfirst through the hole, grunting with the effort, and then he disappears back into the elevator car we fought so hard to get out of.

"Travis!" I cry.

I hear him cursing inside, and I rush to the hole and press my face to it. I pull back immediately, because it is hot and smoky and I can hear Travis coughing.

"What are you doing?" I yell furiously.

I take a deep breath and put my face to the hole again, and see Travis scrabbling around with the lighter in his hand. He finds something on the floor and stuffs it into his pocket. He is coughing badly, and as he comes back out of the hole, his eyes are streaming.

"What are you doing?" I shout at him.

He won't look at me.

"Come on, we need to get out of here," he mumbles as he heads toward the door to the corridor.

"That's what *I* said," I say, but he's already gone.

Out in the hallway, Travis finds a stairwell door and yanks it open. The first thing I hear is running water, like someone decided to run a nice hot bath. Then I see the people, and my heart leaps with joy. Somehow I'd half convinced myself that we were the last people left in the building.

Travis is standing like a stupid statue in the doorway, and when I push by him impatiently, I see why.

It's dark and hot, and water is sliding down walls from the ceiling and pouring down the steps. It's smoky, like maybe there's a bonfire close by that you could char some nice halal marshmallows on, but it's not like any fire I've ever smelled. The stench is rotten, thick with chemicals.

People walk by, barely glancing at us. One man is injured and being helped down by a few of the others.

"What's going on?" I ask loudly.

"We don't know," a man carrying a briefcase says.

For some reason I thought once we found people that everything was going to be all right. But these people, these adults, don't seem to know anything more than we do.

We join the crowd going down, slipping on stairs made slick from all the water.

"How long is this going to take?" I ask.

"This is a piece of cake compared to '93," says an older man with dark strands of hair combed over his bald, freckled head. "When the bomb in the van blew up, a bunch of cars in the parking garage caught fire and it sent this thick, black oily smoke up the stairwells."

A lady with square blue glasses and a pretty dress glances over her shoulder. "I almost stayed in my office, because it took me ten hours to get out last time." She shakes her head. "But this is different. I don't know what's going on, but this is different. At least they put in the emergency lights and *these*"—she points down at the stairs—"so we can see. Last time it was so dark you couldn't see anything."

I hadn't even really noticed the glowing stripes of paint on the stair treads, and I try to imagine what it would have been like to go down these narrow steps in complete darkness. No wonder some people decided to stay in their offices the last time.

"Hey, what's the holdup?" someone yells from behind us, and I realize that we have slowed to a stop.

"The door's stuck," someone calls back, and the crowd around us begins murmuring and jostling.

"*What* door?" the same voice yells. It's a young guy in a suit with an arrogant face and eyes full of fear.

"Calm down, big boy," the older man with the freckled head says. "We're going to get out of here—we just need to stay calm."

"I *am* calm," the young guy yells back, not sounding calm at all.

As we crowd down the stairs, it's so tight that I'm having trouble breathing.

Travis and I have made it to a landing, and below we see a few men beating on a door that inexplicably bars the way.

"What the heck?" someone says. "Why's there a door in the middle of the stairwell?"

"And why's it locked?" a woman asks in a wavering voice, holding a hand to the baby bump of her belly. "Did someone lock it on purpose?"

"It's not locked, it's stuck," a person nearer the door calls back.

"Watch out!" someone yells, and a big man takes a few running steps at the door with a fire extinguisher in his hands. It slams against the door, and white foam spurts out, soaking the people directly behind him and floating up the stairs like a white mist of snow.

But the door doesn't budge.

A woman starts crying.

"Wait, I know another way," someone says, and all of a sudden everyone is turning around. Then we are going *up*, which feels wrong.

"It'll be okay," Travis says, sliding his eyes at me, but he doesn't look like he believes his own words.

We go up and out another door. Small fires are flickering in the ceiling. Pieces of drywall and debris litter the floor, and wires hang from the ceiling like skinny black snakes curling above our heads.

"Don't touch anything," someone says, and I find myself pressing up against Travis as we edge down the hall, the fires burning almost merrily over our heads. Ahead, we see a man with another fire extinguisher dousing the flames. Clouds of fine spray drift down the hall.

"Where are we *going*?" a woman shouts, but nobody answers.

Another door with an exit sign appears through the smoke, and people speed up as the flames begin to flare again.

"Go!" the guy with the extinguisher cries, but instead of following his own advice, he waits until Travis and I are past and then turns back to the flames.

I turn to look at him just before I go through the door into the stairwell. He continues to spray the fire, stopping only long enough for people to pass. His fire extinguisher is the only thing that is keeping this path to freedom passable.

I close my eyes and pray for him as I follow Travis down the stairs.

Chapter Twenty-Eight

Jesse

I listen to Travis's message over and over again.

I make out a few more words after a while, but it's so hard to understand what Travis is saying with all the static and background noise.

At some point I send Hank a message:

Who's the girl?

But he doesn't answer. He's probably out in the field, and who knows how long it will take for him to get my message?

I listen to the last part over and over again. I have a feeling that Travis says the girl's name when he says, "That's . . . with me."

Who was with him? Who was the girl who sounded so

desperate and young? Did she die with Travis, or did she make it out?

I'm shaken by her voice. She sounds like one of my friends. She sounds like me.

Why was she in the World Trade Center with Travis that day?

I hit Play so many times that by three in the morning when I finally give up, my finger is hurting.

When I wake the next morning, I know who I need to call, even though I have no idea whether she will talk to me.

I walk into Starbucks and see her sitting at our favorite table, the one by the window. She is sipping on a coffee, her finger dancing across her tablet screen.

I sit down.

"Hi, Emi," I say.

"Hello, Jesse," she says warily, fiddling with the rings in her ear and sitting up straight, the way she always does when she's nervous.

"I, uh, need help, and I don't have anyone else to ask. I know we're really not friends anymore, and I get it. I wouldn't want to be friends with me either if I were you. All I can say is I'm sorry. And . . . I need your help." I shut up and try to read her expression, but her face remains blank, like an empty page loading for too long.

"I never said I didn't want to be friends with you," she says after a moment. "You pretty much made that choice."

"I was messed up in the head, Emi. I don't know what

happened. I really don't. Everything got so weird with the tagging, and all the secrets, it just seemed easier not to talk to you guys. I didn't know what to say to you."

"The truth," she says simply.

"I'm so, so sorry," I begin. If you say something too much, does it become as meaningless as pennies thrown on the ground? Because this apology is worth a billion pennies, this one I mean with all my heart. "You'll never know how sorry I am, Emi. I don't want to lose you, and Teeny and Myra. I have no explanation, no excuses. But I'm trying to do something good now, and I need help."

"They put my great-grandparents in a camp, you know," she says, and I stare at her in confusion.

"What?"

"My mom told me. During World War II. They rounded up a bunch of Japanese Americans and put them in camps. Not because they did anything wrong, just because of what they were."

"What?" I say again, because while I've heard about this in some class or another, I have no idea why she's telling me about it *now*.

"And when my grandmother was growing up, she remembers her next-door neighbor calling her a Jap and telling her he wished America had nuked all of us, not just those two cities."

She looks at me seriously. "If you don't like Muslims so much, how do you feel about the Japanese?" Which, of course, slashes to the bloody friendship-heart of why she's still mad at me.

"I don't hate Muslims. I don't hate the Japanese. I don't hate *you*." I pull at my ponytail, knowing I deserve this, but desperate for her to believe me. "Why would I have been friends with you for all these years if I didn't like you?"

"I've asked myself that more than once," she answers. "I never could come up with an answer. But what you did . . . writing those ugly words . . . that wasn't who I thought you were. I'm not sure I could ever be friends with that person."

I know I should say something, to explain, but I can't, and I stare down at my lap, defeated.

I wait for her to get up and leave, but she doesn't. After a while, I lift my head and see her calmly watching me.

"What do you need?" she asks.

∞

"This thing is *ancient*," Emi says, holding up a microcassette tape from inside the answering machine. "Wow."

She shakes her head. I sit on her bed as she turns the machine over in her hands, mutters to herself something that sounds like, "Where's the outgoing jack? *Really?*" and then she goes to a shelf over her computer and starts rummaging through neatly labeled boxes.

"Ha!" she says, pulling out a small rectangular device.

"What is that?" I stare at it curiously.

"It's a voice recorder. I used it in school before I got my phone and could record lectures on that."

Of course she did. In the fifth grade. I sigh, happy to be back in Emi's crazy-simple world.

She pops the cassette from the answering machine into the voice recorder and runs a wire from it to her computer. She's just sitting down at her desk when Teeny and Myra come in. They stop when they see me.

"Look what the cat dragged in," Teeny says, yanking her dark hair over her shoulder with a small fist. "Slumming with the minorities, Jesse?"

Myra just glances at me, and then starts typing furiously on her phone, maybe "What to say to your ex-friend when you just wish she'd go the hell away."

"I'm sorry," I say to all of them. "I know what I did was terrible, but you know I'm not like that. Okay, maybe I *was* like that, but it was the worst feeling ever. I don't hate anybody. I screwed up royally. I made a stupid, terrible decision. But we've been friends for a long time, and I hope that if you screwed up as majorly as I did, that I'd at least give you one more chance."

They stare at me in surprise.

"Holy heck, *chica*, what got into you?" Teeny says. "Your time in the slammer turn you into a woman?"

"Oh shut up," I say grumpily.

"Why didn't you just talk to us?" Myra asks. "Why didn't you tell us what was going on?"

"Somehow I thought I couldn't," I say.

"We would've knocked some sense into you. Or tied you up. Something," Teeny says. "You know how many people tell me I need to go back to Mexico? Like that makes any freaking sense. I was *born* here, and my mom is Guatemalan, but some people aren't the sharpest crayons in the box. So what you did . . . it hurt."

I nod, and fix my gaze on the bedspread. "I'm sorry," I say softly. "I never meant to hurt anyone."

"One more thing," Teeny says, and there's something in her voice that makes me look up. "I just think you should know that you might be vanilla-white with a pedigree from the freaking Mayflower, but you still can't dance."

I look at all of them, my gorgeous friends with hearts open as they smile at me, and know I should have realized that true friendship is big enough to leave room for mistakes. Things might not be completely straight between us but they are infinitely better than they were.

"Okay, I've got it," Emi says, turning back to the computer. "I downloaded some free software that's supposed to help us clean up the recording. We'll see." Her fingers fly over the keyboard.

"What's going on?" Teeny asks.

I explain, and Myra says, "Wow, that's sad, and cool, all at the same time."

Teeny curls up on the bed beside me. "So, let's hear it."

Emi types furiously, and we can see graphs on her screen

with lines going up and down. "I'm going to try to reduce the background noise," she says as Travis's first words play over and over again.

Hello? . . . there? I'm . . . World Trade Center.

Hello? Is . . . there? I'm . . . World Trade Center.

Hello? Is . . . there? I'm in . . . World Trade Center.

Each time it gets clearer.

"You're a genius," I exclaim.

"I know. My mother had me tested," Emi says, and her mouth quirks.

"See if you can hear what he says at the end. When he says the girl's name."

Emi nods and turns back to the computer. We sit in silence as she continues to work.

"Okay," she says finally. "Let's see what we have."

She hits the button, and Travis's voice fills the air from her powerful speakers.

It's still static-y and fuzzy, still missing a lot of words, but when we get to the end, when Travis says, *"That's . . . with me,"* this time we can make out the name.

Alia.

That's Alia with me.

My brother was in the towers with a girl named Alia.

"What was she doing in the towers with your brother?" Teeny asks.

"I don't even know why Travis was in the towers," I say.

Myra has been busy on her phone, and she looks up. "If I'm spelling it right, 'Alia' means sublime, lofty, or exalted. Whatever the heck that means. And get this, the name is either Jewish or Muslim."

We stare at her in surprise.

"You've never talked about your brother before," Emi says slowly. "You told me when we were kids that he died on 9/11, but you didn't seem to want to talk about it, so I never asked any questions."

"Why now?" Teeny asks. "What makes you decide to talk about your brother Travis after all these years?"

"It's hard to explain," I say honestly, because how do I explain the barbed wire around my heart that trapped everything in and kept them out? "Everything is so messed up with my family, and it has been for a long time, but it's like I never even noticed, because I didn't know anything different. Travis is dead, but I'm still alive, though my parents don't seem to *get* that. Now they're getting a divorce, or something, and . . . somehow I feel like if I figure out what happened to Travis, maybe it'll help. I know, it's stupid." I twirl my hair and stare determinedly at a wall because I can't meet their eyes.

There's a long silence, and when I finally glance up, the three of them are exchanging a look they all seem to understand.

"As long as you don't go batcrap crazy again, we'll help you," Teeny says. "We want to forgive you, we really do. But what you did was some pretty serious stuff."

"I missed you guys," I say quietly. "I missed you guys so much."

"I prayed that you would come back to us," Teeny says matter-of-factly. She doesn't make a big deal about religion, but the thought of Teeny-prayers coming my way makes me smile, makes me feel stronger.

"Just talk to us when things start going sideways, okay?" Myra says.

"We're here," Emi says simply.

I turn my head so they can't see my tears, but then they pile on for a group hug, and somehow we're all crying, even Emi.

When we finally unwind, Teeny says, "Speaking of batcrap crazy . . . What about your dad? Does he know you've gone all Nancy Drew on your brother?"

"No," I say. "I'm pretty sure if he found out what I was doing, he wouldn't speak to me again. Ever."

At this point, I am the only person in our family that Dad is speaking to.

I wonder how long that will last.

Chapter Twenty-Nine

Alia

We run into more people in the stairwell, and most people seem calm, one lady even joking that she should have worn her running shoes. It's hot though, and the rank, dirty-smelling smoke burns the back of my throat. I pull my shirt over my nose again, and wish I'd thought to bring the half-full bottle of Coke still back in the elevator. I am so thirsty.

Just one sip, one swallow of Coke.

Travis is checking stairwell doors as we pass, and many of them are locked, though a few open. He lets them swing shut, and nods to himself.

A woman ahead of us is having some sort of panic attack. She stops in the middle of the stairs, just crying, and saying, "I can't go any farther. *I just can't.*"

Her friends are urging her along, while people squeeze by

on her left and continue their downward trudge, some with their hands on the shoulders of the people in front of them. The woman in front of me pats the crying lady on the arm as she passes and says, "It gonna be all right, okay, honey? Just keep goin'."

I like that, her patting the stranger. It feels right, like something Lia would do, though Lia would have whisked us all to safety by now.

I touch the crying lady's shoulder as we pass, whispering, "It'll be all right."

Because it *will*. It has to be.

Behind me, I hear people murmuring the same words as they pass the woman. I look up before we turn the next corner, and she is moving again, her face pale and determined.

No one seems to know what is going on, though a few people are talking about a small plane hitting the tower.

"And, really, wasn't it bound to happen?" a woman behind us says. "The towers are so much bigger than everything else around." She sounds like the fact that the towers are so tall reflects on her, like they do the whole city proud by their sheer, unabashed size.

Someone cries, "Move over, move over!" and we squish to the right of the staircase. A man comes down with another man, and he's hurt and bleeding.

I stare in dismay, realizing suddenly that whatever is wrong, is *really, really wrong.*

"Stop using your cell phone!" a woman in front of us yells

at a guy stopped in the stairwell with his phone pressed to his ear.

"What's your problem?" he asks. "It's not even working."

"Maybe the cell phone signals are what's detonating the bombs," the woman says, her voice high and shrill. "You could be setting them off right now."

"Oh, come on," someone else says. "Calm down. I'd kill to find a working cell phone so I can call my husband. The first phone we find working, I'm buying stock in *that* company."

Travis is impatient, stepping around people if they slow too much in front of him, but he always checks to make sure I am still behind him.

We continue walking down, dizzy with the reversals of direction each time we reach a landing. Ten steps to a landing, turn, another ten steps. Over and over again.

I'm already getting tired, and we still have such a long, long way to go. In Lia's world, she goes to the mosque to recharge her superhero energy when she starts to run low, and always comes out stronger and braver after she prays. I think about how I felt when I prayed *Fajr* on the rooftop this morning, the great arc of the blue sky overhead, and it calms me, gives me strength.

Legs aching, thighs trembling, I keep walking.

"What do you do when you're not pickpocketing and saving damsels in distress from elevators?" I ask Travis.

He huffs out an impatient breath.

"By now you should know me well enough to know I

don't do good with silence," I tell him snappishly. "So talk to me."

He sort of smiles, and I think again how cute he is with his too-long hair and distinctive eyes.

"I like to play the saxophone," he says. "My grandfather taught me, and I used to be in a band with my buddies. Greg and Graydon. We called ourselves the Do-Gooders, and we used to do a few gigs around town. The name was kind of a joke."

"Really?" I'm all wide-eyed innocence.

"Really," he says, and throws me a quick grin.

"Is that what you want to do?" I ask. "Play in a band?"

He's quiet for a moment. "I haven't played for a while," he says. "We were never good enough to do anything but play at the local bars anyway. I thought . . . I thought it would be pretty cool to teach kids to love music, the way my gramps did for me. My mom's a teacher, and I see what she does for her kids, and how much she loves it."

"Is that what you're going to school for?"

He laughs shortly, but not like anything is funny. "No, I'm not in college," he says. "I did go for almost a year, but I quit. Since then, I've just been hanging out." There's more, a lot more, but he won't meet my eyes, and for some reason I remember how sad and upset he looked in the elevator just before it fell.

"What about you? What do you want to do when you grow up?" He's changing the subject from himself, and I let him.

"A rodeo clown," I say immediately, because it's what I

always say for the shock value. "I want to dress up in funny clothes, wear lots of makeup, and dodge bulls."

Travis manages to smile. "Sounds about right. Isn't that what everyone does?"

"No, seriously, what I *really* want to do is write comic books," I say, kind of surprising myself, because it's not something I talk about with anyone but my closest friends. "But I can't do that, so I don't know. My parents want me to be something with a bunch of letters after my name."

"Why can't you write comic books?" He acts like it's a serious question.

"Come on. Who actually does that?"

"Somebody does. Why not you?"

I shake my head. "It just sounds like something a little kid would want to do, like be a ballerina, or a princess."

He shrugs. "Sounds like you're too scared to go after something you really want."

We stop talking after that, but I think about what he said.

Am I scared? Is that why I don't take my dream to write comic books seriously? And how can my parents take it seriously if, deep inside me, *I* don't?

A lady in front of us is going slower and slower, her heavy purse drooped down to the crook between her arm and her elbow, almost pulling her over.

"Ma'am?" Travis says. "Are you okay?"

I can tell he's edgy, but his voice is polite.

"I'm just so tired," she whispers.

"Do you want me to carry your purse for you?" he asks.

The exhausted woman gratefully gives him her purse. He slings it over his shoulder, and she continues down the stairs, going faster now.

I pull my shirt back over my nose, because the fumes are getting to me.

A few flights down, the woman begins to slow again. Travis had just checked a stairwell door—locked—and when he turns around, the woman sinks down so she is sitting on the stairs. Both Travis and I crowd around her as people begin moving by us. I see for the first time that she's young, a lot younger than I thought. Her dark hair is pulled back into a messy braid and she has soft brown eyes and freckles on her nose. Even wrenched in pain, with mascara racooning her eyes, her face is pretty and wholesome.

"I have a heart condition. I've had it since I was a kid," she gasps. "Crazy, huh? A twenty-two-year-old with a bad heart. It's like some sort of cosmic joke. I'm not supposed to exert myself too much. I'm not sure—I'm not sure I can keep going."

"Yes, you can," Travis says. He grabs one of her arms and looks at me. I nod, and grab her other arm. We start back down the stairs, and she leans heavily on us.

"I'm sorry, I'm sorry," she says, her teeth clenched, her wide eyes streaming with tears. "Just go on, leave me."

We don't though. Lia wouldn't leave her, and I won't either.

Chapter Thirty

Jesse

I walk home from Emi's house smiling, because it feels so good to be back in with my friends. Emi is going to keep working on the message and save it to a flash drive for me. The biggest surprise is the girl. Alia. Who was she?

I turn onto Main Street and hear laughter. I look up to see Nick, Dave, and Hailey coming toward me.

My stomach plunges into the vicinity of my knees, and I force myself to breathe. I knew Nick must be out of juvenile detention—he only got ten days—but this is the first time I've seen him since he got out.

He's got his hair shaved close to his scalp, and it's dyed white blond. Another tattoo snakes up around his neck, and he looks different, harder, more dangerous. I wanted to believe those good moments between us weren't just my imagination. I've spent months trying to forget what he said to me the first time he saw me in the halls after we'd all been arrested—*You were just like the rest of them. I wanted to see how far a good girl would go.*

"There's our favorite bitch-squealer," Hailey says in a sickly sweet voice as they get closer to me.

Dave's face is red with anger, his fists clenched at his side.

Nick just stares at me with eyes glittering with hate.

How can someone go from caring about you to hating you, like flipping a page in a book? Or had he ever really cared about me at all?

I try to go past them, but Hailey steps in front of me. "You stupid, stupid bitch," she hisses. "Don't think we forgot about you."

Instinctively I glance at Nick, to see whether he's going to stand up for me, but he has that twisted smile on his face like when he talked about getting even with his brother.

Suddenly Dave is in my face. "You're a worthless piece of human garbage. I wish you would just *die.*" His spit flies into my face.

"Nick's dad kicked him out," Hailey says. "Are you proud of yourself?"

I step back from them, and I want to say, "We did it to ourselves! We knew it was wrong, and we did it anyway. Why are you blaming me?"

But I don't say anything.

Nick takes a step toward me, and then he has hold of my

arm. "You're just like us," he says in a hard voice, right in my face. "Nobody cares about you; you're nothing, just like us. If you want to be someone, you have to *make* them notice you. Look at you. You've become like the rest of them, a stupid sheep that just wants to follow the herd."

I know he's wrong, know it bone deep.

"No," I say, the word stuttering like an engine trying to get started. "*No*," I say again, and it roars to life. "What we did was *wrong*. It was wrong to do the tagging, and it was wrong to write what I did on the side of the Peace Center. I knew it was wrong, and I did it anyway. So did you."

But why did we do it? I still don't know for sure, but I think I have an idea. Hate is just fear. Fear that we are powerless, ugly, small, *nothing*, so we hate people to make us feel better about ourselves, so we don't have to be so scared all the time.

"We should have stopped one another," I say quietly.

I am trembling, and suddenly Nick is shaking me. My head whips back and forth as I stare into his eyes and see the hate and rage in them.

"Let her go," a cold voice says from behind me.

Nick's face twists into a sneer.

I yank my arm away from Nick and back away from him. Adam gives me a quick glance, and then looks back at Nick, Dave, and Hailey.

"Stay the hell away from her," Adam says to Nick, stepping forward so he's almost chest to chest with him.

Nick stares at Adam, and you can tell he's thinking about

taking a swing at him, but we've already attracted a small crowd, and he backs away with that creepy smile. I realize suddenly that Nick is a coward. I wanted so badly to see something better in him, but my wishful thinking was never going to make him a different person. He gave me something that felt so big and important at the time, but in the end it was all a fun-house mirror that reflected back the things I hated the most about myself. He pulls the strings of people's emotions from behind the scenes, but he'll never stand up for anything, for *anybody*, ever.

"You better watch your back," Dave says to Adam. "We know where you live. You *and* your sister."

"I'm petrified." Adam sounds bored. "Does that make you feel better?"

Dave is so angry that he's shaking, but the three of them walk away, real slow, as if they haven't just been chased away.

"Are you okay?" Adam's voice is expressionless, but there is a flash of something hot and angry in his eyes.

I nod.

"Come on. I better walk you home," he says.

"Thank you," I say in a small voice. Now that the confrontation is over, I'm trembling like crazy. But there's a small glow of . . . something. Pride? Because for once I said what I needed to say.

If only I could do the same thing with my dad.

"Would you have fought all three of them?" I ask. "They could have hurt you."

"With *both* hands tied behind my back," Adam says. "You don't look this good and not have to fight every once in a while."

He says it deadpan, and I sneak a look at his face, but he doesn't smile. I think that Adam probably *does* know how to fight, not because he's handsome, but because there are so many people like Nick, Dave, and Hailey in the world.

He walks me all the way to the shop, and waits as I go inside.

I turn to look at him, leaning against the rail at the bottom of the steps, his dark hair blowing across his face. He stares at me for a long moment and then walks away without speaking.

ᘉ

That evening, I spend hours combing the Internet. I find a list of names of people who died in the towers, and even though they are in alphabetical order by last name, I don't know Alia's last name, or even how to spell her first name, really. I read each name, almost three thousand of them, one by one.

It takes a long time.

When I get to the *M*'s, I read slower and slower, my stomach clenching with dread. When I finally see Travis's name, I feel dizzy. It's not like I didn't know he died that day, but somehow seeing his name listed with all those other people makes it feel too real.

When I get to the end, I sit back in my chair.

Her name is not on the list.

Whoever Alia was, she didn't die in the towers.

Chapter Thirty-One

Alia

Travis and I help the woman through a stairwell door into a corridor. The lights are working on this floor, and everything looks almost normal, though the alarms are still blaring nonstop overhead. I see a sign for a bathroom and rush toward it. It feels stupid to be thinking about something as ordinary as going to the bathroom right now, but people still have to pee, still have to cry, still have to be human, no matter what else is happening.

As I reach the door, I remember that in my father's office, at least, you need a key to get into the restroom, but the door frame is twisted and the bathroom door is open an inch. When I'm done, the toilet won't flush and the sink won't turn on when I try to wash my hands.

"Come on!" I cry, because I'm so, so thirsty.

When I come out, the dark-haired woman is sitting in a rolling office chair in the middle of the hall. Her purse is in her lap.

"Thank you," she says wearily. "Thank you for helping me. My name's Julia."

"I'm Alia," I say.

She nods, and then pauses a moment to put her hand to her chest. Then she continues. "I got separated from my coworkers in the stairwell. We were all holding hands to stay together, but somehow when I looked up, I didn't see anybody I knew. I appreciate your helping me, but you need to go now. I'll rest here and keep going in a bit."

I shake my head, *no, we're not leaving you,* but I *want* to leave her. I want to run down the stairs as fast as I can, pushing people out of the way if I have to. I want to get out of this building.

I want it so bad, I start walking in circles between the stairwell door and her, just pacing. This feels like life-and-death. Do I really have the time to think about anybody but myself? If staying means I die, do I really want to stay with some woman I only met five minutes ago?

I need to get out.

"Where did Travis go?" I say, suddenly realizing I haven't seen him since I came out of the bathroom.

Julia shakes her head. "I don't know," she says, her voice coming out in gasps. "He was just here . . ."

Did he leave? Abandon us? I was just thinking about it,

and now he's gone, *and maybe Travis was thinking the same thing I was.*

While I've only known Julia for five minutes, I've barely known Travis much longer. Why should he stay with us?

But the thought of him leaving me opens up a yawning gulf of fear so big I almost fall into it.

"I'm going to go see if I can find him," I announce.

"Be careful," Julia murmurs, her eyes closed.

I hear voices shouting nearby and run down the hallway. Around a corner I see several men standing in front of a bank of elevators.

The elevators look like something exploded inside. The thick green marble walls are buckled and black, and the elevator doors are bulging outward. And inside I can hear people calling for help.

"Something's jamming it shut up top," one of the men says, peering up at the elevator door. "We gotta find something to pry it open."

"Let me go see what I can find," a younger guy says and takes off down the hall.

"Just hold on!" the third man, in a royal blue shirt, cups his hands and yells into the elevator doors.

When he steps back to exchange a worried look with the other man, I hear the desperate calls and see the fingers.

My stomach drops sickeningly as I recognize the pale writhing things coming through the cracked elevator doors as the fingers of the people trapped inside. Now I can hear their frantic voices and what they are saying.

"It's so hot, and people are hurt in here!"

"The fireball burned him. I don't think he's breathing!"

"Get us out of here!"

I feel sick.

The two men are talking in low voices, and one of them catches sight of me.

"What are you doing?" he yells at me, and I'm surprised by the ferocity in his voice.

"I'm looking for—" I begin.

"You've got to *get out of here!*" He advances toward me, making shooing motions with his hands. "Get out!"

I back away from him, but my chin comes up. "I'm just looking for my friend," I say loudly, but then I see that he's not angry. He's scared. More scared than I've ever seen anybody in my life.

I take another step back from him, and over his shoulder I see the young guy come out of a door with something in his hand. A leg from an office chair, I realize numbly.

"Two have already hit—do you think there can't be a third?" the man in the blue shirt screams at me. "Go!"

I turn around and go.

Chapter Thirty-Two

Jesse

The Saturday before the Fourth of July is gloomy and dripping, but I hardly notice as I'm sitting on the floor of Hank's closet, going through his and Travis's stuff.

Okay, so I don't feel exactly right about it, but Hank still hasn't gotten back to me, and it's been over a week. I know now that he's avoiding me, and that makes me want to catch a plane to Somalia and kick his ass. But since I can't, I'm going to do some good old-fashioned invasion-of-privacy.

I open an old, battered instrument case, and run my fingers over the tarnished saxophone inside. I'd seen stacks of music scores, and guessed they were Travis's, as his obituary mentioned that he was in a band. I close the music case and put it carefully back where I found it.

There's an entire box of trophies of all shapes and sizes, Travis's and Hank's, and stuck at the bottom of the box is an old stuffed animal of Hank's he kept around even when he got older.

My phone buzzes, and I pull it out and see I have an e-mail from Anne Jonna.

> I found a woman who remembers a young man in the towers who might be your brother. I gave her your contact information. Her name is Julia.

I stare at the message for a moment, feeling a flutter of excitement in my belly, and then turn with renewed determination to the closet. I'm getting closer. I can feel it.

A stack of yearbooks teeters on the top shelf of the closet.

I stand on tiptoe to lift them down. I pick up one from 2000, because that was the year Travis graduated. There are actually two of them, because Hank was a freshman in 2000, but a quick look at the inscriptions inside shows me which one is Travis's. The scrawled notes across the front pages are mainly generic, like *Stay sweet, Travis!* and *Let's keep in touch!* But a few are more interesting: *I'll never forget that party when you rode the pig* and *When you hit the big time don't forget us little guys.*

I turn to the senior section and find Travis's graduation picture, a twin to the smirking, shaggy-haired kid they use every year in the articles. I look up Travis's name in the index and there are two listings for him. One for his senior picture, and one on page 21.

I turn to page 21, and see a picture of Travis holding a saxophone, with two other guys. One is behind a drum set and the other holds a guitar. Travis is in baggy jeans and an over-sized T-shirt, with a small, kind of wistful smile. The caption reads: "The Do-Gooders: Greg Laramore, Travis McLaurin, and Graydon Hunt."

Wait a minute.

I bend over the yearbook, studying the picture until I'm sure. The guy on the left, Greg Laramore, is Mr. Hipster himself, my Entrepreneurship teacher. He's wearing a floppy hat and shades, but it's definitely him.

It's a small town, so I don't know why I'm surprised that I would know one of Travis's old friends. But a teacher? What would Travis be doing if he were still alive? He'd be turning thirty-four this year. What did he want to do when he grew up? Travis had never seemed like me and my friends. He'd been this mythical figure who vanished in smoke and flames. As crazy as it sounds, I am just realizing that he was just a little bit older than I am right now when he died.

Shaken, I run my fingers over the picture of Travis, like I can feel who he was through the cool, glossy picture.

My phone buzzes, and I pull it out of my pocket and see there's a text from Drew about climbing today.

I wonder if he's forgotten I'm on the message list and sent it to me by mistake. He must have heard what I did.

But I haven't been climbing in months, and the thought of being on a mountain, away from it all . . . it's almost too hard to resist.

I stare back down at the picture of my brother. He looks relaxed and happy. A year later, he'd be dead.

I need to talk to Mr. Laramore, but first . . .

First, I need to go climbing.

∽

I'm early, sitting on a blocky boulder on the Undercliff Road trail, with a mist-shrouded view of fields and trees behind me, and the jangle of climbers' gear singing like wind chimes on the cliff in front of me.

"Slime the rock with your feet! Right below you," a guy yells up at his petrified girlfriend.

It's a cloudy day, but even so the trail is full of backpacks and water jugs at the base of the cliff, the climbers swinging above like multicolored metronomes. Hikers with walking sticks and dogs dressed in colorful backpacks saunter by, preferring the horizontal path to the vertical one.

I'm in the process of strangling a light green spicebush when Drew and a couple of people come around a curve in the path. They are laughing and chatting about Fourth of July plans, and I notice with a small shiver that Adam is with them. I'm not surprised, but it doesn't make me feel less nervous.

Adam is wearing jeans and a dark blue stretchy climbing

shirt. The gear on his belt jingles as he walks, and he is laughing at something one of the pretty blond college girls has said. I watch him, unable to stop myself, even when his eyes meet mine and he falls abruptly silent.

Drew is already talking a mile a minute as he approaches. "The third pitch of CCK is one of the best photo-ops on the mountain," he says. "I hope you brought your cameras—this is one you'll want to show the kiddies. Who needs a partner?" Drew's gaze falls on me. I struggle to meet his eyes, and something flickers across his face.

He knows.

Climbing is all about trust. You have to trust your partner. In that one flicker, I know what Drew's thinking: *You're not the person I thought you were, so how can I trust you as a climber?*

It's a small group today, since many of the college kids have gone home for the summer. Everybody here knows I don't have a partner, and people are already pairing up, avoiding my eyes.

I feel the hot prickle of tears, but try to act like the obvious snub isn't bothering me.

"I'll climb with Jesse," Adam says, and the blond girl he was talking to looks at him in surprise.

"Good, fine, I'll climb with Clara," Drew says, obviously relieved.

Adam walks over to me, and I say in a low voice, "You don't have to climb with me. You don't have to do this."

He shrugs. "What if I want to?"

For the first time in months, I see the flash of his dimple.

⌒

Adam leads the first pitch, and I belay him as he moves up the cliff like silk, his muscles rippling in his back as he reaches for the next handhold. I barely know anything about him, but I know everything I need to watching him climb. He is confident, and sure-footed, and careful when he needs to be, and sometimes he stretches farther than he should to get a good handhold, and every once in a while he just goes balls to the wall, like, *Eff it, I'm going all in.*

I lead the last pitch, an exhilarating stretch of white bill-board rock that makes my teeth and spine tingle with fear and excitement. At the top, I kneel on the jutting overhang so I can see Adam on the sheer face of the cliff. I watch his face, knowing that he won't see me, because he's concentrating on finding a foothold. His jaw is clenched, his clear blue eyes shaded by dark eyelashes as he sets his right foot and then reaches up to feel for a crack over his head. His gaze flicks up to mine, and I'm busted. Not that I shouldn't have been watching him, that's my job, but I can tell he sees that it is more than that. I blush and look away, but when I peer back over the edge he's got his eyes closed, and his face is drained of color.

He's not moving.

"Hey," I say. "Adam? Are you okay?"

He nods, but he doesn't open his eyes.

"Adam!" I call again, more sharply.

He doesn't answer.

I tie off his rope and scan for a tree where I can build a second anchor. I find one, and loop the webbing around a tree trunk, twisting the ropes on either side so I can slip a carabiner on the whole thing to equalize the anchor.

Then I walk backward over the edge, my hand tight on the rope coming out of my belay device, and rap down to Adam.

"I'm okay," he says when I reach him, but he doesn't open his eyes and his face is white and sweaty.

"No," I say. "You're not. What's wrong?"

"Just give me a minute. I did something kind of stupid." He leans his forehead against the rock and takes deep breaths.

"I know the feeling," I say. Below us the cliff face drops straight down to the tops of trees.

After a few minutes, he opens his eyes. "I'm feeling better. I just got light-headed for a minute there."

"Are you sick?"

"No, I'm fasting. I thought I'd be okay, but it was hotter than I expected."

"Why are you fasting?" I ask in exasperation. "Are you trying to lose weight or something? That's a stupid thing to do when you're going climbing."

"Tell that to God," he says wryly.

"What?" I stare at him.

"It's Ramadan. We don't eat or drink between sunup and sundown for a month. It's sort of like Lent."

I don't know what to say, so I start moving cams and 'biners around with one hand, clipping and unclipping them like a cowboy in an old western drawing a gun.

"Ready?" Adam says. He slips his sunglasses back on and looks up at the blocky boulder shading us.

"Up or down?"

"I made it this far, I might as well go the distance."

"You first," I say.

We're only a short distance from the top, and Adam takes it slow. I stay beside him as much as I can and still keep out of his way, pointing out cracks for foot- and handholds. When he starts giving me dirty looks, I know he's feeling better.

∞

At the top, we stand on the ledge and the world is at our feet. The sun has come out, and the wind is an orchestra of sound, the lower leaves of the trees tinkling in individual harmony and then building to a great rush of dancing treetops, the steady beat of tires on wet pavement below us keeping time.

"So why'd you do it?" he says as we stand there shoulder to shoulder.

We both know what he's talking about.

"I—" The words get caught in my throat, and I shake my head helplessly. I *need* to answer this question, not only for Adam but for me, and for everybody who cares about me. If I can't explain it now, when I'm standing on the edge of maybe and never, when will I ever?

I take a deep breath. "My dad never talks about my brother Travis. He won't let any of us talk about him either. My mom says it's because it hurts too bad, that he says a lot of horrible things about other people, about . . . Muslims . . . because he's hurting inside. But right before I . . . did what I did . . . I found my father with a photo album full of Travis, and I realized that he did care, and he never told me, and that made me bitter. Because it was like I wasn't supposed to care about my brother, and what happened to him, and here Dad was all these years caring, but not saying anything. It scared me that my dad, who always seems so strong, could be so hurt. I didn't want to be scared. I got angry instead. I was furious that those terrorists, who didn't even know us, could kill my brother and screw up Dad like that, and not only him but my entire family, and . . . me. I didn't know who to be mad at, so I just got mad at everybody."

I can't meet his eyes because I'm afraid of what he'll say. When did I begin to care this much about what he thinks?

"I get being mad because the world isn't the way it's supposed to be," he says.

There's a bitterness in his voice I've never heard before, and I know that somehow he understands what it's like to feel anger that makes you feel powerful and powerless all at the same time.

"It sucks," I say. "Neither of us had anything to do with what happened."

"But we're left dealing with the fallout," he says.

I look out at the valley, the square blocks of houses and plots of land, the summer trees in a million shades of green, and cloud shadows moving slowly across all of it. I wonder why people climb mountains and build towers aiming for the sky. When we are so high, do we feel bigger than everything else? Or does it remind us how small we really are?

"I feel God the most when I'm up here," I say, something I've never admitted to anyone. Sometimes religion seems so messy and full of arbitrary rules, and really, why does it have to be so complicated?

"Me too." He stares out over the world that seems to go on forever. "Have you ever noticed that it somehow feels the same when you're at the bottom looking up at a mountain as it does on the top looking down?"

I take a deep breath. "Can we start over?" I say. "Please?"

He doesn't say anything for a long moment and then he turns to me with a crooked grin. "Hi, I'm Adam, and there's something you should know about me."

I wait.

"I take such great soil samples that my boss insisted I change my middle name to 'the Great' last week. It looks awesome on my license."

I smile. "I bet it does. Hi, Adam, I'm Jesse. Nice to meet you."

Chapter Thirty-Three

Alia

After the man in the blue shirt screams at me, I don't run, exactly, but I walk really fast back to where Julia is still sitting in her office chair.

"Where's Travis?" I say too loud.

"He hasn't come back. What's going on?" Julia's voice is a breathy whisper.

"Nothing," I say. "But we've got to get out of here. Come on, let's go." With or without Travis, it's time to go, but I'm so scared that I want to cry. *I can't do this. I really can't do this by myself.*

"Wait, not yet," Julia gasps.

"Just a minute more," I say, thinking about what the man had said: *Two have already hit—do you think there can't be a third?* Two what? What was he talking about?

"How old are you?" Julia asks, wheezing softly. "You're younger than I first thought. The scarf makes you look older."

"Sixteen," I say, feeling absurdly pleased that the scarf makes me look more grown up.

"Sixteen? Wow. You're one brave girl."

I frown. "I'm not brave." *Lia* is the brave one. I'm always scared inside. Every day, I feel like I'm walking on ice and it's cracking in every direction I turn.

She takes a deep breath and presses her hand to her chest. "My mom used to tell me when I was having one of my attacks that I needed to hold on for just one minute longer than I thought I could bear, and then one more. I think bravery is trusting yourself enough to know you can hold on for that one more minute. I don't know what's going on out there," she says, waving a hand toward the window, "but I've seen what's going on in here, in these stairwells and offices. There are angels walking among us today. And you're one of them."

I shake my head, because I know she's wrong. I'm just trying to get through this.

"I just want to get home," I say. "I just want to see my parents and my brother and my friends."

Travis comes bursting through the stairwell door, and we both startle. He's sweating, his shirt clinging to his chest, and he's breathing hard.

"Hold on," he says, when he sees that I'm getting ready to lift Julia to her feet. "I want to get something first."

Without saying anything about where he had gone, or what he was doing, he runs down the hall. I ease Julia back into the chair, but don't take my eyes off Travis. I'm afraid he's going to disappear again.

He stops in front of a vending machine, which I hadn't even noticed. He messes with it and then comes running back with his arms full of bottled water.

"Thank God," I say, and take the bottle he hands me. I open it, and the first few gulps washes the smoke and gunk out of my throat. I close my eyes and tip my head back, and, *oh*, the slide of smooth, cold water down my throat is wonderful. I can't remember being this thirsty before, even when I was fasting. One of the gates of heaven is called the "Thirst Quencher," and for the first time I really understand why.

When I finish the bottle, I open my eyes and see that Travis is watching me.

"What?" I ask, automatically putting my hand up to my head and tugging my scarf back into place.

"We need to get going," he says, urging Julia to her feet. "I found another stairwell with fewer people."

He swings her purse onto his shoulder, and she clutches his arm. We've stuck several waters into her purse, and I'm carrying three bottles. I'd intended on keeping them for us in case we needed them on the way down, but as soon as I step through the stairwell door and see the tired and desperate faces of the people trudging down the stairs, I hand out the bottles. Travis does the same, and we watch for a moment as people take a few sips and then pass them to the person behind them.

"Let's go," Travis says.

We head back down the stairs.

Chapter Thirty-Four

Jesse

That night, I Skype call Hank fifteen times.

On the sixteenth time, my brother's picture flickers onto the screen.

"Jesus, Jesse." He runs his hand through his short, dark blond hair, and looks pissed and sheepish all at the same time.

"Really, Hank? You taking lessons from Dad?"

"I know, Jesse. I'm sorry I never called you back. I've felt bad about it."

"At least you didn't try to tell me you lost your phone, or your dog ate your computer or something," I say. "But why, Hank?"

"Look, I'm not sure what you want to know. I've spent a lot of time forgetting what happened back then." He shakes his head. "Why do you think I moved over seven thousand miles away? What can I say, Jesse? It's not a time in my life I like to think about."

"I want to understand, Hank," I say. "What happened to Travis? Tell me all the big, loud secrets that have messed up my life and I don't even know why. You know something or you wouldn't be avoiding me."

"Do you really want to know? It's all in the past now. What difference does it make?"

"It makes a *huge* difference," I say fiercely. "I'm sick of all this secrecy. Why won't anybody talk about him?"

Hank sighs. "I don't know the whole story. I was sixteen and pretty heavily invested in my own life. Travis went away to college, and then almost at the end of his first year, he came back, and he was a mess. He holed up in his room, barely coming out to eat. Something happened, but no one would talk about it. It was all whispers and hush-hush. Travis was like the walking wounded, and Dad was seriously pissed. I know it seems strange now that I didn't ask any questions, but it just didn't seem worth getting everyone mad at me."

I can't help but nod, because I certainly understand *that* feeling.

"So, that's it?"

"No, that's *not* it." Joshua crawls onto Hank's lap, sucking his thumb and laying his head on my brother's shoulder. My nephew stares at me unblinkingly for a long moment, and then his eyes drift closed.

"When he finally came out of his room, he had this what-the-hell-ever attitude." Hank's voice is barely above a whisper, and I have to lean in close to the screen to hear him. "He was drinking and staying out all night, and he started hanging around Topher McCall and those kids. Bad news, you know? Travis was getting in all these fights, and there was a rumor he was stealing. I mean, just stupid stuff. He and Dad got into this huge fight while I was at a party one night. I heard about it from one of the neighbors the next day after Travis moved out. After that, I only saw him once before he died. He was visiting Gramps in the nursing home, and I couldn't hear what he was saying, but he was crying. I was only sixteen, okay? I didn't want my big brother to know I saw him like that, so I left. And that was the last time I saw him."

He looks down at Joshua, and the sleeping boy curls an arm around Hank's neck and snuggles closer.

"So, Travis was what? Some kind of juvenile delinquent?"

"No, that's the thing. He wasn't. Actually, he was a pretty smart dude—he even skipped a grade. I always admired him, because I could never get my crap together, not while I was in high school."

"But why," I say, "don't any of you want to know what he was doing in the towers that day?"

Hank stares down at Joshua for a long time. I have time to think the screen must have frozen before he looks back up at me.

"I guess, some people want to know every detail of what happened to the ones who died. But for us . . . you don't know what it was like back then. Mom and Dad were getting calls for interviews, and everyone was talking about Travis, Travis, Travis. I just wanted to forget, you know?

"One day I came home and Dad was screaming at someone on the phone. I thought he was going to have a heart attack, his face was so freaking red. He was almost hysterical, and when he slammed down the phone he yelled at me, 'Don't you think I *know* he was a coward?' Which was the worst thing Dad could say about anyone. I have no idea who he was talking to, but after that Dad changed our number and refused to talk about Travis. There was a compensation fund set up for the victims and families, and he wouldn't even take any money. It was crazy. *He* was crazy."

"Say that again, in present tense," I say, and he grins.

"I hear you. But . . . you can't understand what it was like after it happened. I just . . . disappeared, and all anybody could think of when they saw me was Travis. I halfway expected them to play the National Anthem whenever I walked into a room. The whole country was so messed up for a while. We went to war, and I remember cheering when we started bombing. But then it all just spiraled. It seemed like we were willing to do about anything to make us feel safer, and it led to a lot of bad things."

He's quiet for a moment. "We were at the cemetery that day. On 9/11. Gramps's memorial service was getting ready to start, the honor guard was there, and I remember thinking how weird it was that Gramps, who loved his apartment in the Bronx, liked to play music, and who told really bad jokes, was in a little metal vase. I mean, he was sick for a while before he died, but still, how do you end up in a freaking vase? People were coming in and talking about what was going on with all the planes, and Dad was so mad because Travis wasn't there, but we went ahead and had the service anyway.

"Afterward, we heard about the towers falling, and the planes that flew into the Pentagon and crashed into the field in Pennsylvania. We didn't know Travis was in the towers then. Why would he be there? It was days later that someone called and told us they found a body—Jesus, or part of a body, I don't know—with Travis's wallet. We didn't even know he was missing. They sent Travis's dental records to the city and they confirmed it was him. By then we already knew because of Travis's message. The house phone and the shop used the same line in those days, and no one had bothered listening to the messages because Dad had closed the shop. Mom was the one who thought to check the answering machine and . . . it was awful. We were lucky, because there *was* a body to bury, though I always wondered how much of him was in the coffin." He is silent for a long moment. "We got a form letter a while later about Travis's stuff, and Dad went into the city and brought back a zippered plastic bag. Things they found with him. Gramps's knife was in the bag, and Travis's wallet. Some of the plastic had melted together inside the wallet. I remember that made it so real.

"I only listened to Travis's message once. I couldn't listen to it again. Mom used to listen to it over and over again. I think she was trying to figure out what Travis was saying because you couldn't hear all of it. She unplugged it from the telephone line so that new calls wouldn't erase it by mistake. After a year or so she stopped, but by that time Dad had gotten so violent about *not* talking about Travis, I was afraid he would just up and throw the answering machine out the window one day. So I took it and put it in my closet. No one ever said a word about it. I think at that point we were all just numb.

"We didn't ask a lot of questions after Travis died. I know it sounds strange, but we were too busy forgetting. It was easier that way."

"Spoken like a true son of Gerald McLaurin," I say, but I say it softly. "What do you think all that forgetting has done to us?"

"Is it bad, Jesse? It must be. Mom told me what you did. I guess I hoped that things would be better after a while. I let you down, Jesse, I know I did, but I was too busy trying to save myself."

I shake my head, understanding, but not wanting to.

"I got a friend to clean up the message so I could hear more of it," I say. "At the end Travis said he was in the towers with a girl named Alia. Do you know who she was?"

"Alia?" Hank says, and frowns. "I never heard Travis mention a girl named Alia. Who was she?"

"I'm trying to find out," I say.

He is silent for a moment.

"That's weird," he says, "because there was something else in the bag with Travis's stuff. Something that didn't make any sense."

I grip the edge of the desk as I stare at my brother's face seven thousand miles away.

"What was it?" I ask.

"There was a girl's scarf in the bag. A white scarf with red and green flowers on it. We never knew why he had it."

Chapter Thirty-Five

Alia

I remember sitting with my mother and Nenek when I was six or seven years old.

My grandmother was making a batik scarf, and I sat beside her on the floor and touched the edge of the long, silky fabric, loving the way it slid slippery and smooth between my fingers.

"This is for you, Lala," Nenek said. "I am making it just for you."

The scarf was stretched across a frame, wide swaths of wax already covering it. I breathed in the light scent of beeswax.

Nenek touched the dried wax. "This is so the original color of the scarf stays pure and true. Remember, Lala, that no matter what life writes on your soul that you will always be Alia inside."

Mama poured wax from the pot on the burner into the canting, a small copper container with a long narrow spout. Nenek held the canting over the scarf, then tipped the cup and with swift, graceful movements poured the wax across the cloth already marked with pencil lines.

Mama sat on the floor next to me and put her arm around me. I snuggled back into her arms and watched Nenek's quick, deft movements.

"Each piece of batik contains influences from many people and cultures," she said, biting her lips as she worked. "See this? This is a lotus blossom."

Only the outline was there right now, but I could see the beginnings of a beautiful flower.

"The lotus lives in the deep mud, but eventually it grows to meet the sun and blooms into a beautiful flower. It is a message of hope, that the potential we hold deep inside us will triumph."

Mama got up to pour more wax for Nenek, and I was content to sit and watch. I knew that making batik cloth was a long process, and that there would be more applications of wax and dye before it was complete, but when it was done it would be all mine, imbued with the love of my mother and grandmother.

∽

Someone starts singing, and after a moment, others join in. It makes me smile as I concentrate on getting down the stairs.

Amazing Grace, how sweet the sound,
That saved a wretch like me.
I once was lost, but now am found,
Was blind, but now I see.

The song ends, and someone starts crying, big gulping sobs.

"Gramps used to rock 'Amazing Grace' on his sax," Travis says. He's breathing hard because he's carrying the bulk of Julia's weight. She isn't talking anymore, and I don't even know if she hears us. "They were going to play it at his . . . at his memorial service today."

"It's a beautiful song," I say gently.

The stairs are never ending, and while the lights are on in this part of the stairwell, it's still hot.

"We would go to church and Gramps would start singing," Travis continues, "and all I could hear was him. His voice all deep and low, and I remember it tickled the inside of my chest." He blinks, his jaw working.

"It sounds like you really loved him," I say.

"I did," he says, and his voice is flat and heavy. "I wish I could be more like him."

We continue on in silence. I slide my hand down the rail, feeling the slick dampness and knowing it's the sweat of the thousands of people who have come down these steps in front of me.

As strange as it seems, and as scared as everybody is, walking down the flights of stairs has gotten boring.

"Anybody want a Mountain Dew?" someone calls, appearing in a stairwell door with a bunch of sodas. People reach for the drinks, but I shake my head, smiling my thanks.

Travis plods down next to me, his head lowered, and I wonder what he is thinking. With one hand, the one not holding Julia, I adjust my scarf, pulling it tighter around my head, and try to think about happier things.

I decided to fast full-time for Ramadan when I was eleven. I was determined to do it for the entire month, because I was saving for a Game Boy and if I broke the fast I'd have to give my money to the poor. Ayah took it very seriously when I told him I wanted to try, and sat down with me to make sure I understood why we were doing it, that it was during Ramadan that God first revealed the Quran to the Prophet Muhammad, peace be upon him, and that we were not only refraining from eating and drinking but also from evil actions, words, and deeds. "Live as if every day is a miracle," he told me, and then hugged me hard.

Fasting that month was the hardest thing I'd ever done, but thankfully Ramadan was in January that year, so the days weren't so long. I haven't done a summer Ramadan yet, when the sun rises so early and sets so late that we could be fasting for fifteen hours.

I felt so grown up getting up with Mama and Ayah and Ridwan before dawn so we could eat, and I could never wait for the elaborate, noisy iftar dinners to break our fast at night. When we got word that the moon had been sighted, and that we would be celebrating the end of Ramadan the next day, I could barely contain myself. The next morning, I got dressed up in my new pink dress, and made sloppy handmade cards for my family, and we asked for forgiveness for any bad things we had done to one another that year. All our friends and family came over, and I remember Mama and Ayah hugging me and telling me they loved me, and were so proud of me.

I wanted to feel like that forever. What had changed?

When was the last time I told my parents I loved them?

It wasn't that I didn't love them, of course I did, but "I love you" regularly got steamrolled by loud words and stupid arguments. Their expectations were like carrying around something delicate and unwieldy, something way too heavy for me. I always thought I'd go to college, and they'd accept me for who I was, and we would go back to being friends like we used to be.

But what if I never made it down these stairs?

What if I never saw them again?

"My parents and I fought this morning," I blurt out. "Why of all mornings did I have to fight with them *today*?"

"My dad and I haven't talked in over a month," Travis says, and adjusts Julia's weight on his shoulder. "I don't know if he'll ever forgive me."

"Forgive you for what?" I ask.

But he doesn't answer.

Chapter Thirty-Six

Jesse

I can hear the crackle of Fourth of July fireworks as I search my parents' room. Emi, Teeny, and Myra invited me to go to the fairgrounds to watch them, but I can't get the thought of the scarf out of my head. Dad left a while ago, and I know he might be back anytime, so I'm trying to hurry.

Yes, I could have just asked Mom about the scarf, but lately my mother has seemed so fractured that I've stopped myself every time I've wanted to ask the questions that are piled up inside me. I'm afraid that just one more thing will break her open at the fault lines.

I find the scarf tucked into the bottom drawer of my mother's dresser inside a plastic grocery bag, and it would be funny if it all weren't so stupid. What is wrong with my family? It's like we're all carrying around puzzle pieces of

Travis, hugging them jealously to our chests, trying to keep our small part of him to ourselves.

The scarf is yellowed with age, and the delicate red and green flowers and yellow designs are faded. Streaks of dirt mar its surface, and other, darker stains, which I'm afraid might be blood.

I shake it out, and dust flies up, lingering in a thick shaft of light from the lamp. The faint smell of smoke wafts through the air.

I run my fingers over the silky material, tracing the swirling patterns.

Was this Alia's?

Who was she though, and why did my brother have her scarf?

∽

"Jesse! Can you check on the lasagna?" Yalda calls to me.

I nod and maneuver my way through a crowd of chattering people intent on their own culinary tasks to peer into the oven. The lasagna isn't bubbling yet, so I close the door and go back to helping Sabeen spread tablecloths over the tables.

The Peace Center has been transformed. Green tablecloths cover the tables, twinkling Christmas lights hang from the ceiling, and a pile of wrapped gifts sits on a table. Tonight is Eid al-Fitr, which I've gathered is to celebrate the end of Ramadan, and the Peace Center has invited people in the community to come celebrate. I've been here since four helping set up, and as Sabeen and I billow the last tablecloth onto a table, she says worriedly, "The thing about parties is you never know if people are going to show up, you know?"

"They'll show up," I say.

"Are you staying?" she asks, her eyes direct.

"I'm not sure anyone would want me here," I say honestly. "I was just going to help set up and leave." I didn't have to be here tonight but I'd volunteered anyway.

"You can't set up for a party and then not attend." She smiles. "I'd like you to stay."

I nod, trying not to show how good her acceptance makes me feel. I straighten and stretch my hands over my head. I catch Adam's eye. He is standing on a ladder fixing a strand of lights, and he smiles.

Sabeen sees him, and he looks away, his smile fading. I'm embarrassed for some reason.

"Sometimes I think I have it easier, wearing the hijab," Sabeen says, lighting the candle in the colorful lamp being used as the table's centerpiece.

"Why?" My eyes are drawn back to Adam, and he looks so *good* with his jumble of dark hair and deep blue eyes that I swallow hard.

"Adam doesn't look different; he got Mom's light skin and blue eyes. I've always wondered if that makes it harder for him to be Muslim. People don't expect it from him, so he has to go out of his way to prove what he is."

I think about Adam's cocky attitude and easy confidence and realize maybe it's not easy at all, but a defense against a world that insists on seeing him as something he's not.

"Anyway," she continues. "I like wearing the hijab, so there's no doubt about exactly what I am. When I cover myself"—she holds out her arms to indicate her long-sleeved sparkly shirt and matching ankle-length skirt—"no one can judge me by what I'm wearing, or the way I look, or by my bra size. You either like me for me, or you don't. It's as simple as that."

"Do you date?" I ask suddenly, and she smiles at me almost in sympathy.

"No, Muslims don't date. They marry." She gives me a level look, and I realize she's telling me something. "The way I see it, teenage dating sucks," she continues. "It never lasts, and then you break up, and you mope around writing crappy poetry and generally feeling awful about yourself. After a while you find another guy, and it starts all over again. Why is all that pain worth it if you know it's not going to work out?"

I'd heard some version of this from Teeny. She doesn't seem to mind not dating, says it's all BS that never ends *well*. Are they right? I cried about Nick for weeks, and while I didn't write crappy poetry, I'd spent hours curled up in my closet listening to my sad song list and feeling sorry for myself. I never thought I was going to marry him or anything, so were the months with him worth the pain of the breakup?

"But how will you know what kind of guy is right for you if you don't—you know—try out a few?" I ask.

"You make it sound like test driving a car! This is my heart, my body, we're talking about. After I graduate from college, there will be time to think about the man I want to marry, and he'll know I waited just for him, and I'll know he waited for me."

"But what if you fall in love without meaning to?" I ask, and I can't help glancing over toward Adam who is laughing at something Jade has said.

Sabeen follows my gaze. "We can fall in love. We're human, and it's not like we have control over things like that, but . . ."

She looks at me steadily. "You just can't do anything about it."

∾

"Can I talk to you?" I ask Adam a while later. People are starting to arrive, and Yalda and Adam and Sabeen's father, a tall man with skin the color of light rust and salt-and-pepper hair, are greeting people at the door with a hearty "Eid Mubarak!"

We're both trying to stay out the way of the last-minute frantic effort to cram all the food, some familiar, most deliciously exotic smelling, onto a long table, and I lean on the wall beside him.

"Sure, as long as you don't talk to me about a big, juicy hamburger. Or pasta," he says. He's dressed in khakis and a long-sleeved green shirt that still has straight-from-the-store creases in it, and I can't help but notice the warm, deep boy-smell of him, soap, and something spicy.

I hesitate, wondering where to start. After our talk on top of the mountain, I feel better with him, but I'm still not sure we're completely okay.

He turns to me. "What's up?"

And I find myself pouring the story out to him, about finding the answering machine, and about Alia, and how if I could find her, maybe she could tell me what Travis was doing in those last hours before he died.

"Alia could be either a Jewish or Muslim name," I finish. "If I knew which, maybe it could help me find her."

"How old did you say she was?" Adam asks thoughtfully.

"On the tape, she sounds young, like my age."

"I would say Muslim, then, if it *is* her scarf. A lot of Orthodox Jewish women cover their hair, but not until after they're married. Or maybe it was just an ordinary scarf she decided to wear that morning and she wasn't religious at all."

"I suppose," I say in frustration, "that her name might not mean anything either. People name their kids all sorts of things. I mean, you're 'Adam,' which isn't a Muslim name. Maybe she's Christian, and her parents just liked the name 'Alia.'"

"But Adam is a Muslim name," Adam says, amused. "You've heard of Adam and Eve, right?"

"But that's in the Bible," I say.

"Adam and Eve are in the Quran too," he says. "Muslims respect the original Jewish Torah and the Christian Psalms and Gospel, and believe that all three religions worship the same God. Basically Islam just continues where Judaism and Christianity left off. The Quran talks about a lot of the same stuff as the Bible, like Abraham, Moses, Noah and his ark, and John the Baptist. Even Jesus. *Especially* Jesus. We don't believe he was the son of God, but we do believe he was a very important prophet."

"Oh." I'd never really thought about what Muslims believed, but somehow I'd thought their religion was completely different from Christianity. "So who the heck is Allah, then?"

He laughs. "What's the Spanish word for 'hello'?"

"*Hola.*" I stare at him in confusion.

"The Spanish word for God?"

I think a moment, and then shrug.

"It's *Dios.* In French it's *Dieu.* In Arabic, it's *Allah.* It's all the same God."

I nod, wondering if my dad knows this. How could he not? How could I not, before?

"So how do I find this Alia? Assuming she's Muslim?"

"What, just because I'm Muslim, and she's Muslim, you think I know her? There's like 1.6 billion Muslims in the world, you know."

"I'm sorry, I didn't mean—"

"Joking, Jesse, I'm joking." He puts his head back against

the wall and closes his eyes. "You said Alia was from New York City, right?"

"I'm guessing she was, since she was in the towers so early that day."

"Well, we used to live there, before . . . we had to leave. My dad still knows a lot of people in New York. He's always going there. I'll see if he can ask around about her."

"You'd do that?"

"Sure." He flashes me his dimple. "Why not?"

We both know why not, and I smile gratefully.

A chorus of phones begin ringing, many of them with a strange, haunting trill. People stir and reach for them, a murmur of excitement filling the air.

I raise my eyebrows at Adam as he takes out his phone and hits a button.

"It's an app," he says, showing it to me. "It has alarms to let us know when we can eat, and when to pray."

His screen shows a compass with an arrow pointing toward the front of the building.

"When we pray, all Muslims face Mecca," Adam says. "While Muslims may be pretty cool, we're not geographic prodigies, so the arrow tells us which direction to pray, no matter where we are. Sabeen's got a prayer rug with a compass in it that she keeps in our car because she's always losing her phone."

A woman offers me a bowl, and I reach for a fat, juicy date.

"Think fast!" Sabeen cries, and tosses a water bottle at Adam, who catches it easily.

Around me, people are uncapping the bottles and chugging thirstily.

"I could maybe not eat all day, but I can't imagine not drinking," I say.

"You get used to it," Sabeen says cheerfully, coming up to us. "Honestly"—she lowers her voice and leans close to me—"the worst is at the end of the day when your breath starts stinking and you can't even eat a mint. You just *know* you're gross, but there's nothing you can do."

She glances at Adam, and suddenly they say in a chorus, "The smell of a fasting man's breath is like perfume to God!"

"It's what my dad always says when we complain," Adam explains.

"Feel free to eat, my friends," Adam and Sabeen's father calls, but most of the group follows him to the front of the room, the women with uncovered hair winding scarves around their heads.

"First, we pray," Adam says, and grins widely at me. "Then we eat."

Chapter Thirty-Seven

Alia

We stop in a corner of the stairwell for Julia to rest for a moment, kicking aside abandoned stiletto heels, jackets, and a coffee cup so we can stand out of the way against the wall.

Someone has a radio, and we hear the murmur of "planes, planes hit *both* towers" go through the crowd.

"That explains the smell," one man says as he passes us, typing furiously into his BlackBerry as he walks. "It's jet fuel."

"My God, we're breathing jet fuel?" someone else asks.

I reflexively pull my shirt up over my mouth and nose. I wish I'd thought to dump water on my shirt before I gave it all away. Travis has already told me that I should take my scarf off and wrap it around my face, but I won't. Not now, when I need to feel brave and strong more than ever.

"How could planes hit both towers?" I ask as we start down again with Julia. "It's a beautiful clear day. It doesn't make any sense."

"Accidents happen," Travis says under his breath. He looks exhausted, his blond hair plastered to his forehead with sweat.

"How could it be an accident?" the man with the Black-Berry asks. "It's not like they could miss seeing the towers. One plane, *maybe*, but not two."

I'm silent, because I know he's right. Someone must have deliberately flown those planes into the towers. How could someone do something like that?

"It's those damn Muslims again," someone says angrily from behind us.

I say loudly, "You don't know that. Why would Muslims do something like this? It's against everything we believe."

A woman in a no-nonsense suit with tennis shoes over her panty hose glances back at me, and her eyes widen as if I just sprouted horns and a tail. Suddenly I'm a danger because I'm wearing a head scarf?

Is this the way it's going to be?

Please God, please don't let it be Muslims.

Julia sags against us.

"Just leave me, *please just leave me*," she has been murmuring over and over again for the last couple of flights.

I hear the scattered clapping and hum of excitement ahead of us a full flight before I see the first fireman. We all drop to single file as a group of them comes up the stairs. They look exhausted, in heavy pants and boots, their coats open to show blue sweat-soaked T-shirts emblazoned with the FDNY shield, lugging axes, hoses, crowbars, and oxygen tanks.

I lock eyes with one of them, a young guy, probably in his twenties, and he has clear blue eyes and gingery bangs matted with sweat, and his helmet keeps slipping over his eyes. He's breathing hard, but he manages to nod at me. I feel scared for him, but so, so happy that he's here with me on the stairs, even though he doesn't say anything.

None of them say anything, they're all so tired. One older firefighter has a hand clasped to his chest and he's gasping raggedly for air, leaning heavily on the rail.

One of the last in the group notices Travis and me catch Julia as she abruptly sags in our arms.

"What's wrong?" he asks. He's not young, and even though he looks nothing like my father, he reminds me of Ayah with his steady voice and calm gaze. "What's wrong with her?"

"She's got some sort of heart condition," I say.

He leans down over Julia, and for the first time I notice her face is stark white and her lips are blue. Her eyes flutter as she presses a hand to her chest.

He calls up to the other firemen who have already trudged out of sight. "Lieu, I got a woman here having a heart attack or something. Whatcha want me to do?"

There's a flurry of activity above as someone snaps an order, and another firefighter comes back down and helps lift Julia out of our arms.

"Let's go," the older firefighter says, and though his voice is unflappable, I can sense his urgency.

Impulsively I hug him, and his helmet bumps against my head, and his ax pokes into my leg, but he hugs me back, one-armed and without speaking.

"Wait, wait," Julia whispers, her eyes closed. She opens her eyes and looks straight at us. "Thank you," she says, and her voice is clear.

We nod, and her eyes drift closed. "Thank you," she murmurs again.

And then they are gone. The two firemen charge down the stairs, Julia dangling between them, her head resting on one of their shoulders. I frame the picture in my head, because I don't want to forget.

I notice that Travis is still carrying Julia's purse, and he sees me noticing.

"I didn't think the firemen would want to carry it," he says defensively. "I'm going to make sure it gets back to her."

"I believe you," I say softly, and I do. Maybe he *was* thinking about stealing the maintenance guy's wallet earlier in the sky lobby, but I know beyond a shadow of a doubt that's not what he's thinking about now.

"I'm not like you think I am," he says. "I mean, sure, I've gotten into some trouble lately, but it's not like I'm some sort of career criminal or anything. It's just . . . nothing seemed to matter. My dad thinks I'm a pretty horrible excuse for a human being, and it's hard not to agree with him."

"You were in college. You said you wanted to be a music teacher." I stare at him curiously. "How do you go from that to, you know. *That.*" I gesture at the purse he's carrying, meaning him trying to steal from the guy in the sky lobby, which is a little oblique, but he seems to get it.

He shakes his head. "You'd be surprised how easy it is for everything good about yourself to slip away. I know it was stupid, I always knew it really wasn't me, but I just couldn't seem to care enough to stop."

"Your dad really thinks that about you? That you're horrible?" I can't even imagine. No matter what I did, what I said, I know that Ayah will always love me. Even now, when I'm still a little angry at him for not letting me go to the NYU program, I know that he truly believes that he has my best interests at heart.

"When I was a kid," Travis says slowly, "and it would storm, I used to sneak into bed with my parents. My dad would put his arms around me, and I'd feel so safe, like a kid taco. He'd kiss my forehead, and it felt all scratchy and rough, but still good, you know? I knew he loved me, then. He's just not a real huggy-feely type of guy. He doesn't give out praise very often, but when he does, you know he means it. But he is so sure he's right. He hears what he wants to hear, and thinks what he wants to think. He used to tell me, 'I get up every morning and get on the side of that mountain and prove I'm a man. What are you going to do to prove what kind of man you are, Travis?' Like I had an answer; I was ten years old. But that's how he sees the world. And now, I know I've disappointed him. And I don't know if he'll be able to look at me the same way. Mom tells me to just wait, that he'll come around, but I'm not sure he will."

I open my mouth, but what on earth is there to say to *that*?

All of a sudden, there's a call from above us, an urgent command to "move right, move right!"

Travis and I squeeze up against the wall and see the woman coming down the stairs, her eyes wide open and unseeing. "Don't touch her!" the man behind her yells, and we squeeze back tighter against the wall.

Oh God, oh God, please help me, please help her! I scream silently in my mind as she drifts toward us silently, like a ghost.

She has what looks like gobs of dirty bubble gum on her face, but I know with a kind of dumb horror that it is her *skin*, blackened by fire, peeling away from her flesh.

She walks by, her eyes unseeing, not even touching the railing. Several people hover around her, afraid to touch her, but still making sure she doesn't fall.

As she passes me, I see that she has no skin on her back, none at all; it's just raw, charred flesh. Her skin has rolled up to the back of her neck, like an obscene pink turtleneck.

After she's gone, I put my hands on my knees because I feel like I'm going to throw up. Travis's face is pale, his eyes wider.

"Let's go, let's go," someone calls from above us, and I realize that Travis and I are holding up the line.

We start down again.

Chapter Thirty-Eight

Jesse

Adam walks me home from the Peace Center through the heavy night air, swollen mosquitoes buzzing past our ears. His hands are stuffed into his pockets, and he's not walking particularly close to me, but I feel almost magnetized, like my entire body is being pulled toward him.

"What are you thinking about?" he asks, and the question opens something in me, like my heart has been unfolded and shaken out in the clean, summer air.

"Have you ever kissed a girl?" I ask before I lose my courage.

He doesn't say anything for a minute, and I feel so stupid.

"Never mind," I say quickly. "Forget I asked."

"You've been talking to Sabeen, huh?"

"We talked for a while." I look at the rich, red henna design

Sabeen painted on my palms, an elaborate floral drawing. I like Adam's sister, even if I get the feeling that she's worried about Adam and me. The fact that she thinks there's something to worry *about* makes me feel warm and jittery inside.

"Well, Sabeen thinks she knows what's best for me, and maybe she does, but what *I choose to do*," he says and shivers race up and down my arms, "is none of her business."

How can words have this effect on me, like I jumped into a lake so icy that it burns and makes me feel heady and alive? His eyes are on me, and something tells me that he can see what I'm feeling.

We walk in silence for a few minutes.

"What else do you have? I'm almost afraid to ask," he says, and turns to smile at me.

It's like he is handing me a key to himself, and the unexpected power of it makes me brave. "Do you ever regret being Muslim? I've been thinking about how we're born into this world with no control of *what* we are, and it seems like we spend the rest of our lives trying to make people see *who* we are."

He gives me a quick glance, but whatever he sees in my face seems to reassure him.

"My father says that coming to America made him a better Muslim," he says, kicking some leaves off the road. "When he was in college, things had gotten pretty bad in Syria, and people were being arrested and killed by the thousands. One day Dad and his brother helped some people who were being attacked in the street. That night he got a call telling him not to go to his finals at the university the next day, that there would be people waiting for him. He left that night and eventually made his way to America. His brother didn't believe the warning, and was never seen again. When my dad first got here, he applied for political asylum, but he said he was determined to hate pizza and jeans because he thought somehow that would keep him from forgetting his home country."

"Pizza and jeans?" I ask, and a small burble of laughter escapes me.

"I know." Adam laughs. "Now pizza is his favorite food. But he didn't want to lose himself here, so for a while he did everything he could to not forget where he came from. But after he graduated from college and got a job, he decided it was pretty cool to live in a country where you didn't have to be worried about just disappearing one night, like his brother did. He married my mom, a good southern girl from Louisiana, and by the time my sister and I were born, he had hired a lawyer to try to move the immigration proceedings along, but then 9/11 happened . . ." He stops.

"What?" I put my hand on his arm, and he stares down at it and then up at me, and something kind of breaks in his eyes. I hold my breath, my gaze locked with his for a long moment, and then he grabs my hand and squeezes it.

We continue walking, hand in hand, something big and unsaid filling the space between us.

Adam clears his throat and continues, his voice husky. "I only remember some of it. I was only three, but Sabeen remembers more. We were living in New York City, and my sister remembers my mother carrying her out to the living room and seeing my father in handcuffs. Both Sabeen and I were crying, and there were all these strangers in the house, some of them with guns. They were all talking in loud voices, even to my mother, who had converted and changed her name by then. They took my dad to jail. He was there for two months, like he was a common criminal, not an engineer with a job and a family, who had never done anything wrong in his entire life. They said it was because he was here illegally, but it's not like he was hiding or anything. He had a lawyer, he'd put in an appeal, he was just waiting to hear back. I remember being scared, and my mom telling me it would be okay, that, God willing, my father would come home soon. Then one day they let him out of jail. No apologies or explanations, just *you're free to go*."

"That's terrible," I say, and squeeze his fingers.

He looks down at our linked hands. "My dad said it made him a better Muslim, because he saw how important it was for him to show Americans that all Muslims weren't like the ones who hijacked those planes. His citizenship application was eventually approved, we moved to Michigan, and my parents became involved in outreach for the Muslim American community. It's not like they were the only ones that happened to. A ton of Muslims were arrested after 9/11, some of them for less reason than my dad. It's always been like that and always *is* going to be like that, one group singled out for one reason or another. It's just our turn."

He says this so matter-of-factly that my stomach turns.

"What?" He sees my face, and shrugs. "Yeah, I know, it sucks. But eventually there'll be another group to hate on. Most people don't give me a hard time because my dad is from another country, or that I'm Muslim. It's hard though, because I want to believe the best in people, but time and time again, I get proved wrong." He looks away, but he grips my hand, and tiny trembles course through my stomach and chest.

"I'm sorry," I whisper.

We're standing outside the shop. Fireflies are swirling around, and we watch them for a few minutes, shining their tiny lights in all that darkness.

"You better go in," he says.

"Okay," I say, but I don't want to let go of his hand.

We stand for a few moments and then he releases my hand and I go up the stairs.

It's only after I'm inside that I realize he never answered my question about whether or not he'd ever kissed anybody.

∽

That night, Dad and I watch a show about someone doing a makeover on her kitchen. We don't talk much, but it's a good silence, not the awful, bottomless pit that it used to be. The hopeful part of me thinks *maybe things can change. Maybe they can get better.*

Later, my cell phone rings and it flashes an unknown number. I almost don't answer it, but I sigh and go stand by my window where I have better reception.

"Hello?"

"Is this Jesse?" a woman's voice says. Her voice is breathy, as if she's excited, or having trouble breathing.

"This is she," I answer automatically, leaning against the windowsill and looking up at the moon rising over the tops of the trees.

"My name is Julia Harris. Anne Jonna gave me your number. She said you wanted to talk to me about my experience in the World Trade Center."

I feel a surge of excitement. "Yes! Thank you for calling. You see, my brother Travis, he died in the towers and—"

"Travis McLaurin? So he was your brother?" she interrupts me.

"Yes." My pulse is *thump-thumping.* "Travis was my brother."

"I'm so sorry he didn't make it." She pauses, and when she speaks again, her voice is choked. "I tried to call several times—"

"You called my parents?" I think about what Hank said about someone calling, and Dad getting so upset that he refused to talk about Travis again after that.

"I tried, but the number had been changed. I found the number on my cell phone bill, and I really wanted to—"

"Wait. Your cell phone bill?"

"There was a strange number on my cell phone bill. I didn't see it until months later, but when I saw it . . . I knew it was them calling out. Travis was carrying my purse, and he must have found the phone. I'm glad it worked. Do you know if he got through? From the towers?"

"Yes," I say numbly. "He left a message."

She is silent for a moment. "Well, I guess that's something," she says. "I suppose . . . I suppose I was hoping he was able to talk to someone. I liked thinking I helped him do that, at least, after all the two of them did for me."

"The two of them?" I press my phone tightly to my ear, feeling the rounded edges of the case pressing into my skin.

"Travis and Alia," Julia says. "Do you know what happened to Alia?"

"No," I say, feeling a crushing sense of disappointment. It's not like I even knew Alia, but somehow she's gotten all wrapped up with Travis in my mind. "I was hoping you could tell me about her. I'd like to contact her. Can you tell me what happened in the towers?"

I listen with fascination and rising dread as she tells me about Travis and Alia with her in the north tower, helping her down the stairs, giving her water, waiting as she recovered enough to go on. In my head, all I can think is: *102 minutes. They had 102 minutes from the time the first plane hit until the north tower came down. How long did they spend helping Julia? How much time did that leave them?*

"Do you know anything else about Alia that might help me find her?" I ask when she finishes telling me how the firemen helped her down and put her in an ambulance, getting out right before the first tower fell. "I'd like to know what happened to her and Travis after that."

"Me too," Julia says, and sighs. "I thank God for the two of them every day. I moved away from the city after the attacks. I thought I could stay, but every time I heard a loud noise or saw a plane fly overhead, I felt so sick and scared. I moved back to New Mexico, and now I raise schnauzers. I looked for their names in the papers when they were doing the stories on all the victims, and I found Travis's, but I never could find Alia's. I like to think she made it out, but . . ."

"But what?" I ask.

"I think they would have stayed together," she says. "The two of them."

The thought is beautiful and horrifying all at the same time.

"But even if they didn't find her—and I know they didn't find a lot of the bodies—they still would have known that she was there," I say. "She still would have been listed among the dead."

"Sure," she says. "That's true. If anyone knew she was there in the first place."

Chapter Thirty-Nine

Alia

"Be careful," Travis says to me. There's water on the stairs, and he turns to give me his hand. I hesitate, and then take it.

His hand is warm as he carefully closes his fingers around mine. He makes sure I get past the water without slipping, and then we continue down. We pass an abandoned wheelchair at the top of a landing, and below we can see a woman being carried by several men. I wonder if they know her.

I think about what Julia had said: *There are angels walking among us today.*

The stairway is so narrow, and there are so many frightened people jammed into this small space, and the *woo-ah-woo-ah* of the sirens is screaming in our ears, so loud it makes you feel like you're going out of your mind. The funny thing, though, is that everyone is pretty calm. Nobody is shoving to get ahead and everyone is just walking steadily down. When someone starts getting panicky, there has always been someone with a calming word. Both fear and bravery are contagious, I realize.

Travis is still holding my hand, and I know that he's worried about me slipping, and maybe my touch is helping *him* feel better. I wonder suddenly what my parents would think about him.

"Will you tell me what happened?" I ask when there is a lull in the walking as something or someone in front of us holds up the line. "With your father?"

He looks over at me, his jaw working, and rubs the back of his neck.

"I was a coward," he says in a flat voice. "And my grandfather died for it."

"What?" My voice rises, and a few people glance over their shoulders at us. But the line is moving again, and we begin shuffling back down the stairs.

"Gramps had a group of guys he jammed with on Wednesday nights. They'd known one another since 'Nam, and they'd get together every week and play, drink beer, and hang out. Just like kids, except they were all like in their fifties and sixties. I went with him that night, and we left late, and a couple of punks came out of nowhere. One of them started slapping Gramps around, just punching him for no reason, you know? Gramps was trying to talk them down, to stay calm, but one of them pulled a knife . . . and I freaked out. I ran. I left Gramps, and by the time I found someone to help, and came back, he was almost dead."

He swallows and traces a finger down a thin crack in the wall. A woman in front of us is praying and working rosary beads, and their tiny clicking somehow feels reassuring.

Travis turns his head back to me, and his eyes are stark. "He was in the hospital for weeks. He was in a coma, and they said he might come out of it, but they didn't know. So Dad moved him to a nursing home in our town, and he just wasted away, month after month, until finally he died. By the end, I was *praying* he would die. Isn't that messed up? But I knew he wouldn't want to live like that. He was always so full of life. He never would have wanted to just lie there like that. Never. But I put him there, and he never even opened his eyes so I could tell him *I was sorry*. God, I was so sorry."

"It's not your fault," I say, when I can talk, my eyes full of tears for him. "You have to know that."

"My dad says I'm a coward," Travis says. "And he's right, I know he is. I almost ran away from *you*, back there in the corridor. I started thinking, 'I'll just go down one flight, see if I can find somebody to help,' and the next thing I knew, I was down two flights and all I could think about was getting out."

"But you came back," I say.

"Yeah. I did. But I didn't want to, so I know my dad's right about me. He hasn't forgiven me for Gramps, and I can't blame him, because I can't forgive me either."

"That's terrible," I say quietly, but suddenly I'm mad at Travis's father. How could he make this good, kind boy feel like this?

"I got so angry," he says in a low voice. "I wanted to *kill* those guys, but the police never found them, and sometimes I just wanted to kick someone's ass, *anybody's*."

I don't know what to say, so I squeeze his fingers and keep walking.

A little while later, I ask, "We're going to get out of here, right?"

"Yeah, we're going to get out of here." He grips my hand hard as we follow the line of people moving quietly down the stairs.

"Doesn't it feel like things will be different when we get out?" I'm not real sure what I'm trying to say, but how could you go through something like this and it not change everything?

Travis takes a piece of paper towel from a guy standing in a stairwell door holding a roll he had dunked in water, and hands it to me.

"Yeah, things will be different," he says hoarsely as I press the paper towel to my face.

I see a heavyset man ahead of us being helped down the stairs by two men. Something about him is familiar, and I realize that it is Mr. Morowitz, my dad's friend from his office, the one I talked to what seems like a lifetime ago.

"Mr. Morowitz!" I call. "Mr. Morowitz!"

The people in front of us let us by so we can catch up with him.

"Alia!" His eyes widen in surprise. "I'm so happy to see you! Did you find your father?"

"My father?" I frown. "No, you said he wasn't in the building."

"I need to rest a minute," he tells his coworkers, and they guide him to a stairwell door, which thankfully is unlocked.

Travis and I follow them inside the office, which is quiet and empty. Mr. Morowitz's coworkers, a big guy who looks like he played pro football and a tall man with short, neat dreads, help him slide to the floor. Mr. Morowitz takes several big breaths, and the tall man gently takes off Mr. Morowitz's glasses, which have become fogged with sweat, and slips them into his front pocket.

"Thank you, my friend," Mr. Morowitz gasps, and closes his eyes. He looks exhausted.

"Mr. Morowitz? Did you see my father?" I ask impatiently. Suddenly, I'm having trouble breathing.

"He must have . . . forgotten something . . . because I saw him come in soon after you left," Mr. Morowitz says, fighting for breath. "I was just getting up to tell him I saw you when there was a whirring sound, and this big explosion, and the entire building just . . . lurched. Like in an earthquake, just shuddering back and forth. It sways in the wind," he says, almost dreamily. "Up there, you get used to the window blinds going *clack-clack-clack* on a windy day, and the water sloshing around in the toilet bowls. But this was different. The building leaned over to the side, and at first I didn't think it would bounce back. I braced myself to keep from sliding. The windows shattered, and I could see all this paper floating outside, like a ticker-tape parade. And then the building careened back the other way. All I could do was hang on. As soon as I could, I ran for a doorway like they tell you to do in an earthquake. It got hot almost immediately, and smoke started pouring in. When the building stopped moving, I knew it was time to get out of there. All of us did. We didn't talk much, just headed for the stairs. We've been coming down ever since. Slow and steady, right, gentlemen?"

"But my father," I say, and there are black spots in front of my eyes. "What happened to my father?"

"I don't know, Alia." Mr. Morowitz's voice is thick with regret as he stares up at me. "He was standing near the door, and then I didn't see him again."

"He might still be up there? He might be hurt, and not be able to get down?" I cry. "How could you just leave him like that? Why didn't you check to make sure if he got out?"

Mr. Morowitz closes his eyes. "You don't understand, Alia," he says almost in a whisper. "It all happened so fast . . . we did the best we could. Andrew, here"—he nods at the tall man—"he went around and checked, but he couldn't find anyone else. Only our receptionist, and she . . . she didn't make it." He swallows hard. "You have to understand, it was very smoky and hard to see."

"But he could be hurt!" I'm shaking his shoulder, and I can't seem to stop.

"Alia," Travis says, and pulls me away. "Alia. Calm down. He's probably fine. If we got out of an elevator, don't you think your dad was able to get out of his own office?"

But I'm thinking about the woman we just saw coming down the stairs, burned terribly, and *what if Ayah is up there too hurt to move?*

I see in Travis's haunted eyes that he is remembering the same thing.

"I've got to go see," I say.

"Alia . . ."

"He could be hurt and can't move!" I turn and grab the knob on the stairwell door.

"Alia, no. He'd want you to get out!" Travis grabs my arm.

"It's my father! I'm not going to be a coward and pretend like my father might not be up there needing help!"

Immediately, I realize what I've said, but it's too late to take back the words. It's always too late to take back the words. Travis looks like I have hit him, his face white, his eyes staring.

"Let me go," I say in a softer voice, tugging away from his iron grip on my arm, and his fingers fall away, and his mouth opens but nothing comes out.

"I've got to go," I say. "I've got to go find him."

I open the door, and it swings shut behind me.

I take a deep breath and start up the stairs.

Alone.

Chapter Forty

Jesse

It's the middle of August when Mr. Laramore finally comes home.

The day after I found his picture in the yearbook with Travis, I knocked on his door and a neighbor came out and told me he was gone for the summer.

After getting off work, I drove the truck by his house like I've been doing almost every day, and this time I see a car in the driveway, lights on in the windows.

I go up to the door and knock.

"Jesse?" Mr. Laramore is dressed the same at home as he is in school, and I don't know why I'm surprised. It's not like jeans and high-tops on a thirty-something guy isn't a fashion statement *anywhere.*

I'd gotten a C in his Entrepreneurship class, which I was

actually pretty proud of. I'd been so screwed up with Nick, and the fallout from getting arrested, that I barely remembered the last couple of months of school.

"How are you, Jesse?" His tone is friendly, if a little guarded. Of course it is. He's thinking about what I painted on the side of the Peace Center.

"You knew my brother Travis," I say without preamble. "Why didn't you tell me that you knew my brother?"

His face freezes, and then he recovers. "Let's sit down."

We sit on the rocking chairs on his front porch, but I keep my feet planted on the floor so the chair won't rock. I don't need the ground feeling any more precarious and unstable than it already does.

"I knew you were Travis's sister," Mr. Laramore says. "Of course I did. I still think about him all the time: whether he'd have a family, if we would have gone to Little League games together, barbecued in my backyard. He wanted to be a music teacher, and maybe we would have hung out together in the teachers' lounge. Yes, I think about him, but I didn't see any reason to bring up something that was so painful for your family. For *all* of us."

"You could have at least said, 'Hey, Jesse, I knew your brother,'" I say quietly. "I wish people would stop acting like Travis dying in the towers is the only thing important about him."

Mr. Laramore looks at me for a moment. "Hey, Jesse," he says softly. "I knew your brother."

"Thank you." I swallow and trace my fingers along the wood grain of the chair's armrest. "You were his friend, right? What can you tell me about him?"

He leans his head against the back of the rocking chair. "We kind of lost touch after high school. I left to go to Syracuse, and Travis got into Columbia, which surprised no one because he was sharp. I knew he dropped out before the end of the school year and moved home, but I didn't see him until I returned for the summer. We tried hanging out a couple of times, but it just didn't work out. He'd changed so much after what happened with your grandfather."

"With my grandfather?" I ask. "What happened?"

Mr. Laramore doesn't answer, just rocks on the creaking porch boards like he's some freaking old lady.

"*What happened with Gramps?*" I say.

He sighs. "Your grandfather and Travis were mugged. Travis ran, and your grandfather was badly hurt."

I shake my head mutely. I don't want to hear this. Not about my brother.

"Not many people knew, but Travis couldn't forgive himself for not doing more to help his—your—grandfather. They never caught the guys who did it. By the time I really talked to him about what happened, he was hanging around Topher and his bunch of lowlifes, and he'd already gotten into some trouble. A bunch of fights, some minor larceny. I couldn't understand it. I didn't like his new friends, and I don't think he really wanted to hang around me anymore.

"That's why I was surprised when he showed up at my house the night before he died. I was home from school for a long weekend, visiting my girlfriend, and your grandfather had just died. Your parents brought him here to a nursing home after the mugging, and he hung on for a while, but it was inevitable. Travis was blaming himself, saying it was his fault. He was so angry that his dad was burying his grandfather's ashes in town, rather than taking him back to New York City. Travis said his grandfather had lived his whole life in the city, and he'd want to be buried there, where he'd been the happiest. I tried talking him down, but he was a mess. Your grandfather's memorial service was the next day, and Travis was all hyped up."

"Did he say anything about going to the towers on the day of Gramps's memorial service? That was on 9/11, right?" I ask, and the words seem to vibrate in the warm summer night air.

"He was talking crazy. You've got to understand. But he did say . . . he did say he'd like to take some of your grandfather's ashes to the city."

My mind is spinning, trying to figure all of this out. "So that's why he was there? He took my grandfather's ashes to the city? But why didn't you ever *tell* someone?"

He's quiet for a long time. "The easy answer is no one asked. The harder one is . . . I couldn't bring myself to talk to your parents. I should have been a better friend to Travis, and I wasn't. Hell, I should have gone *with* him if he felt like that was something he needed to do. Maybe things would have turned out differently. But I didn't. And I can't change that."

Friends are sometimes the only thing that keep us from plunging into the abyss. But you have to reach for them, and they have to be there on the side of the cliff reaching out to you too. I think of Emi, Teeny, and Myra, and squeeze my eyes shut because I almost fell all the way.

"But why," I say slowly, "did Travis go to the World Trade Center? With the ashes?"

Mr. Laramore is surprised. "That's where your grandfather worked, all the way up to when . . . when he got hurt. Your grandfather helped build the towers, then he worked there as some kind of maintenance guy for like thirty years. Travis said it was the place your grandfather liked best in the entire world."

Chapter Forty-One

Alia

I'm charging up the stairs like I have Lia-strength propelling me. I was so tired before, but my exhaustion seems to have vanished, because all I can think of is my father upstairs, hurt, unable to move. My feet feel light, and I don't even notice as people press out of my way, murmuring in confusion as I push past without bothering to say excuse me.

"Alia! Alia!" I hear someone behind me calling my name.

At first I don't stop. I *hear* it, but I really don't. I'm too focused on getting up, up, up as fast as I can.

But eventually I realize that I am panting hard, and that I have a major stitch in my side. I'm in good shape, but I know I need to pace myself or I'm never going to reach where I need to go.

I stop in the corner of a stairwell, gasping, as people continue to walk down past me, though there aren't nearly as many people as there were earlier.

They're getting out.

A few people ask me if I'm okay, and someone else pours water over my head as they pass. I must look bad.

I hear someone calling my name again. I turn, my hand on the rail, and peer down the stairs. My heart surges as I see Travis coming up behind me, his face determined.

"Holy crap, I didn't think you'd ever slow down. What are you, a professional stair climber?" he gasps as he reaches me.

"I run," I say, though I'm breathing hard too.

He nods, leaning over and putting his hands on his knees as he tries to catch his breath.

"What are you doing?" I ask.

"What does it look like?"

I smile at him, feeling grateful and overwhelmed. "You don't even know me. Why would you come with me?"

"I didn't want to, believe me," he pants, "but I'm so tired of regretting the things I didn't do."

I wait with him as he gets his wind back, leaning against the railing because my thighs are trembling and my heart is pounding.

Travis looks up at me. "I have his ashes," he says.

"What?" I ask, confused and desperate to continue my race back up the stairs.

"My grandfather's ashes. He would have wanted to be

here. I wanted to throw his ashes from the roof and they never would have let me do it from the observation deck of the other tower. I had Gramps's ID card, and it still worked, so I just walked right in with the rest of the people who work here." He's still breathing hard, and he concentrates on that for a moment. "I waited in the sky lobby until I saw a maintenance guy. I hoped he would have the electronic swipe card to the roof. But—"

"I stopped you," I say in realization. "You weren't trying to steal that guy's wallet. You wanted his swipe card."

"After you left, I hoped that I would find someone else, but then a security guard got suspicious and made me leave. I never made it to the roof. Even with a card, security officers watch on a camera and have to buzz you through the door. I brought Gramps's uniform shirt"—he gestures to his shirt, and I realize that somewhere along the line he has stripped off the baggy jersey and is wearing a short-sleeved button-down shirt with "McLaurin" embroidered across the pocket—"and I was hoping they'd just buzz me through. It was stupid, but . . ."

"No," I say. "It's not stupid. It's beautiful. I'm sorry you weren't able to do it."

We both try to regain our breath, but I'm itching to go and I turn back to the stairs.

"Alia," he says.

He's one step below me, with his messy hair and mismatched eyes.

"I couldn't let you go by yourself," he says. "We started this together, we'll finish it together."

"Thank you," I say, and take his hand.

Together, we turn to go up the stairs.

Chapter Forty-Two

Jesse

Adam and I talk about everything. *What was your first pet's name? What was your favorite cartoon when you were a kid? If you could go anywhere not all touristy and obvious, where would you go?* It's like we are devouring each other, story by story, and this need to know *everything* feels voracious and almost desperate, like we are kissing with our words and can't get enough.

His dad is still asking around about a Muslim girl named Alia who was in the towers on 9/11, and after talking to Mr. Laramore yesterday, I can't help but feel we are getting closer to finding out what happened to Travis that day. Alia still remains elusive, however. I can't find anything about her on the Internet, and I'd even e-mailed Anne Jonna again to ask if she could put out word on her survivor network, but so far I've heard nothing back.

I can't help but remember what Julia said, that she thought Alia and Travis would have stayed together. And as much as I want to believe that *someone* must have known Alia was in the towers that day, the reality is that if Travis had not been found with his wallet, or not left a message, my parents would never have known he was there.

Adam and I have been down at the river, listening to the frogs sing and talking in the safety of the shadowy darkness. Now he pulls his new car into a parking space down the street from my apartment. The car isn't really new, far from it, but he paid for it himself with the money he earned working this summer. He starts college in a couple of weeks, and I ache thinking about him being gone, though he'll only be a few hours away.

We're holding hands as he walks me back toward my apartment, the street full of tourists finding restaurants and bars. So far, we've not done more than hold hands, though the electricity between us sizzles.

"So, at least I know *why* Travis was there," I say as my building comes into view. We stop by a streetlight, far enough away so that no one in the apartment over the shop can see us. As much as we've been together over the past month, I've been careful not to let my dad ever see us. And, I've noticed, Adam isn't exactly inviting me back to his house either. It makes me want to laugh, or weep, or hit something.

"That's what you wanted to know, right?" Adam says. "Why your brother was in the towers?"

"Yes," I say slowly. "But now I want to know all of it. How

did he meet Alia? What happened to her? What happened to *him*? The more I've discovered the more I want to know."

He laughs, a small huff of breath. "That's life, right?" He reaches for a strand of my hair and rolls it between his fingers.

"I just want to know what happened," I say, but the words get caught in my throat as he looks at me.

I want to kiss him, but I know that it's something that will mean way more than it would if he were any other guy. I'm still not sure he's kissed anyone before, and the thought makes my blood run thick and slow. I reach my finger to touch the dimple in his cheek, the small indention that's there even when he's not smiling.

"I lost my faith for a while," he says suddenly, his voice low, and quivers run along my arms, because of all the things we talked about, we never talked about *this*. "I lost it when my parents moved here with my sister and I stayed behind with my cousin to finish high school. I did some stuff I'm not proud of, trusted people I shouldn't have. That's why I left to come here. I needed to remind myself who I am. But now . . . now, I don't know what I'm doing again."

I stay silent as he runs the back of his knuckles over my cheek and my breath catches.

"I tried to stay away from you," he says. "The first time I saw you, when we climbed the falls that day, I knew it was going to be hard. And then after you did what you did, I tried to stay angry at you. It felt safer that way. But even that couldn't keep me away from you." He laughs a little.

"You don't have to lose your faith to be with me, do you?" I ask, running my hand across his cheek and then down his neck. He rolls his head to the side, and I feel the soft hair at the back of his neck.

"I think I do," he says. "Right now anyway. I have trouble doing things half-ass, you know? If I'd already finished college and was thinking about a wife, then we'd be golden."

Neither one of us moves to step away, to untangle our hands, our hearts.

"I don't understand why you can't have both right now," I say.

"That's just the way it works," he says, but doesn't let go of me.

My neighbor comes out of her door, Mrs. Lawrence walking her dog, and we finally separate slowly and reluctantly. Lightning is flashing far away, and I can feel the faint strum of thunder in my bones.

"Climbing tomorrow, right?"

"Yep." He grins crookedly before turning and walking away, whistling under his breath.

My phone buzzes as I fumble for my keys, and I pull it out of my bag.

It's an e-mail from Anne Jonna.

There's a missing persons poster at the 9/11 museum. A girl named Alia. I think you should go check it out.

Chapter Forty-Three

Alia

I'm leading the way up the stairs, and Travis follows without complaining.

The jet fuel smell is stronger as we go higher, and the smoke is thicker. We run into small groups of people here and there, and while Travis may talk to them, I don't really notice. I don't stop. I slow when I just can't take it anymore, and once I have my wind back, I start up again faster. I concentrate on the glowing paint lines on the stairs and lifting my feet to take one more step.

"I don't know if we can keep going, Alia," Travis gasps. "The smoke is getting worse."

"If my father is up there, it's getting worse for him too," I gasp back without stopping.

Travis is still checking doors as we pass, and it scares me

that some open and some don't. What if the door to Ayah's floor doesn't open? It's still a long way up, but what would we do then?

The stairwell walls are creaking, and cracked in places, and somehow I know that the tower is dying, little by little. It makes me want to turn around and race back the way we've come, but I have to make sure Ayah is okay.

We turn a corner of the stairwell and see the firemen, and I want to jump with joy.

"My father," I gasp as I stumble to a stop in front of the two firemen who are standing in the stairway, their faces red. "My father is up there! I think he's hurt. We need to go find him!"

"What floor?" one of them says immediately, while the other one leans against the wall, his head down. I tell them, and the fireman says nothing for a moment. He's young, with a thick head of messy hair, a dusting of fuzz across his upper lip, and red-rimmed and exhausted eyes.

"We're working our way up," says the other fireman, a heavyset older man with a crew cut. "We'll find him. You need to go back down. You need to leave the building as quickly as possible."

"I have to go to him!" I can hear the hysteria in my voice, and Travis puts his hand on my arm.

"How old are you?" the older firemen says. "Sixteen, seventeen? What are you even doing here? If I were your father, I would want you to get to safety. We'll find him, I promise."

"Can't you call someone?" I ask desperately. "Please, call someone and tell them that my father is up there!"

The firemen exchange looks. "Our radio signals aren't getting through," the younger one says. "We can't call out."

"You need to turn around and go. Right now!" the older one says harshly.

"No!" I cry. "I can't leave him!"

"Alia," Travis says quietly.

I ignore him and take a step up the stairs, but the older fireman pushes off the wall and stands beside his younger partner, and they are blocking the stairs. They are not going to let me go up, and, oh God, *I need to find Ayah!*

"Please! He could be dying!" I want to push past them, I want superhero strength, but I am so tired, and they won't move, and then Travis has me by the arm, tugging me back down the stairs. I start crying because I didn't say good-bye to Ayah this morning, I did not kiss his cheek like I usually do, and why didn't I tell him I loved him?

As I look back, the two firefighters are starting up the stairs again.

Chapter Forty-Four

Jesse

"Who was that?" a voice asks from inside the dark, empty shop.

I jump, still reeling from the e-mail Anne just sent me about the missing persons poster.

"God, you scared me, Dad," I say, trying to make my voice light. "Why are you sitting in the dark?"

My chest feels tight. He's sitting behind the counter, and I know he has a clear view of the street. He could have seen me and Adam. I never thought he would be in the shop and *how could we be so stupid? How had we gotten so careless?*

"Who was that?" he asks again, and I know he knows.

"Adam," I say, hoping that will be enough.

"Adam who?" He knows who he is. I can tell by his voice. There's no use in lying. "Adam Ayoub."

"Did you know he's Muslim?" I wish I could see Dad's face, because I'm pretty sure it doesn't match up with the weird cheery tone of his voice. It's a small town. I should have known he'd find out.

"Yes, I knew, but he's not one of *them*, Dad, he doesn't want to hurt anyone—"

"He doesn't want to hurt anyone." His tone is flat.

I want so badly to say something about how I feel about Adam, but how do I say the words? Not saying them feels like a kind of betrayal of Adam, and saying them is a betrayal of Dad, and which one is worse?

"So, let me get this straight," Dad says, and his voice is rising, but still with that false, almost *happy*, tone. "You've decided it would be a good idea to hang out with *one of the people who killed your brother*?" This last part he roars like machine gun spray across the room.

I back up fast until I run into the glass front door and the bells jingle merrily above me.

"Adam was only three when 9/11 happened, Dad, he didn't have anything to do with—"

"*I don't care how old he was!*" He stands up with a clatter, the stool falling away behind him. "Those people want to destroy us! They hate everything we stand for! They don't eat, they don't drink, they *live* on hate for America!"

I don't say anything, but I can't help but think he lives on hate too, and how is it any different?

I feel his rage pressing outward like a big pressure bubble

against my chest. I put my hand on the door handle, wondering if I should run, because while he's never laid a finger on me before, I've never seen him this angry before either. .

"Adam and his family are good people." I'm talking loudly, trying to make him understand. *And I think I might love him, Dad, and, oh God, what would you say if I told you* that? "Adam and his dad are even helping me find out what Travis was doing in the towers that day. They're *helping* me!"

As soon as the words come out of my mouth, I know it is a mistake, an unrecoverable failure.

With a shatter of glass, the stand holding expensive designer sunglasses goes crashing to the floor.

"*They are not good people!* Those people won't stop until they have killed every one of us, and you want to talk to them about your *brother*? The one they *killed*?"

"They didn't kill him," I try to keep control of my voice. "You can't blame almost two billion people for what just a few of them did!"

He is silent, and I continue in a softer tone. "You never talk about Travis, and you won't let any of us talk about him either. How do you think that makes me feel?"

He doesn't say anything for a long time, and it's like we are both clinging to a rope that can only hold one of us, and I wonder which one will let go first.

"You're not my daughter anymore," he says, and his words echo in the cool stillness of the shop. "Do you hear me? *You're not my daughter anymore.*"

Chapter Forty-Five

Alia

Travis is talking as he pulls me down the stairs, but I'm not listening to him, I'm not listening to anything but the frantic beat of my thoughts, a constant drumming of *you need to find him, you need to find Ayah.* I'm crying, big choking sobs that bring in gasps of thick, smoky air. I'm overcome with coughing, and have to stop.

"Alia, you need to calm down," Travis says, and finally I hear him, and I know he's right, but *I cannot leave my father up there.* But all of a sudden I can't breathe, and I lean forward with my hands on my knees and Travis is saying, *Breathe, Alia, breathe.* I try to, but I catch another lungful of acrid, burning air, and my vision starts to go black at the edges.

Breathe, Alia, breathe.

And suddenly, I can again. I stand up, still coughing, but not as bad.

"There's got to be another way up," I say to Travis when I can talk again. "We'll find another stairwell."

Travis doesn't say anything, but he looks weary and somehow defeated.

"There's got to be another way up!" I scream at him, and start back down the stairwell. After a moment, I hear him follow.

The next door I try is locked, but the one below it swings open easily, and I breathe a small prayer of thanks.

Bookcases lay on the ground, manuals scattering under my feet as I stumble past desks. For some reason small details stand out: floor tiles that are skewed at a weird angle; a paper floating up in front of me so slowly that I can see that it is a memo about keeping the bathrooms clean; a wall with a perfect Z ripped through it.

I make my way past overturned furniture, stepping around big gray worms of air-conditioning ducts that have fallen from the ceiling. There has to be another stairwell, but where?

"Alia, we need to go," Travis says.

I feel a gust of wind and turn instinctively toward it. I suddenly, desperately want to feel the cool wind on my face, need to take a few deep breaths of air that is clean and good. I go into an office, and some of the windows are blown out. I can feel glass crunching under my feet, and the wind whips at the smoke, tossing it around like a gray, ragged flag. The wind gets stronger, and I lean my head out the narrow window, gulping down air.

And then I freeze in shock.

"Alia, we have to go—" Travis is saying as he comes up beside me, and then, "Oh my God."

The other tower, the south one, is burning, and orange molten metal is pouring out of one side like a waterfall of lava. Papers and burning bits of things float through the air like some kind of crazy flaming confetti. A large piece of metal floats and wobbles past our window, and then a fiery shower of debris spills down.

Horrified, I look down, and see smoke and the dim blaze of red lights spiraling crazily.

Holding on tight to the edge of the window, I lean out and look up. Flames flicker along the side of the building far above us. People have their heads out the window, waving something white—a tablecloth, a chef's coat?—at several helicopters that are circling the top of the building.

I feel Travis's hand on my back as he steadies me.

I turn to him, speechless.

"The firefighters will get to them," Travis says.

But I don't believe him.

Chapter Forty-Six

Jesse

I'm fleeing, not thinking, as I run. I see Dad's truck and jump inside, feeling under his seat for the spare key. I crank the engine, and back out of the driveway, gravel flying as I spin the truck onto the road and hit the gas.

I don't know where I'm going, just away, away from my father and his endless rage and his terrible words that he can never take back.

I accelerate and fly down the empty road. I turn onto Main Street and see the Gunks, shining silver in the moonlight. Suddenly I know where I need to go, and head over the bridge, and then open up on the road that leads through fields and then swoops up into the dark forest.

I'm crying as I drive, and I know I should stop, or at least slow down, that this is dangerous driving these narrow roads and sharp curves like this, but I don't.

How could he say that to me? How could his hate be so big that it leaves no room for me?

I reach the base of the Gunks and turn to make the steep climb to the top. The moon has disappeared behind the clouds, and it's just my headlights cutting a heavy swath through the green trees as I wind higher and higher.

Near the top, I pull off the side of the road and get out. The wind has picked up, and even though it's August, it's a cool wind and I shiver. I run across the deserted road and find the trail that I know is there, though it's hard to see in the darkness.

I scramble up the steep path, holding on to trees to keep my balance, and gingerly cross a wide rock face to the spot I want. It's the edge of the sky, a cliff dropping off steeply below me, but from here I can see in almost every direction. I stand on the mountaintop and feel the freshening wind on my face and take deep gulps of air, trying to calm myself.

I stand, feeling the rock under my feet, the night sky stretching endlessly above me, in a cathedral that echoes in every part of me.

༄

A while later, I hear the rustle of something big in the bushes and I step back against a tree. It could be a bear. It could be anything.

The rumbling of thunder I heard earlier has gotten closer, and I can see the play of lightning in the tops of the clouds.

I need to go, I need to get down off this cliff, but now something big is coming toward me.

"Jesse!" someone shouts, and then Adam comes into view, scrabbling across the rock face toward me.

"What are you doing here?" I ask dumbly.

"You left your earbuds in my car. I came back to see if I could peg your window with a pebble or something, and I saw you come running out. You looked so upset, I followed you. Why were you driving like that?"

I tell him quickly about the fight and what my dad said, and his face turns grim.

"We should have been more careful," he says. "We should have known this was coming." A bolt of thunder cracks across the sky, and he looks around. "Come on, let's get off this cliff," he says, and reaches out to grab my wrist. "If it starts raining, we'll never make it across that rock face in the dark."

But it's too late. The sky opens up, and rain falls in swirling, battering sheets. Lightning is dancing around us now, and I yank at his hand. "Come on!" I shout. "I know a place."

We slip and slide down the path, and Adam swears as he stumbles. It starts hailing, tiny pellets hitting my face and back, but I finally see the overhang.

"Here," I gasp as I pull him in under it, out of the rain and the hail.

I turn to look at Adam. It's dark, but he takes out his phone and turns on the flashlight app.

"You're bleeding!" I exclaim, seeing the rivulet of blood running down his face from a cut in his forehead.

"I am?"

"Right here." I touch the spot on his forehead, and his breath catches.

I freeze, and I can feel the cold drops of rain on my suddenly burning skin.

I trace around the cut on his forehead, pretending my fingers aren't trembling, and that his eyes haven't closed as he takes a deep breath.

I'm shivering but I have never felt so warm in my life, my skin humming with heat and yearning.

"Adam—" I start to say, and a rush of mud and leaves come crashing down over the overhang. Adam presses me against the rock and holds my face against his shoulder as more mud and now rocks come cascading down. I can feel his body against every inch of me, his leg wedged between mine, the tenseness of his muscles as he braces himself. I know that he's getting the worst of it, and I shut my eyes, feeling the rapid beating of his heart and smelling the warm, soap-soft smell of his shirt against my face.

Thunder cracks right above us, and I jump. He rubs his fingers into the back of my neck, saying, "*Shhh, shhh.*" I can feel the warm dampness of his breath against my ear, and goose pimples race down my arms, which have nothing to do with the cold and the rain, and everything to do with him.

"It's going to be okay." He pulls away so he can look down at me.

His eyes are almost black in the shadows, and his face is splattered with mud and blood, but I've never seen anything so beautiful in my life. I want to kiss him, suddenly and desperately, and his face goes quiet. Then he leans forward, his lips brushing mine, and it's fire and ice, and I want to crawl inside him as I catch his shoulders and bring his lips down harder on mine. He cups one hand against the back of my head and braces himself against the wall with the other, pressing me hard against the rock. I suck in my breath, tasting him and me, all intermingled. The feel of him against me, the white-hot fury of the storm, all of it blurs into need and hunger and now.

We kiss for what seems like forever, and when we pull apart, the mudslide has stopped and it's just rain falling in a steady stream outside the overhang.

"You're still bleeding," I say softly, reaching both my hands up and rubbing his cheeks, feeling the graze of stubble under my palms.

"I don't think I'd notice if my arm was amputated right now." We stand chest to chest for a long moment, breathing together.

"Is it always like that?" His voice brushes against my ear.

"No," I say, and he nods, like he knew that but just wanted to make sure.

∽

We sit with our backs against the wall, watching the rain slow. We're sitting thigh to thigh, our arms and hands intertwined.

"I knew it," I say suddenly.

"Knew what?"

"That you hadn't kissed anyone before." There's a sunshiny little window in my heart because of it.

He smiles, but his eyes are shadowed. "I was just waiting for you," he says. "If I'd known it was going to be like that . . . well, let's just say I'm not sure I would have held out as long as I did."

I close my eyes as he brushes the hair back from my face, feeling powerful in an elemental, earth-mother kind of way.

"I'm glad your first kiss was with me," I say.

"Me too," he says, and squeezes my fingers.

In the quiet darkness of our small haven, the rain misting in the air, I tell him the rest of it.

About the missing poster that Anne found at the 9/11 museum.

That I'm afraid Alia might be dead.

Chapter Forty-Seven

Alia

I'm just turning away from the terrible scene outside the window when something catches my eye. I turn back and watch numbly as a woman falls past our window.

"Nooooo!" I scream, and turn to Travis. He puts his arms around me and holds me tightly.

No, no, no, no, no, no.

Please, no.

"Why did she do that?" I whisper into Travis's chest. Why would someone jump out the window?

But as I see flames begin licking along the edge of the ceiling above us, I know. She jumped because her choices were monstrous, were unbearable. Which would I choose? To burn alive or to jump?

I shudder because I can't even imagine having to make

that choice, can't even imagine what it must be like on the floors above us.

Where Ayah may still be.

"I've got to find him," I say, and draw away from Travis, but he suddenly pulls me back.

"Don't look," he says, and crushes my face against his chest. I start crying, because even without seeing, I know. Another person has fallen, or jumped, plummeting to the ground so very far below.

"Don't they know if they just hang on someone will come help them?" But even as I say the words, I know that whatever is going on upstairs has left these people with no other options.

Travis doesn't say anything, but he is trembling so hard that I put my arms around him and hug him fiercely. In my mind, the words in the narration box over our heads read:

They cling together as the world falls apart, filling each other's cracks with bits of themselves.

I see a phone on the desk and with a small yelp, I lunge toward it. But when I put the receiver to my ear, there's only silence.

"It's not working!" I wanted to let someone, *anyone*, know that we are here, and what's going on. Do people know how bad this is?

Travis starts to say something, and then he looks down at Julia's purse that he has carried up all those stairs. He pulls it off his shoulder and dumps it onto the desk. A wallet, keys, pens, a card on a cord just like the one Dad carries to work every day, subway tokens, and . . .

A cell phone.

With shaking fingers, Travis flips open the phone and dials three numbers.

9-1-1.

He listens, his face full of hope, but immediately it fades.

"Busy," he says briefly.

"Try someone else," I urge. "Maybe if you call someone else, it'll work."

He dials again, listens, and then shakes his head.

"Still busy. Alia, we need to go." Travis looks up at the flames spreading out like hungry vines in the ceiling above us. "We need to go *now*."

The smoke is getting thicker, and I know he is right.

"One more time," I say, because I can't let go of my belief that if only people understood what was going on here they would be here, helping.

More people are jumping now, and I'm trying to not look out the narrow windows. I close my eyes, but I see them anyway.

I force myself to concentrate on Travis's face, the strong line of his jaw, the way his straight blond hair sweeps across his forehead as he holds the phone to his ear.

I move closer to him.

"It's ringing," he says.

Chapter Forty-Eight

Jesse

Adam follows me to Emi's house, where he waits patiently as I run in, and then follows me to the climbing shop so I can drop off Dad's truck. There are no lights on in the apartment over the shop when I slip the key back under the seat and walk over to Adam's car.

We don't speak, lost in our own thoughts, as he drives me to where Mom's staying, a small apartment in her friend Mary's garage. Mary sometimes rents it out to budget-minded climbers, luring them in with the promise of a home-cooked breakfast.

"We're going to do this, right?" I ask as we stand in the driveway. "Tomorrow morning?"

"Just promise you won't go tonight. There's nothing to see tonight."

I hesitate, because I want to run, run, run as fast as I can. But he's right, there won't be anything to see until tomorrow morning.

"Early," I say.

"Early," he agrees and presses a kiss to my forehead.

I lean my head against him for a moment, and then step away.

"You sure you don't want me to come in with you?"

It's tempting, but I know I need to do this myself.

He nods and turns to get back into his car. I watch him go, and then take a deep breath and go into my mother's apartment.

As late as it is, Mom is sitting on the couch watching *I Love Lucy*.

"Jesse!" She's surprised to see me, but recovers quickly. "I made breakfast for dinner, if you want a feta and sausage omelet."

She winces a little, and I know that she's thinking of Dad, because that's his favorite kind of omelet.

I never really realized how much she loved my father until she left him. I look over at the small refrigerator where she's got September 11 circled on the calendar, and has written the time of the memorial the town is planning for Travis. It's something she never would have dared to do when she was still living with Dad. In the past, it was like September 11 didn't exist, though as the anniversary approached, Dad would get quieter and drink more, and Mom would work herself up like some sort of windup doll, leaving a path of casseroles and a sparkling-clean apartment in her wake.

You really don't think about your parents loving each other. Those big displays of love like you see in the movies are hidden, maybe behind closed doors, or maybe just so buried under the minutia of life that they even forget. But in the beginning, did they all start with the same big, fiery explosion of feeling I have for Adam?

I squeeze the small USB flash drive I hold in my hand and take a deep breath.

I need to do this. For them, for me, for all of us.

"Mom," I say. "I have something to tell you."

I tell her all of it, why Travis was in the towers, about Alia, and what I've been able to piece together about what they were doing in those desperate minutes. When I'm done, all that is left is the ending. She's crying, and I'm shaking, because it's such a relief to tell her, but at the same time her grief is tearing me apart.

I think about how busy she always stays. It reminds me of that cartoon character that starts running so fast he's this big blur and you just know he's worried about stopping and all his pieces just flying apart. That's the way she has been for fifteen years, and it breaks my heart.

"There's one more thing," I say, and the words feel like glass in my mouth because I don't want to do this, but I have to. This is too big for me to carry by myself.

I go to the spindly desk where she keeps her laptop and

carry it over to the coffee table. She watches without speaking as I turn it on and slip in the USB drive.

"Emi cleaned it up so we can hear the whole message. Listen," I say, and click Play.

Travis's voice comes out of the speakers.

"Hello? Is anyone there? I'm inside the World Trade Center."

Chapter Forty-Nine

Alia

"Hello? Is anyone there? I'm inside the World Trade Center."

Travis closes his eyes in disappointment, and I know immediately that he's gotten an answering machine.

"Hello? Anyone there? Hello?"

He lowers his voice and turns away from me.

"Listen, it's bad. I don't know if we're going to make it out. I wanted to tell you . . . I wanted to tell all of you I love you. I love you, Mom, and Hank and Jesse and . . . Dad, I know you hate me, but I love you too, okay?"

In a horrible instant I understand what Travis has been hiding from me, and what I must have known too. He's not sure we're getting out of here.

We may not get out of here.

I clutch my stomach and rock back and forth, my mouth open, but no sound comes out.

And then it does.

"Tell them to call my mother!" I cry, an explosion of pain and sound. "Tell them that Ayah is here, and I'm trying to find him, and that I love her and Ayah so much! Tell her that!"

"That's Alia with me." Travis puts his arm around me as he continues to talk into the phone. "Hello? Hello?"

He curses and pulls the phone away from his ear.

"Come on," he says. "We're going. *Now.*"

I open my mouth to argue, to tell him that I need to find Ayah, but suddenly we hear a horrifying rumbling sound like a thousand trains approaching the station and the entire building begins to tremble.

Chapter Fifty

Jesse

The recording ends. My mother started to cry as soon as she heard Travis's voice, tears slipping down her cheeks as she grips the side of the laptop with both hands, as if that would bring her dead son closer.

"I never knew what he said," she whispers. "I never knew exactly what his last words to us were."

She bows her head and weeps for the son she will never see again. And suddenly, I am crying too, for my mom, for Travis, for Alia. For myself. I wonder what kind of big brother Travis would have been. I wonder what he would have become.

I wonder what the world would be like if 9/11 never happened.

My mother and I rock in each other's arms for a long, long time.

❧

The next morning, when Adam picks me up, she hugs me hard at the door.

"Jesse, I love you," she says. "Remember that. Always remember that."

"Yeah, but Dad doesn't," I say bitterly. We stayed up almost all night talking, and I've told her about Adam, and the fight with Dad.

"You know that's not true." She gives me a gentle shake. "It's just easier for him to get angry than to deal with the pain."

"Then he's going to die a lonely old man," I say. "It's not my job to put you two back together, okay? That was too much for me to take on. You guys have to do it yourselves."

❧

Three hours later, Adam and I enter the light-filled entrance atrium of the 9/11 Memorial Museum. Two rusted steel tridents that used to be part of the outside wall of the north tower stand tall against the glass.

I'm feeling a sense of urgency that is out of proportion to the solemnity of the museum, and Adam follows me without complaint as I head toward the stairs instead of taking the slow escalator filled with chattering people. As we start down the long flight of steps, I see a photograph of the Twin Towers standing tall and proud, and something turns painfully in my stomach.

Head down, I hurry down the stairs, from daylight into darkness.

The exhibit begins with a series of overlapping panels showing how people reacted to the news of planes run amok in the skies: people staring upward, people crying, pointing, their expressions scared, angry, confused. So many emotions soaking a wick that shines bright and horrifying even all these years later.

We follow the ramps deeper into the basement of the old towers, listening to the ghostly voices jumbled together in fear and confusion as the tragedy unfolds, their faces silent and horror-stricken.

We continue to an overlook of a cavernous hall. Adam and I stop to read the display in front of us. The massive wall to our left is a surviving retaining wall from the original World Trade Center, which held back the Hudson River as the towers fell. In the middle of the hall stands a tall, rusting column covered with painted numbers and letters, mementos and posters.

"It's the last column they removed from the original Twin Towers site," Adam says.

I nod, thinking about how hard it must have been to let that final piece go so they could build something new.

We continue down the ramp, going deeper. I start to breathe too fast, because while I can hang onto the side of a cliff with nothing but air and sky around me, I feel crushed under the weight of all this concrete and steel.

Missing persons posters are projected in light onto a dark wall, gradually fading in and out. Thousands of these posters plastered Lower Manhattan after the towers went down. In the confusion of the first couple of days, people held out hope that their missing loved ones were walking the street dazed, or had been taken to a hospital. But the hospitals were mostly empty, and the people on the posters were dead. So few of the missing were ever found alive. As the days passed, the posters fluttered on walls, lampposts, and subway entrances, a cry of desperate yearning and misplaced hope.

I search for one with Alia's name on it, but there isn't one.

Adam grabs my hand and we continue on, but I'm thinking: *Where is the poster Anne e-mailed me about?*

At the bottom of the ramp, we reach the Survivors' Stairs, part of one of the sprawling World Trade Center's many staircases. Hundreds of people had used these stairs as an escape route, and it had somehow survived the towers falling.

"Do you think we're going to find the poster?" I ask Adam as we stand at the top of the stairs. "Do you think we'll ever know what happened to them?"

Chapter Fifty-One

Alia

The screeching, tearing, thundering noise gets louder, and as we watch, the other tower slowly begins to drop, the floors at the top pancaking onto the ones below them, the top of the building disappearing into smoke. Then, all of a sudden, the entire building just falls, rushing past our window with a horrendous roar.

The building trembles, and a great cloud explodes toward us, dark and boiling.

"Get down," Travis yells. "Get down!"

He pushes me to the floor and draws my face into his chest as the smoke engulfs us. Every breath hurts, and I close my eyes and pray as hard as I ever have in my life.

The other tower fell, it fell straight down like a waterfall of concrete and steel, and, oh God, please help me, because is this one going to fall too?

Travis tightens his arms around me, shielding me as parts of the ceiling fall. It doesn't feel like it will ever end, and I hold on to him with all my strength.

Eventually the terrible roaring, clanking noises subside, and Travis unwinds his arms. I sit up, coughing and spitting. The smoke has begun to clear, and I can make out the corner of the desk, and then the chair, and then bookcases farther away as the smoke continues to spiral out the window. I rub my eyes with the palms of my hands, and Travis coughs, his forehead on his knees.

"No, no, no, no, no," I keep saying, but I'm not sure if I'm saying it out loud or if it's in my head. I feel numb, and somehow unattached from myself, as if my mind has floated free like a balloon.

The smoke above us swirls slowly out the broken windows. We are hundreds of feet in the air, and as much as I wish I could just fly out the window, I'm not Lia, I'm not a superhero, and the only way I'm going to survive is to get up and walk down hundreds of steps.

"Gramps always used to say that they would never fall," Travis says, but he's not really talking to me.

He starts crawling across the floor, pulling me with him. He is leaving tracks of blood on the floor, and when I glance down at my hands, I see my palms are speckled with glass. I don't feel any pain.

"We need to get out," Travis says. "If the other tower fell, this one could too."

I crawl faster, trying to keep my head below the smoke, but it's still so thick that I have to stop every couple of seconds to cough. Travis reaches up to a desk and grabs a vase. He yanks out the flowers and, before I can protest, puts a hand to my hijab.

"What—? No!" I grab the ends of the scarf and clutch it to my head.

"You need to use it to wrap around your face so you can breathe," he says hoarsely.

I shake my head back and forth, tears spilling down my cheeks.

It seems like forever ago that I put it on, even though it was only a few hours ago. I'd give anything to go back to earlier this morning before planes started crashing into towers, and entire buildings dropped out of the sky.

Without speaking, Travis lets go of the scarf and dumps the water at the bottom of the vase over the front of my shirt.

"Pull it up over your face, then," he says, his voice husky with smoke. "Come on. We're going to get out of here alive, okay? We're going to make it."

Chapter Fifty-Two

Jesse

We go down the modern-day stairs beside the chipped and crumbled Survivors' Stairs. What did it look like before? I imagine Travis and Alia on a similar staircase, deep within the World Trade Center, their hands sliding down the railing as they flee the smoke and the flames.

At the bottom, we wander through a vast hall, looking at the "impact steel," bent unimaginably when American Airlines Flight 11 crashed into the north tower. In just a little over an hour and a half it would all be over. I wonder what Travis and Alia were thinking. I wonder what they thought had happened. Because how could you ever imagine the truth?

No one could.

An elevator motor, as big as a small car, sits near a crumpled fire truck.

"It's amazing anything at all survived," Adam says, his voice quiet.

Inside the memorial exhibition, the sight of the thousands of faces on the wall, the faces of people who died on this very spot, freezes me.

"I can't do this," I say in a small voice.

I know Travis's picture is probably there. Is it the same picture that has shown up in every article since he died? But that's not the Travis I'm searching for, the eighteen-year-old boy with a cocky grin, an entire lifetime stretching before him. I'm looking for the Travis who was here that day, desperate and scared, whose remaining lifetime was measured in minutes.

I'm looking for a girl named Alia.

Outside the exhibit, I try calling Anne Jonna again, but get the same recording that she would be out of town until Monday. I wish I'd thought to ask her earlier where she saw the missing persons poster of Alia in this huge, echoing museum, but it's too late now.

"Come on," Adam says, tugging me over a small bridge toward the glass doors of the historical exhibit.

We wind through the exhibits, following a timeline outlining the terrible events of that day, passing artifacts found in the rubble: baseball tickets, shoes, wallets, eyeglasses, an old-fashioned Rolodex; a wheel of a plane; an in-flight magazine from one of the doomed flights. We hear voices of people from answering machines leaving their last messages, and pass a secluded room with photos of people jumping or falling from the top floors of the buildings. We pause in front of a fireman's hat, battered but still recognizable. There is a pay phone from the observation deck of the south tower, a bike rack with bikes like faithful steeds still waiting for their owners to come back.

Inside a glass case is part of a store, shirts hanging on racks, a sign reading $29.99. It looks like any other store display, except everything is covered in a thick layer of dust and the people who worked here, shopped here, left and never returned.

So many things, and while they are just things, they belonged to people who had lived and breathed and loved. They are tangible symbols of the innocent people who were caught up in a day of horror and fear. How twisted is the world when your shoe could become part of a museum exhibit?

I go faster and faster, searching for some trace of Alia, of Travis.

Chapter Fifty-Three

Alia

I crawl after Travis.

It's hard to see where we're going, and as we get farther away from the window, it gets harder to breathe. We can hear the fire crackling now, and see a dull orange glow as we make our way slowly toward the stairwell door. My hands slip and slide across cards from a broken Rolodex, and a picture taken at Disney World—of a girl probably eight years old and smiling happily—is smoldering.

"I forgot her purse," Travis says and stops, shaking his head and coughing.

"You can't go back," I say, and a moment later he keeps crawling.

Please God, please get me out of this, I say over and over in my head.

As we get closer to the reception desk, part of the ceiling and wall right in front of us crashes to the floor.

"Run!" Travis says, leaping to his feet and grabbing my hand.

We run to the stairwell door, and when Travis slams the door open, I see that the entire stairwell is covered with dust. Inches of it cake the floor and walls, and float lazily in the air.

Travis starts down the stairs, and I follow.

I want to go up, to find Ayah, but I understand now that he would want me to go down.

To get out.

To stay alive.

∽

There's no one in the stairwells as we race down the stairs, sometimes skipping three or four steps at a time. Our feet slip and slide in the dust, and the constant turning on the landings makes me dizzy. My hand is sliding down the railing so fast that my palm burns. We are both coughing, but Travis is almost choking, and I realize that while I have my shirt pulled up around my mouth, Travis's grandfather's shirt is too small for him, and he's having trouble keeping it over his mouth.

"Wait," I say. "*Wait*."

Travis stops in a landing beside an abandoned coil of fire hose and two fire extinguishers. I wonder if we are all alone in the exhausted, dying tower.

I realize Travis is crying.

"I lost them," he says.

"What?"

"I lost his ashes." He coughs. "They must have fallen out of my pocket."

I take his hand. "He was here when they built the towers," I say. "He'll be here when they die."

Tears streak the dark ashes on his cheeks, and ash and dust crowd the air. All of it is becoming ashes now.

Travis coughs again, and I unwind the scarf from around my head. For a moment, my hands are tangled in the ends of it and I pull it to my face, because even through the smoke I can smell my mother's citrus scent on it, and the faint scent of beeswax that always reminds me of Nenek.

"Take it," I say, offering it to Travis.

His eyelashes are caked with dust and his eyes are red, and at first he doesn't make a move to take it.

"You need it," I tell him, and wind it gently around his neck and mouth, my fingers brushing his cheek, and he closes his eyes briefly.

I don't need the scarf to be strong, to be Lia. Today, despite all the fear and chaos, I *was* Lia. She's always been there inside me. Faith and strength aren't something you wear like some sort of costume; they come from inside you.

"Thank you," he says, his voice cracking.

"You're welcome."

I turn and lead the way down.

Chapter Fifty-Four

Jesse

If we hadn't been searching for it, we never would have noticed it.

My breath catches, and Adam pulls me close, wrapping his arm around my shoulders.

MISSING

ALIA SUSANTO

There's a black-and-white picture of a young, laughing girl in a head scarf, trees and brownstones behind her. How did her parents pick which picture to use? How do you make that choice?

She's wearing the scarf, the one found with Travis.

I'm trying not to cry, and Adam pulls me tight against him.

I feel like I'm a leaf fluttering in the wind, shuddering and falling down, down, down. I'm crying in earnest now, because it is all so senseless. All those people died, people who got up in the morning and went to work, laughed and cried, loved and dreamed. All of them gone, and for what? My brother was a kid who liked to play music with his friends. And Alia. She looks my age, small and feisty with a happy smile.

How did they deserve to die?

Chapter Fifty-Five

Alia

Everything is burning. Small fires race across the tops of doorways, and it's so hot that I feel like I'm in an oven. We've slowed down because the stairs are so dark and slippery with water and dust. If we break an ankle, we'll never get out of here. But we're getting close. We're almost there.

Below us we can hear shouting—*go, go, go!*—and the pounding of running feet. Some people are still in here with us, and somehow that knowledge comforts me, because we're not the only ones left.

Travis is behind me, and I look back over my shoulder and his face is focused, grim.

That's when we hear the sound.

The sound of a thousand trains coming all at once.

"No!" Because I know what it is; I heard the same sound right before the other tower fell.

I start running, Travis right behind me, but now I can hear a banging sound, like a gigantic metal ball bouncing down the stairwell above us. The entire building is shaking, concrete falling in chunks out of the walls.

Travis sprints past me to one of the stairwell doors and tries to open it as the entire building twists. He yanks on the door, and it suddenly flies open, slamming him against the wall. A gust of wind comes down the stairwell, a hurricane of dust and wind that sweeps up both of us and sends us flying down the stairs. We end up in a corner of the landing, and I hear a screeching sound, like a million banshees, and the winds gets stronger as the building comes rushing down at us.

I love you, Ayah.

Travis curses and shoves me into the corner, using his body to shield me.

I love you, Mama.

I can hear Travis praying.

I love you, I love you, I love—

Chapter Fifty-Six

Jesse

It's the last weekend before my senior year starts. My friends and I have driven out to the lake and are lying out on towels, sneaking sips of wine coolers that Myra snagged from her parents' fridge.

"Seniors rule," Teeny says lazily, digging her toes in the water and accidentally flipping some at Myra, who yelps.

"When's Hank coming in?" Emi asks me, her lips blue. She's dressed in a sleek black Speedo, back from a marathon swim.

"Tonight," I say, feeling a frisson of happiness. It'll be the first time I've seen Hank in almost four years, and he's bringing Deka and Joshua.

Things have changed in the couple of weeks since I returned from the museum. I was devastated when we got back, and Adam and I spent hours at our picnic table by the river as I talked and talked, trying to make sense of everything, trying to understand *why.*

But there's no understanding why. It's like trying to understand why lightning strikes where it does, or why mothers buckle their toddlers in their car seats and drive them into the ocean. There is no why. There is only incomprehension.

I'm not sure what my mom said to Dad, but they are talking again, and he's even agreed to see Hank. Mom and I still live in the small apartment in Mary's garage, and we've grown closer. She cried when I told her about finding Alia's missing persons poster, and I realize that what had started as my quest had become hers too.

She says Dad wants to talk to me, but so far I've refused. I'm not ready.

I'm not sure I'll ever be ready.

"Where's Mr. Hottie? I thought you said he was coming," Myra asks. She dropped her phone in the lake when we first got here, and we've been laughing at her all day because she's so lost without it.

"He'll be here," I say, taking a pull from the wine cooler and handing it to Emi, who wrinkles up her nose but takes a drink anyway.

"I can't believe you're dating him," Teeny says. "I mean, how can you have a normal conversation with him? I'd be like, 'Dude, don't move. Don't talk. Just *sit* there so I can look at you.'"

I laugh. "We're not exactly dating," I say. "It's complicated."

It *is* complicated. Adam isn't supposed to be dating, and though he's told his parents that he has feelings for me, he is still struggling with his faith.

But he's worth waiting for, and I'll be patient while he figures out how to balance religion and love in this messy, mixed-up world.

"Your dad really is going to go to the 9/11 thing?" Emi asks curiously.

I shrug. "I guess so."

Mom has evidently told him everything that I discovered about Travis, and something has changed in him. My mom keeps telling me he's trying, and she thinks I should be trying too, but I tried for seventeen years. I'm done trying.

Although I've kept searching, I haven't been able to find out anything else about what Travis and Alia were doing in those last minutes in the towers. I tried calling the number on Alia's missing persons poster, but it is a pizza delivery store now. I've found no trace of Alia Susanto. Late at night, I wonder if Alia's parents knew she was in the towers. There were thousands of remains that were never identified; they rest now in a repository inside the 9/11 Museum. Could Alia be among them?

I ache to think that when my mother gets up to talk about Travis at the fifteenth anniversary memorial, she will not know the exact shape and texture of my brother's death. It's not only the loss that burns but the open-endedness of it. How can we accept that we will simply never know the end of the story?

I see Adam walking across the sand, and I get up to meet him. He waves at my friends, who giggle, and we walk hand in hand along the shore, the pebbly sand crunching under our feet, the blue water gleaming beside us.

"Hey, you," I say, and he twines his fingers tight around mine.

Summer is slowly sliding into fall, and the tips of a few trees are starting to glow gold. Everything changes, no matter how much you want it to stay the same.

"How was your first week?" I ask.

Adam started college last week, and it's far enough away that he's in the dorms but close enough that he can come back and visit every weekend.

"It's lonely without you," he says.

"What, you miss me or something up there at the big university? You better not be practicing your newfound kissing skills on anyone else," I tease.

He laughs. "No, I think we need to practice more before I showcase my skills to the public."

I grin. "You could take it on the road. I shouldn't tell you, but you're a seriously natural talent."

He laughs again. "Of course I am."

We walk in companionable silence, and I work on treasuring *right here, right now*, because that's important.

"You going to talk to him?" he asks after a while.

"I'm not sure why you're so gung-ho about me talking to my dad, since you're the reason we're not talking, and the last time we had any type of conversation, he called you a terrorist."

He shrugs. "He's still your dad. What's between you and him has nothing to do with me."

"But it does," I say, though in some ways it's not true. What's going on with me and my father has been going on for as long as I can remember.

"The last time we fought, I was too scared to tell him about my feelings for you. It was like I denied you, and I'm afraid I'll do it again. And that makes everything that's between us mean nothing," I say, not able to look at him.

"You know it's not nothing," he says, and pulls me closer so we are walking shoulder to shoulder.

"But what is it?"

"What I feel for you . . . that can't be wrong," he says after a moment. "Other than that I don't know."

"I don't know either," I say, "but we'll figure it out."

∾

Mom has gone to pick up Hank and his family at the airport, so I know my dad will be alone.

When I come up the stairs, I feel myself tensing, because I'm listening for the TV, I'm listening for him yelling, and this is exactly how I don't want to feel. This is why I have been avoiding him.

I almost turn around and leave, but as I stand on the stairs I realize that if I don't do this, for the rest of my life I will wonder if I can be brave enough to do all the other things I want to do.

When I get upstairs, the apartment is dark and quiet. I think that I was wrong, that he's not here, and my courage begins to fade.

"Dad?" I call, and my voice echoes.

"Jesse?" I hear movement in the back, and a moment later he comes out, freshly showered and shaved, a towel around his neck. He's shaved off his beard, and he looks younger, more vulnerable.

I stand by the counter, and a lifetime of hurt and pain and unsaid words swirls between us.

I take a deep breath. "I'm tired of living my life scared that you're going to stop loving me. I did things, and I regret them, but I was just too afraid to say the things I needed to say. I can't live like that anymore, keeping everything locked up inside. I'm in love with Adam, and I really don't know where that's going to take me, but I'm your daughter and it shouldn't matter. You should love me just the way I am."

He stands there for a long moment.

"I do," he says finally, and his voice cracks. He clears his throat. "I do love you, Jesse. I'm sorry that you ever doubted that."

His eyes are glistening, and I realize that he's crying, he's crying for *me*, and this is how a waterfall thaws, one small drop at a time, until the whole thing tumbles to life again.

"I can't live my life as small as possible anymore," I say.

"I don't want you to," he says, and he scrubs his eyes with the end of the towel.

We stand on opposite sides of the room, and there's not going to be an emotional reunion, me sobbing in my father's arms, because that's not who either one of us is, but I think, maybe, there's hope.

Chapter Fifty-Seven

Jesse

The reunion with my brother is rocky, but good. Hank isn't ready to forgive Dad completely either, but we're all trying, and in the end I suppose that's all we can do. You can forgive, but it's impossible to forget, and the trick is how to live with that.

The apartment over the shop has been filled with my nephew's ringing laughter and the big, warm lightness of my mother's smiles. My father has not said much, but he sits and watches his grandson with eyes that are happy and sad, and when Joshua climbed into his lap, he held him tight and pressed a scratchy kiss to his forehead.

Hank and his family are staying in my old room, and my mother and I go back to her apartment at night and make hot chocolate and watch her sappy reruns.

"I'm proud of you, Jesse," she says a few days after Hank arrives.

"For what?" I ask, looking at her in surprise.

"For being you."

She goes to bed, and I pull up a search engine and scroll through the hundreds of stories of people who were there the day the towers fell. So many different perspectives on the same day.

While Adam and I were in the museum, we saw a wall made up of 2,983 squares painted every shade of blue. It's supposed to represent how people remember the color of the September sky the morning the towers fell. No shade is the same, but they make a perfect montage of color. Every person has a unique experience to add to that day, building a wall of memory that will never fall down.

I google "Alia Susanto 9/11" as I have many times over the past weeks, more out of habit than anything, because it's hard to stop searching.

There's something new at the top of the page, and I stare in disbelief before clicking on the link.

It's a recent news article entitled "Muslim Graphic Novelist Tackles the Difficult Subject of 9/11 as 15th Anniversary Approaches."

Beside the article is the cover of a comic book, a hellish vision of the towers burning as the second plane hits, and in the forefront is a girl in traditional Muslim garb. It appears that she is flying, and lightning bolts shoot from her fingertips.

On her head is a white scarf covered with swirling red and green flowers.

Chapter Fifty-Eight

Jesse

Parking is hard to find in the Brooklyn neighborhood, but I eventually find a spot and walk up to the building with a bright green awning shading the front steps. It's a cloudy September morning, and people are on their way to work and school, oblivious to me as I stand staring up at the building and wondering what I'm going to find inside.

I had texted Adam at school when I found Alia's scarf on the cover of a comic book, and the name of the woman who wrote it.

Adam called his father, and by the next day his father had an address for me.

I ring the buzzer, and a woman's voice answers and buzzes me up.

She wanted to see me, Adam's father had said. She wanted to see me as soon as possible.

Upstairs the door opens before I get there.

A woman stands there, dark curly hair bouncing around her pretty face. She looks solemn, but when she sees me, she lights up.

"You look just like him," she says, and pulls me in for a hug as if it's the most natural thing in the whole world.

"I thought you were dead," I say to Alia Peterson.

That's why I couldn't find her. The girl in the towers with my brother had become a woman with a different name and a different life.

I follow her into the high-ceilinged apartment, full of light and color and a bin of kids' toys in the corner.

"This was my parents' apartment, but they moved back to California to be near my nenek when she was dying." She sits on the couch, wrapping her arms around her knees, and nods for me to sit. "John and I were married by then, and there was no question that we wanted it."

"You weren't easy to find," I say.

"I'm so glad you did," she says simply.

There's a silence, but not uncomfortable, and I feel like she is drinking me whole with her wide, depthless eyes. After a moment she nods, and smiles.

"I've always thought of you as a baby. I don't know why you never grew up in my head," she says.

I reach into my purse and pull out the scarf, yellowed and faded, and hold it out to her.

She doesn't take it, and then she does, bringing it to her

face and closing her eyes. She sits for a long time with her eyes shut, and I wonder what she's thinking about.

Finally she opens her eyes.

"Can you tell me about Travis?" I ask. "I want to know everything."

She sits, and her gaze, while still on me, is not seeing me anymore.

"I'll start at the beginning," she says. "That's where you always have to start to really understand."

She leans her head back against the couch and begins.

"I wake that morning thinking about what to wear, the taste of candied dreams lingering even after I open my eyes . . ."

Chapter Fifty-Nine

Alia

Travis is lying on top of me, and I pray with him as the wind whips at us and the banging sound gets louder, picking up speed.

"Nooooooo!" I scream as the wind tears me out of Travis's arms.

The blast of air sweeps past all that was and never will be again. Gone is the endless view from the Windows on the World, and the 198 elevators that raced up and down like zippers. Gone are the people settling into a workday, the computers and Rolodexes, the pictures of smiling kids, wives, and husbands, the cardboard box prayer mats in the 106th-floor stairwell. Gone are the thousands upon thousands of pulse beats that made up the heart of the towers. All of it is being swept away in a few terrible seconds, wiped away in a rush of wind and a cascade of concrete and steel.

I reach out my hands toward Travis, and he lunges at me with both arms, but a cloud of dust and smoke comes rushing down the stairwell at us, and *I'm flying through the air* . . .

∽

"That was the last time I saw him," I say to Travis's sister, with her wide blue eyes wet with tears. The angle of the sun has changed while I've talked, and thick golden light full of swirling dust motes falls on the side of her face. I study her, trying to imprint her face in my mind so I can draw it later.

So young. She's so young, but then, so was I. In a way, we were all so young when we woke up that September morning.

"I don't think I could have done all that stuff you guys did," Jesse says. "I would have run out as fast as I could."

"You never know," I say. "You never know until it happens."

"So what happened then? How did you make it out? There weren't a whole lot of people who survived inside when the towers fell. It must have been a miracle."

"I used to get mad when people said that," I say, and smile slightly at that long-ago Alia, self-righteous and hurting. "I had no idea how, or *why*, I made it out, and so many other people didn't."

People called it a miracle, but they never did again when I screamed that why weren't there miracles for *all of them*? For all those people who died?

Why wasn't there a miracle for Travis?

"When I woke up, the sky was the first thing I saw. I was coughing, and these waves of smoke kept billowing around me, but as I lay there, the smoke would clear for a moment and I could see the blue sky. I was on top of a smoking heap of rubble, and the tower around me was gone." Despite everything that happened, that memory is the one I revisit the most often. The blue sky shining over all that destruction.

"Wait," Jesse says. "How? How could you have survived?"

I shake my head, because only God knows how and why. There is no explanation. It took years before I could accept that simple fact.

"I don't remember a lot about what happened after that. I remember bits and pieces, scrambling down a mountain of rubble, full of tall spikes of metal, and fire. I was limping because my knee hurt, every *bit* of me hurt. I—I don't know how I got down from there. The next thing I remember, I was in a wasteland and nothing looked right. Smoke and dust were everywhere, and I waded through dust that came up almost to my knees, and I coughed up black stuff that tasted like death. I almost ran into a crumpled fire truck before I saw it. I reached a street, but I was so disoriented, I didn't even know what street it was. I saw a few people, just ghosts that moved slow and dazed in the smoke."

It's hard to explain to this girl who was barely alive when all this happened what my memories of that day are like. Some are rock hard and crystal clear, but some are ephemeral and slip out of my grasp every time I reach for them. The doctors said it was because I suffered a concussion, and they were so dismissive that I never told anyone the rest of it. That I felt someone beside me as I clambered through contorted metal beams and smoking rubble to get out. The sensation was so strong that I could almost feel a hand in mine, but when I looked no one was there.

"Later," I continue, "I found myself walking with a crowd of people. I remember them being completely silent, but I'm not sure that I hadn't just shut down at that point. It seemed like people were walking slowly and almost aimlessly, as if we were going someplace but no one knew where. People were lined up in long lines in front of pay phones, so desperate to reach across the horror to find someone they loved on the other side.

"The last thing I really remember is just standing and watching the ash fall like snow, and thinking it looked so pretty."

I clear my throat and check my watch. John will be back soon, but I don't want to rush this no matter how worn out I suddenly feel. Jesse has curled up on the couch, a forgotten soda in her hand, and I think for a moment how much she looks like Travis, something about the arch of her cheekbone, the way one corner of her mouth tilts ever so slightly upward.

"I woke up in the hospital with a concussion, three broken ribs, and a badly sprained knee. I had been unconscious for two days, and no one at the hospital knew who I was. My parents were frantic with worry. Thank God, my father had made it out, helping a coworker who had been injured when the first plane hit, but my parents didn't know I was in the towers until the hospital called them. My parents thought I might have run away, and made a poster using a picture my friend had taken of me that morning." I smile thinking of Kaitlin and Tanjia. "It was the only recent picture they had of me in the scarf. Everyone—everyone who knew I was at the World Trade Center died that day."

Poor sweet Mr. Morowitz with his funny suits and big smile never made it out, nor did the coworkers who were helping him, and there is nothing in this world that can explain how I survived and he didn't. Nothing at all.

"My parents asked the hospital to keep my identity a secret. By that time, the anger toward Muslims was growing and my parents were frightened. I was in a fog for a long time. I cried, and drew, and my parents let me grieve.

"I cried for a week straight when Travis's picture and mini-obituary appeared in the *New York Times'* 'Portraits of Grief.' I had known he was dead, of course I did, but seeing that made it more final than I could bear.

"I was so sad, but I was also angry at Travis's dad. Your dad. I was so angry at everything and everybody. I didn't realize it then, but when something terrible happens, all we have left is choice. You can fill that awful void inside you with anger, or you can fill it with love for the ones who remain beside you, with hope for the future."

"But why were you mad at my dad?" Jesse asks. "Not that my dad doesn't piss me off, don't get me wrong, but why were *you* mad at him? It takes a superior level of jerkiness to piss off people who don't even know you." She grins and I smile back, my heart aching as I see another piece of Travis in her.

"It's hard to explain now, but at the time I was upset that he had made Travis feel like a coward. That Travis died the way he did knowing his father felt like that about him. I called him, you know. One day about a month after it happened. I found the number, and I was literally shaking with rage when he answered. I think I said something like, 'I know you think your son was a coward but I want to tell you what he did in the towers.' I meant to tell him the whole story. For almost fifteen years I've been *wanting* to tell the story to someone who knew and loved Travis. But I was foggy on pain medication, and it all went wrong somehow. He was screaming, and I was screaming back, and then he hung up on me. I never called back."

"Dad hears what he wants to hear," Jesse says slowly. "He always has."

Her old-young eyes are so full of pain that I have to look away. I think about Ayah, and feel so lucky to have him still in my life, and so thankful that I had a father like him when I was growing up.

"After that were the gray days. The city smelled like smoke and ashes; exhausted police walked the streets, and people carried flowers and left scribbled poetry on lampposts. I spent hours at the makeshift memorial at Union Square, holding candles as I stood shoulder to shoulder with thousands of other grieving people. I insisted on wearing a scarf, even though my mother was petrified every time I left the apartment. Bad things were happening to Muslims, but I was too caught up in my own grief to notice. In fact, all I felt was the unity and accord of my bewildered city. It became *my* city after that, even though when I moved here I didn't want to stay."

In those months, my eyes would trace the shape of the towers in the sky over and over again, my mind refusing to believe that they were gone, the absence of them so much bigger than they ever were in real life. I cried the night I first saw the ghostly tribute of light outlining where the towers used to stand, pillars of pure light reaching up into the sky and pushing back the darkness.

Time passed, dragging a trowel across my memories, leveling out the pain and horror, pulling radiant nuggets of grace to the surface: the people in the stairwell who were able to put aside their fear and make room for the injured, who offered a kind word when someone faltered, and helped a stranger. The determination of the firefighters and policemen as they charged up the stairs. It was meeting the eyes of a random person in the weeks after the towers fell, the phoenix of fierce solidarity that rose from the ashes of that day.

"The city and I began to heal," I say, "though I still dropped into deep depressions sometimes, and the sound of a car backfiring or a door slamming could send me into a panic. I would get spectacularly angry for no reason, and sometimes I would catch a phantom whiff of burning jet fuel. My drawing got me past the worst of it. Seeing a therapist also helped, and she talked me through the incredible guilt I felt for simply surviving. How do you think about what clothes to wear, about school, or watch the sunlight glittering off the river, when so many people could no longer do those simple things? Eventually, though, things went back to some semblance of normality. I graduated, and I went to NYU to study art."

"And your parents? You said they didn't want you to be a comic book artist, and that's exactly what you did," Jesse says, gesturing at the poster-sized magazine covers of Lia on the walls, which John insists on hanging though I wish he wouldn't.

I smile. "For a while, the important things became important. It was like we all hit an invisible reset button. My parents were so happy I was alive that I think I could have told them I wanted to be a—a rodeo clown, and they still would have been okay with my career choice."

Jesse is silent for a long time, playing with her golden ponytail, and I sit quietly.

"Do you ever think about why?" she asks finally. "Why this all happened?"

I nod, because of course I have. At times it was the *only* thing I could think about.

"People do terrible things. People do beautiful things. It's against the black backdrop of evil that the shining light of good shows the brightest. We can't just focus on the darkness of the night, or we'll miss out on the stars," I say.

"I know you're religious," she says after a moment. "My . . . friend is pretty religious too, but sometimes I think that so many people die in the name of religion and I just don't understand how we can keep believing in things that seem to tear us apart."

I was here once, when I was her age. I remember what it felt like.

"We're all going in the same direction," I say gently. "It may not feel like it at times, but we all want the same things. We're just on different paths."

She nods, and the door opens, and John wheels in the stroller. He stops when he sees Jesse and raises his eyebrow at me.

I remember the first time I saw John, with his mess of curly blond hair and laughing brown eyes. It was right after I sold the first of my Lia stories, and he was sitting in the park throwing a Frisbee to his dog. I immediately began sketching him, and when he turned and smiled at me, I knew I'd found him.

In my happiest times, like when I held my baby daughter for the first time, I feel Travis there. He is there in the unfinished part of my childhood, in the cocky smile of a young teenage boy I see on the subway. He is there in the potential of my daughter who would not be here today if it weren't for a shaggy-haired boy who died too soon.

I get up to kiss my husband and lift my daughter out of the stroller. They've been at the park, and she's sweaty and bright-eyed, and her chubby arms reach for me.

Jesse has followed me over and smiles at my little girl as I bounce her up and down in my arms.

"What's her name?" she asks.

"Hope," I say. "Her name is Hope."

Chapter Sixty

Jesse

Alia and I sit near the reflecting pools, two enormous water-falls that flow into the ground where the Twin Towers used to stand. Around the edge of the pools are bronze panels inscribed with the names of the fallen, and above our heads the peak of One World Trade Center disappears into the clouds.

Alia, in a pretty patterned scarf, uses her foot to rock the stroller holding her sleeping daughter.

I look down at the glossy comic book in my hands. It is Alia's tribute to 9/11, and all that happened that day.

As I flip through the pages, I see Alia has drawn my brother with eloquent, sure strokes: the strong edge of his clenched jaw, his slightly mismatched eyes. I see my brother in the elevator, with his shaggy hair and eyes wide with pain.

I see him climbing through a hole in the wall into a bath-room, and helping Julia down the stairs. I see him dragging Alia away from the windows as the south tower fell.

I'm crying as I finish.

"It's a prologue," Alia says quietly. "It's how ordinary Alia became Lia the Superhero. Because after that day, she knew she could do anything."

I nod.

We sit in a silence of mutual grief, a small shared space of sorrow.

I stare at the black pools, the water falling like endless tears into the place where the towers used to stand.

My brother died here. The towers fell here. Close to three thousand people died in pain and terror while the world watched in horror. I thought about what it must have been like that day, to be watching on TV as the towers fell. How could you bear to watch?

How could you bear not to?

The clouds have cleared up, and it is a sparkling-clear early September afternoon. Children are running around, and people are taking selfies with the reflecting pools in the background.

We sit for a long time, and I think about Adam. I hope that we can work it out, that we can navigate all the obstacles facing us. It might take some time, but if he and I can't make it work, with all the love that is between us, what hope is there?

"Are you ready?" Alia says to me. "Are you ready to see his name?"

She stands, and I stand with her.

A leaf of the Survivor Tree, found broken and burned at ground zero and nursed back to life, drifts softly down and lands on the pavement in front of us.

"I'm ready," I say.

Alia reaches into the stroller and lifts her sleeping daughter, cuddling her against her chest as she leads me to the edge of the waterfall. She shows me how to slide my hand underneath the bronze panel and dip it into the shallow pool of water. I lay my hand on Travis's name, and a perfect imprint of my hand shows up dark and watery on the bronze panel.

"Good-bye," I whisper.

Alia and I stand together as the imprint of my hand on my brother's name fades until there is nothing left, except hope and love and the blue forever of the September sky.

Author's Note

There are so many accounts of bravery in the towers, shown not only by first responders, but by ordinary people as well. I wanted Alia and Travis's story to do justice to as many of them as possible. Their story is not based on one person's experience, but rather on a montage of experiences, to try to capture the fullest extent of what was going on inside the Twin Towers that fateful day. In most instances I stayed true to actuality, but in a few cases it was necessary to stretch that to include what I thought Alia and Travis's narrative needed to show. Their escape from the elevator was based on the experiences of six men who were trapped in an elevator on the fiftieth floor and freed themselves with the help of a window washer's squeegee. Alia's miraculous escape was based on what happened to Pasquale Buzzelli, who became known as the 9/11 surfer. You can read his story in his book, *We All Fall Down: The True Story of the 9/11 Surfer.*

In the original version of this story, Alia did not survive. After long conversations with my editor, we decided that Alia's survival was important, because while almost three thousand people died, most people in the towers that day *did* make it out. During the days after 9/11, people came together in amazing ways to make sure that those inside the towers and the first responders who died trying to save them would never be forgotten. That decision helped shape this book into what I had always intended it to be: a message of hope even in the midst of tragedy.

You will not find Travis McLaurin's name on the bronze panels surrounding the reflecting pools at the 9/11 Memorial, just as you will not find a missing persons poster for Alia Susanto in the 9/11 Memorial Museum. While *All We Have Left* is based on extensive research, the people depicted are my own creations. For anyone looking to read more about the tragic events on 9/11 at the World Trade Center, I highly recommend: *City in the Sky: The Rise and Fall of the World Trade Center* by James Glanz and Eric Lipton; *102 Minutes: The Unforgettable Story of the Fight to Survive Inside the Twin Towers* by Jim Dwyer and Kevin Flynn; and *September 11: An Oral History* by Dean Murphy. These books were invaluable to me as I wrote this book.

As with any religion, there are many different ways in which a Muslim approaches the practice of his or her faith. It is impossible to capture the full breadth and scope of any religion, and the words and actions of my characters are not necessarily reflective of every Muslim's beliefs. I think it is also important to remember that 9/11 happened to all Americans, no matter what their religious affiliations. People of all faiths died together that day.

The more I read about the profound courage displayed that day, not only in the towers, but at the Pentagon, and in the air over that Pennsylvania field near Shanksville, the more I realized that *this* is what needs to be remembered about 9/11. Even in the face of incomprehensible evil, the human spirit prevailed. This is what I hope the children of today and tomorrow will understand about the day the world changed.

Acknowledgments

A big shout-out to my editor, Mary Kate Castellani. This is a much stronger, better book because of your thoughtful suggestions, Mary Kate. Thank you! Also, my thanks to *all* of the awesome people at Bloomsbury who have worked hard to make my books look so pretty inside and out, and to get my stories into the hands of readers.

I met every week for nine months with a delightful group of people as I researched and wrote this book. I appreciate you all for taking me into your homes and hearts, and showing me what real-life Islam looks like.

Thank you, Bapak, for your patience as I bombarded you with questions about Indonesia, and an increasingly frantic list of questions about names and pronunciations. Also, thank you, Jill Nelson, for reading my climbing scenes over and over. I am so lucky to have friends and family with such diverse, interesting life experiences. As always, any mistakes are my own.

If you ever get the chance to visit the 9/11 Memorial Museum, I would highly recommend it. The staff is helpful and informed, and the experience left me both humbled and uplifted. I would also like to thank the staff at the Rock and Snow in New Paltz for answering all of my nosy questions.

Thank you to my agent, Sarah Davies, who is the best agent an author could have. Truly. Also, thank you to Bettina Restrepo for reading this book in its early stages.

Thank you, Mom and Aunt Joyce, as always. I don't know how I could do it without you.

And to my readers, including the many dedicated book bloggers: You guys rock! Thank you so much for supporting my books.

Finally, to the loves of my life: Zack, Gavin, and Eddie. You are my world.

Wendy Mills is the author of *Positively Beautiful* and *All We Have Left*. She was born on the edge of the water and has never left it. She now lives with her family on a tropical island off the southwest coast of Florida, where she spends her time writing and dodging hurricanes.

www.wendymillsbooks.com
@WendyMillsBooks

Let love
take flight . . .

Let love take flight . . .

positively
beautiful

WENDY MILLS

BLOOMSBURY

Erin Bailey's life changes forever the day her mom is
diagnosed with a rare, genetic form of breast cancer. Now,
Erin must decide whether or not to have her DNA tested
to find out her own potential fate. As her world turns
upside down, Erin must summon courage she never
knew she had . . .

www.bloomsbury.com
Twitter: BloomsburyKids
Snapchat: BloomsburyYA